BOULDER CITY LIBRARY
3 1432 00182 9918

D0090419

SILENCE

SILENCE

DEBORAH LYTTON

For my daughters, Ava and Caroline

Who inspire me with their faith, courage and grace

Visit us at ShadowMountain.com

Library of Congress Cataloging-in-Publication Data

Lytton, Deborah A., author.
Silence / Deborah Lytton.
pages cm
After an accident robs Stella of her hearing and her dream of going to Broadway, she meets Hayden, a boy who stutters, and comes to learn what it truly means to connect and communicate in a world filled with silence.
ISBN 978-1-60907-945-1 (hardbound : alk. paper)
[1. Communication—Fiction. 2. Love—Fiction. 3. Deaf—Fiction 4. Stuttering—Fiction. 5. Self-acceptance—Fiction. 6. People with disabilities—Fiction.] I. Title.
PZ7.L9959Si 2015
[Fic]—dc23 2014019063

Printed in the United States of America
R. R. Donnelley, Harrisonburg, VA

10 9 8 7 6 5 4 3 2 1

Music is the silence between the notes.

—CLAUDE DEBUSSY

ME

STELLA

I hear the thunder of feet moving across concrete floors. Lockers clanging. Cell phones ringing. Flirtatious laughter. Hollered greetings. Books dropping. Doors slamming.

The melody of Monday morning at Richmond High School. It plays in my ears like a soundtrack to a movie about someone else's life. I watch from the outside. Listen from the outside. Moving through the noisy hallways without making a single sound. Because I am a nobody. Invisible. Silent.

I walk down the crowded corridor, wrapped in anonymity.

My best friend, Lily, waits for me in front of my locker.

"The cast list is going up right now," she tells me in her soft voice. A hopeful smile lights up her pretty face. She is wearing mascara. And lip gloss. I'm not sure whether I like it or whether it makes me feel like Lily is becoming someone else. Someone I don't know. Lily tosses her head so her blonde curls dip in front of her face. She grins as two football players pass by. It looks like a move she has practiced in the mirror. Then Lily turns back to me, expectantly. "I'm sure your name will be on it." And there is the Lily who is my best friend. The kind of friend who really believes in me, even when I don't believe in myself.

"I hope so," I answer as we turn toward the hallway that houses the drama department.

I am quiet and unheard. Most of the time. Except when I sing. Then I feel like a nightingale sharing my song. My voice reaches out to the world because in those moments, I can fly. I am suspended in the air. Like magic. When I sing, I'm no longer invisible. I'm no longer the fifteen-year-old who never raises her hand in class, who only has one friend and never volunteers to be first for anything.

When I sing, I make my own soundtrack. I believe anything is possible. Miracles can happen.

Lily is talking about some gossip involving people at school I don't even know. I tune out. I am more nervous than I imagined I would be.

I remember the exact moment I knew I could sing. I was in first grade. My teacher asked each of us to sing a part in the school performance—alone. My teacher, Mrs. Fisher, was looking down at her notes when I opened my mouth. I felt the notes soar out of me like feathers floating on a soft summer breeze. I curved the notes, held them out, kept them in time. I made the feathers dance on the wind. I was so happy to be singing, I didn't notice anything else at first. But then Mrs. Fisher's eyes were on me, not on her papers. A bright smile lit up her face. Every other head in the room turned to watch me. And I got my very first solo.

All of the kids at school knew I was the girl with the voice. I was seen, I was heard, I was somebody. Maybe I still didn't quite fit in, but I had a place. And I felt safe there. That was before my parents split up our family, before my mother moved my sister and me to new schools. Before everything changed. Nothing like starting high school without one single friend. It's like entering a cave of lions completely unprotected. Only one thing you can do: hide.

That's why it's been over a year since I've had the courage to sing outside my bedroom. No one here knows me as the girl with the voice. They don't know me at all.

But last Friday, I took my chance. I auditioned for the school musical because *West Side Story* happens to be my favorite musical of all time. And because Lily said she would never forgive me if I didn't try. But mostly because I knew I would never forgive myself.

"Walk faster," Lily urges as she grabs my hand to pull me along.

"I don't know why I'm so excited," she tells me. "It's not like *I* auditioned."

I give her a sideways grin. Lily has the worst singing voice I've ever heard, but she can speak French and Italian fluently, and she does math problems for fun. Still, she wants to change all that. She wants to be seen as more than a brain. I guess you could say that she just wants to be seen.

"On the outside," I say, "you're a sophomore, but inside . . . you're a stage mother looking for your daughter's big break."

Lily giggles at my teasing. "I'm calling myself Stage Mom from now on."

We've reached the drama room. The entry to the theater is marked by crimson double doors. Above them is a wooden sign: DRAMA. Around the doors are posters from theater performances at Richmond from the past twenty years: *Oklahoma, My Fair Lady, Pippin, Grease, Hairspray, The Music Man, The Phantom of the Opera, Les Misérables.*

The red doors are like a stop sign.

Stop. Are you talented enough to enter?

The cast list for the musical is posted on one of the doors. A crowd is gathered in front of it. I can hear emotions circling around me, polarized into two distinct sounds. Shrieks of joy. Moans of disappointment.

Lily squeezes my arm. "I'll wait here," she tells me as she finds a spot near the poster of *My Fair Lady.*

"Be right back," I say.

I wade into the melee. Look for my name.

A supporting role is the best a sophomore can expect. The top part of the list will be the leads. I fix my eyes on the bottom half of the list. Scan it quickly. My name isn't there.

I wasn't good enough. Rejection is the painful reality of every performer. I know this, but it hurts just the same. Disappointment tastes bitter in my mouth. I had placed more hope in this audition than I realized. I swallow and turn away from the list. I promise myself I will not cry. Not here. Not now.

I try to make my way back to Lily. I will have to tell her. I will have to say the words aloud. She will probably be able to tell from one look at my face.

The crowd presses in on me. Roaring in my ears. I can't break free. I am pushed back toward the door as I try to move away from it. Everyone clamors to see if their name is listed. Tears burn my throat. I will not let them release.

I will try again next year, I promise myself. The promise wants to make me feel better. It doesn't. I want to go home, but I can't break free from the crowd.

Then I hear it—my name. "Stella Layne? As Maria?"

I turn to look in their direction.

"Who is Stella Layne?"

"I have no idea."

"Isn't she a *sophomore*?"

The words whirl around me like leaves in a hurricane. I can't grasp them.

Suddenly, I turn around again. The list is directly in front of me. That's when I see it.

My name *is* there.

Not in the supporting cast list.

But as the lead.

As Maria.

The lead in the school musical.

Me.

Stella Layne.

I can't believe something so wonderful is happening to me. I don't deserve it. I must be dreaming. The tears that threatened seconds earlier dry up as though they have been heated by the sun. I feel warm all over. Golden.

Joy fills my heart so full I can't contain it, like a bright light seeping through the cracks of a closed door. I can't stop smiling.

This is the best day of my life.

LIFE

STELLA

The next day, I can't wait to go to school. I walk to class, chatting with Lily. I obsess about my geometry test. Lily obsesses about boys. Boys equal trouble. Look at my mom and my dad. He's on to wife number two, family number two. We've been left behind. An every third Saturday commitment, like a golf game.

Better to focus on schoolwork. And singing. Always on singing. My dream keeps me going. Broadway. Someday I will sing on a Broadway stage. I can imagine the orchestra playing. The bright spotlight. The hush of the crowd as they wait to hear my voice.

I can communicate through music—feelings, emotions. Things I can't share in any other way. People feel them when I sing. And somehow, in those moments, I feel connected to the world around me, to the people around me. Imagine being able to do that every day. Forever.

Someday.

Someday Broadway. I say it over and over in my head.

And it keeps me going when I feel lost, adrift. My dreams anchor me to the present. They give me hope. And that hope is what propels me forward each day, knowing that there is something bigger and better in my future. Something worth believing in.

Someday Broadway.

Warmth on my skin stops me suddenly. It shifts across my face like sunshine. Someone is watching me. I can sense it. I glance around. And I see him. Tall, slender. With tousled caramel-colored hair that touches his shoulders. A pale scar runs across his chin. It stands out against the sun-kissed shade of his skin. I've never seen him before. Something about him seems familiar. His eyes catch mine and keep me there. Eyes that glow like they are lit from within. A golden-blue spotlight. My skin is still warm from his gaze. He can't be looking at me; it must be a mistake. I glance around to see if he is looking at someone else. Someone behind me, perhaps, but there is no one. No one except me. I am caught again in the spotlight of his eyes. And I cannot move. I watch him. Watching me.

The bell rings, startling me.

Lily grabs my arm. "Stella, we'll be late for class," she says. She looks at him. At me.

"Right," I answer. But I don't move. I am held captive.

"Stella!" Lily shakes me again, forcing me to look at her. "Come on." She rolls her eyes—her signal that this is someone we should dismiss as unimportant. Not good-looking enough. Not a football player. Not special.

But somehow, though I can't explain it, I know he is special. I don't know how. I just do.

"Right," I say again. "Let's go," I manage as I break free and move with Lily, heading to class.

I look over my shoulder one last time. He's still watching me.

Rehearsals begin right away. The cast sits in a circle on stage. We hold our scripts. Read our lines. I love it. I am meant to do this forever.

Tony is played by a senior, Kace Maxwell. He stars in every school play and basically rules the drama department. I know who he is, but we've never spoken. I doubt he knew my name before I appeared on the cast list as Maria. The other students worship him, hang on his every word, follow him around, compliment him. Kace has black hair and bright hazel eyes that sparkle like he has a secret. My mother would say he has charisma, that indefinable something that makes people stand out from the rest.

I wonder if I have charisma.

Kace is friends with everyone. He is nice, but reserved. I can tell he wishes his best friend, Quinn, had been chosen instead of me. Quinn is always the lead. If Kace is the king of the drama department, Quinn is queen. Everyone expected her to play Maria. She auditioned for the role, but was cast as one of the Jet girlfriends. She is also my understudy.

"Stella is a sophomore. I'm a senior," I overhear her complaining. "This is my last chance. She'll have other years to be the lead."

That's how it usually works; seniors usually do play the leads. Her words shake my confidence and make me wonder why Mr. Preston chose me.

Quinn smiles my way, but her smile doesn't reach her eyes. It's like a clown smile someone drew on her face with pink lipstick.

I try not to let it distract me. I have a job to do. I look down at my script. Highlight my lines.

Someday Broadway.

The next afternoon, we run songs next to the piano. Nerves tingle in my hands and feet. I hear my heart beating in my ears as I wait for my turn. I can do this. I know I can.

I listen to the first song. Kace sings "Something's Coming." His pitch is perfect, his tone smooth and pure. Kace has a voice that draws you in and makes you want to listen. He doesn't miss a note. As I sit on stage and listen, my hands become clammy, my throat parched. I have never been so nervous to sing.

I reach for my water bottle. Take a sip. Breathe in and out. Try to focus.

The atmosphere in the room changes. Crackles. An electricity surrounds me like lightning. I sense him before I see him.

Hair like a lion's mane. Chaos and order at the same time. Soulful eyes with stories to tell. Though he is at the back of the theater, I know who he is. The same as before. It's as if I know him.

I close my water bottle. Pretend to look at my script. Instead, I watch him. He wears jeans and a long-sleeved T-shirt with a blue backpack slung over one shoulder. Sneakers. He is lanky, like he doesn't eat much. He moves gracefully and slowly, taking a seat in the first row.

What does his voice sound like? I imagine it to be deep, smooth. His lips are round, in contrast to the sloping arches of his cheekbones. I find myself looking again at the scar on his chin. It must have been painful.

I am awakened from my hypnotism by applause. Everyone is clapping for Kace. I hear my hands clap together. It sounds overly loud. I try to soften them so my clapping isn't so jarring. But I am not thinking about Kace and his song.

When Mr. Preston calls my name, I don't hear him at first. Someone next to me pokes me in the side. "Stella, that's you."

Embarrassed, I stand quickly and move toward the piano.

Mr. Preston nods. "I want to run your solo of 'Somewhere.' Then you can work on it at home. Try to layer it with emotion. Remember, you close the show. I want to feel your pain, your loss."

"I understand," I tell him. My throat is so dry. I swallow, gulp air. I hope I can deliver. I've practiced at home, but I've never performed this song in front of anyone.

Just then, Mr. Preston notices him and steps to the other side of me, closer to the edge of the stage. "Ah, Mr. Rivers. Thank you for coming. Please, join us."

Everyone turns and watches as the stranger moves toward the steps on the left of the stage. Whispers swirl around me like the gnats that come out before sunset and hover in masses over the grass, waiting to bite.

"Who is he?"

"Why is he here?"

"He's new."

"Is his name on the cast list?"

"I don't know."

I watch him as he comes closer. His eyes should be on Mr. Preston, but they are locked with mine. They are the color of the sky on a summer day. I can't breathe. How in the world will I sing?

Mr. Preston stops him by throwing an arm around his shoulders as though they are old friends. "People, this is Hayden Rivers."

Hayden Rivers.

Hayden. I have a name for him now.

Mr. Preston is still speaking. "Hayden is a new student here, and thankfully, he plays the piano. Much better than I do!" Everyone erupts in laughter at that. When Mr. Preston plays, he bangs on the keys as if he is fighting with the piano. He butchers Rodgers and Hammerstein and Leonard Bernstein and Stephen Schwartz, turning their classic songs into commercial jingles.

Mr. Preston raises one hand for silence, but he is laughing with us. "So I've begged and pleaded, and Hayden agreed to help us out." He holds up his hand to his mouth in a conspiratorial manner and says to Hayden in a stage whisper, so it is loud enough for everyone to hear, "Don't tell them how much I have to pay you!"

Hayden smiles shyly, seemingly at the group. But he only looks at me.

I hold my breath and wait for him to speak. I anticipate the smooth, deep voice I have imagined.

"Th-thank . . . you. Gl-glad . . . to . . . help." Hayden's voice is halting. Staggered. Slow. As though it is difficult for him to form the words. His voice is nothing like I expected.

I'm disappointed, somehow. I look down at my hands and weave my fingers together. Hold on tight.

Some students whisper to one another. Judge him. Words like "weird" and "strange" reach my ears. One comment is louder than the rest. It booms in my ears like a loudspeaker.

"Is he an alien?" This provokes laughter. For some inexplicable reason, I feel protective. So much so that it overcomes my shyness, my disappointment. Everything. I want to cover Hayden's ears so he can't hear their words. I look at him, hoping to help somehow. And I find myself caught in his stare. I don't look away.

"Okay then. Introduction's over." If Mr. Preston heard the comments, he doesn't show it. He points at me instead. "Stella over there is our Maria. She's next."

I watch as Hayden glides toward me with a smooth gait, seemingly oblivious to the stares and whispers. Our eyes lock as though neither of us wants to be the first to look away.

When he steps behind me to sit at the piano, my skin tingles. A shiver runs through my stomach. The air shifts around me as though it has been rearranged.

I wait to hear the notes of the introduction. I expect to hear the song I have rehearsed. But when Hayden begins to play, the room spins. I am captivated by the emotion in the music. The notes dance in the air, as Hayden breathes life into the song.

His head is bent over the piano keys. Hair hides his face. I watch in wonder as Hayden's fingers create a story without words. Somehow, at the right moment, I open my mouth and sing. I find the rhythm, the hills and valleys of the melody. The pain and anguish of loss in the song. I pour everything I have into my performance.

I am no longer myself. I am Maria. Every inch of my being is filled with her sorrow. I don't think about the lyrics or the sound of my own voice. I am lost in the music. The moment.

The last note is soft. Filled with heartache. I hear the sound disappear. The silence slaps me. I startle awake, as though I slipped out of my own skin and have now returned. My first instinct is to look at Hayden.

Our eyes meet. It is as if we have just danced together. I smile, thanking him. He grins back like we share a secret. In that split second, we are the only two people on the stage. The only two people in the world. No one has ever looked at me like this before. I am hot and cold at the same time, but I have never felt so present. There is nothing but this moment. It is only then that I notice the applause.

"That's what I'm talking about, people," Mr. Preston tells us. "Nice work, Stella. Sing it that way opening night, and we'll get a standing ovation."

It's the biggest compliment I can imagine. I duck my head and thank Mr. Preston softly.

Kace is called up next with the Jets. As he passes me, he bows slightly. Bestows a leading man smile. I have earned his respect. I may be a sophomore, but Kace now believes I am worthy of standing beside him on stage.

I am released while the Jets rehearse. I can go home. But I wish to stay just a bit longer. I linger over my backpack. Try to sneak one more look at the piano, except students block my view. I can't see him.

But I can hear the music as I leave the stage.

Touching my heart with the language of sound. Magical.

NEW

STELLA

I walk through the halls, suddenly popular. Everyone knows my name now. I am instantly elevated. Just like that. I am the star of the school musical.

"You are über famous," Lily says.

The third cheerleader in a row calls, "Hi, Stella."

"Who knew being your BFF was going to land me a spot on the varsity squad?"

I shrug, downplaying my own happiness at finally being noticed. "I'm just the flavor of the month. No big deal."

Lily nods and forces a grin. For a split second, I think I spot jealousy lurking in the shadows of her smile. Then it is gone. And I can't be sure if I imagined it.

"Nada importante," Lily agrees. I hear sarcasm hiding in the syllables. Little drops of envy mixed with bitterness. I hope I am wrong. That I am overly sensitive to being the center of attention.

I spot Hayden leaning against his locker. His eyes are almost hidden under a canopy of tangled hair. But they find mine like a guiding star. I am drawn to him. So much that it takes me by surprise. I catch my breath. Wonder what I am doing. Mesmerized by a boy.

I must stay on course. I have a goal. A focus. Someday Broadway.

My mother lost her focus when she met my dad. She abandoned her goal of becoming an actress. She never went to New York, London, or Hollywood. She never lived her dream. Instead, she became an accountant in suburbia. And then he left her. For his twenty-something trainer with flat abs and a spray tan. Love breaks your heart and leaves you sobbing on the kitchen floor.

So I keep walking. I don't stop.

Every day, I stand on stage, reciting my lines. Singing my songs. I think I am acting. Pretending I am Maria. That I love Tony. Kace looks into my eyes. Holds my hand. But I don't see him. I am thinking of Hayden. I am not acting. I know this. I am singing my songs to Hayden. I am afraid he knows this. So I stop looking at him.

Lily has US History with Hayden. She's nicknamed him SC for the Scarecrow in *The Wizard of Oz.* She rattles off a list of all the things that are wrong with him.

"He's awkward, has perpetual bedhead, and a speech problem. His fashion sense is très horrible. Y.C.D.B."

Lily likes to say things in code. Y.C.D.B. means "You Can Do Better."

"Kace is perfect for you," she announces at lunch. "You could be like a Hollywood It couple. The stars of the musical, falling in love." Her voice gets all romantic and dreamy.

I roll my eyes, take a bite out of my apple. I want to tell her that I'm not interested in Kace. I sing my songs to Hayden, I want to say. But I don't. Because Hayden's never even spoken to me. He looks at me like he knows me, like I mean something to him. When I sing, he plays the piano. That's all, but it's better that way.

After my parents split up, I vowed that I will never fall in love. I will never feel the pain of betrayal my mother has felt. I will never trust a boy with my heart. Yet somehow, I find myself wanting the something I vowed never to want. And wanting it with Hayden.

Dress rehearsal. I love my costume. It's flowing and white, feminine and graceful. It makes me feel immortal. I think of the words my mother says all the time to Emerson, my younger sister, and me.

"These are some of the best moments of your life. Embrace them."

I embrace this moment. Spinning around in the mirror, entranced by my reflection, I am a whirling ring of white light. My life has endless possibilities. I breathe deep. Hold tight to this moment. Smile at myself.

I know all my lines. Hit every note. I feel like I am outside myself and inside myself all at the same time. Emerson sneaks into the auditorium to watch. She sits in the middle of the theater with her freshman friends. Waves at me. It makes me happy to know she is there.

Today, Kace and I will kiss on stage for the first time. Before now, we have just marked it. This is Maria and Tony's first kiss. The one that declares their love for each other. The kiss that changes everything.

This won't be my first stage kiss. I've been in *Beauty and the Beast* and *Hairspray.* I've had to pretend kiss before. It's like pretend holding hands, like walking and talking in character. It doesn't mean anything. This I know. But I've never real kissed. Not where it means something—everything.

So when Kace leans in to kiss me, I force my mind blank. I am Maria. Not Stella. This means nothing to me. It is like walking and talking. I am playing a role. I am Maria, he is Tony. I expect to feel nothing. Only his kiss surprises me. It isn't nothing. His kiss is soft and gentle. Sweet.

He watches me as we break apart at the exact same moment, as we have been directed. But I notice that his forest-colored eyes have ribbons of gold running through them, and that his hand lingers on mine for a second longer than necessary. I don't have time to think about it, though, because I have to finish the scene. I click into performance mode and am Maria once again.

Before I know it, I am singing my last song. The first piece Hayden ever played for me. Kace lies on the floor. Still. Silent. I kneel beside him, and I fill the song with Maria's despair. Her love for Tony. Her grief. Tears fall from my eyes as I hold my last note. And then the curtain drops.

A wide grin breaks out over Kace's face. He opens his eyes. Looks right at me. Nods his approval. I meet his smile with one of my own. I have earned my place here, I know that now. A wave of confidence rushes through me, grounding me and giving me strength. Adrenaline sends tingles through my body—the after-shocks of performance. I can't think straight. I am half Maria and half Stella. Not quite myself.

The cast begins rushing to the wings, taking their places for the curtain call. My head is still muddled as I move off-stage. Kace and I will enter from opposite sides for the curtain call. And we will be the last ones to take our bows.

Moments later, I cross the stage to take my place beside Kace. I can almost hear the thundering applause, see the standing ovation. I imagine my mother sitting beside my sister in the audience. Someone bringing me a bouquet of red roses tied with a gold ribbon. I take my bow. And the curtain drops.

The cast turns to one another and cheers. We have worked hard to get here. Every single one of us deserves the imagined applause. I turn to Kace.

"You're going to be amazing."

"And you will take their breath away," he says softly, his hazel eyes resting on mine.

There is a brief second of something unsaid. It trickles through his words, but I can't quite grasp it. He turns and quickly walks away. I watch him go. Wonder if his complimenting me is disloyal to Quinn. Or if there is something else. I realize my hands are clasped together. As if they hold the compliment tight.

Later, we all gather in a circle on the floor of the green room, sharing a celebratory pizza. Hayden sits on the other side of the circle between two senior girls. They are talking to him. They make it look so easy. Like Lily. I wonder why it is so hard for me.

Quinn starts a game. "Name your dream vacation." We go around calling out our answers.

"Hawaii."

"Paris," Kace says and sends one of his leading-man grins my way.

I feel my cheeks burn hot. Quinn glares at me. I don't dare look at Hayden. I reach for my water.

"Australia."

"London."

"New York."

"Bahamas."

Now it is my turn. I haven't yet decided what I will say. As I look around the circle, I catch Hayden watching me. I don't look away. Instead, I lock eyes with him. And I say the first thought that comes to my mind.

"The beach."

Hayden grins. His teeth are blinding against the copper of his skin. Does he think my answer is silly? Is he laughing at me? The beach is fifteen minutes away. It's not exotic. But it is the truth; I would rather be at the beach than anywhere else on earth. I love the roar of the waves pounding in my ears. The screeching of the seagulls. The endless expanse of the sea. It makes me feel peaceful and happy. My parents used to take us to the beach as a family. My happiest memories aren't of Christmas mornings or birthday presents. My happiest memories are of long summer days at the beach.

I look down at my pizza as the rest of the cast calls out

exotic destinations. I wish I had come up with something unique. Exciting.

"Hayden, you're up," someone calls.

Only then do I look up from studying every pocket of grease on my slice of cheese pizza. I look up to see him.

Hayden looks right at me. And says two words. "The . . . beach."

Later, Mr. Preston stands in the middle of the circle and gives us notes. I write them on a notepad. When I finish, I notice Quinn staring at me. Her eyes are narrowed. I imagine she is hoping I get sick tomorrow so she can have her chance. I glance away, pretending I don't see.

At the end of the notes, Mr. Preston claps his hands together. "I am so proud of you all. I can't wait for your friends and families to see this magnificent performance. In all my years here . . ." He pretend-coughs to hide the number 25. "I have never worked with such a talented group. This show is worthy of Broadway. I want you all to know that. You are tremendous. Each and every one of you." Mr. Preston's voice shakes a little at this last part. Then he covers it by clearing his throat. "Now go home and rest up. I'll see you here tomorrow at five for costumes and makeup."

We scatter. I head to the wings to retrieve my backpack and sweatshirt. As I lean over to get them, I realize I am right next to Hayden. He is turned away from me. Looking for his own backpack, probably.

The wings are the darkest part of the theater tonight, meant for hiding entrances and exits. We have to learn to see in the shadows. He doesn't know I am here. I study him, memorize everything about him: the pattern of his plaid shirt, the rip in the knee of his jeans, a woven leather bracelet he wears on his right wrist, the keychain dangling from his pocket in the shape of a silver knot.

He turns suddenly, as though he can sense me. I shift my eyes quickly, not wanting him to catch me staring. I wonder, not for the first time, what in the world is wrong with me.

"St-st-el-la," Hayden says in his jarred speech.

Yet my name sounds beautiful the way he says it, each letter drawn out. Melodic.

I glance back at him and catch my breath. His gaze holds me. Standing here alone, in the shadows, time seems to stop. Sound fades away. All I know is Hayden.

"Stella!" My sister's voice startles me. I take a small step backward, away from Hayden, from this moment. Emerson is still talking. "I've been looking for you. Mom's waiting."

"Okay, I'm ready to go."

She looks from me to Hayden and back again. I can tell she is trying to figure out what she missed.

Nothing, I want to tell her. And everything.

"Bye," I say softly as I walk away. I try to see his eyes, his expression, but he has turned away. The shadows close in around him. He doesn't answer.

"What happened?" Emerson asks me before we are out of earshot.

"Hayden," is my only answer.

I turn to look at him once more. But he has already disappeared.

IT

STELLA

Tomorrow is opening night. I should be at home drinking tea in my pajamas. Resting my voice. Reading over my lines. Instead, I'm at a party with Lily. I never say no to Lily. No one says no to Lily.

Music throbs in my ears. I want to go home. I need to sleep. Meditate on my performance. This is the last place I want to be.

Lily drags me around. We're looking for someone. Connor Williams, her latest obsession. "He is très fabulous," she tells me. "We are M.F.E.O." Made For Each Other.

I roll my eyes. Last week, she thought she and a guy who plays drums in the school band were M.F.E.O. He never even learned her name.

I want to tell her about Hayden, about what happened today. Hearing him speak my name. Suddenly, my world has changed. Shifted. Only I can't explain it. Or that it scares me, enough that I've spent the past few hours reminding myself of my pledge.

No boys. No distractions. Someday Broadway.

The party is a sea of bodies. All of them blend into one wave of popularity, the wave Lily wants to ride. She carries me along with her into the current whether I like it or not. I can't breathe here. I can't seem to keep my head above water. I just want to go home.

And then I see him. Hayden leans against the back gate. His blond curls brush his shoulder. I want to touch them. He stares at me. I don't look away.

I can't.

I'm captivated by him.

Lily sees him too. "Imagine that. SC is here. Staring. At. You. Again. Très predictable."

And that's when I see the flicker in her eyes. It is gone almost as quickly as it appears. But not before I understand.

Hayden is "nada importante" in Lily's world. She doesn't want him.

But no, it's not that. She doesn't like him being interested in me. Not one bit. In Lily's world, she should have a boyfriend before I do. Before the shy new girl. The girl who doesn't even want a boyfriend.

Lily rolls her eyes. Annoyed with this game of silence. "Speak," she tells me. "Say something. Anything!"

I look into his eyes, into the depths below the surface. I want to know more—need to know more—but I don't say a word. Neither does Hayden.

"N.B.," I remind her softly. *No boys.*

She knows my mantra, but she doesn't agree with it. She gives me a long look. The kind only a best friend can give you. The kind of look that tells you they don't believe you. I meet her eyes, and she sees it there. She squeezes my hand.

She can tell that I am afraid of this feeling, of what it means. Someday Broadway, I tell myself. I let Lily pull me away.

We find Connor. Lily isn't silent. Lily isn't afraid. She makes jokes, gives compliments. I watch in awe. She giggles, tilts her head to the side so her hair falls across her face. Lily looks so pretty when she smiles. She has perfect teeth and a wide, inviting grin. She tries on his baseball cap, poses in it. Then she plays with his hair, dubbing it "hat head." She puts the cap back on Connor, leaving her perfectly manicured hand resting lightly on his shoulder.

Other girls walk by and look at her enviously. She is where they want to be. Connor is handsome, super popular, with a deep, rich baritone voice. Captain of the football team. He has olive skin and dark hair that contrasts with Lily's blondeness. Together they look like a Homecoming couple.

I stand next to her, feeling like the frumpy best friend, listening to Lily speak to Connor in French. The lilting language sounds like a love song. He doesn't understand a single word, of course, which makes it even more charming. He looks at her like she is a brand-new toy he wants. I stand there, bored, ignored. Wondering where Hayden is now. Wishing I wasn't afraid. Wishing I had a little bit of Lily's courage.

Connor's friends from the football team start joking around.

"Who's the hottie?" one asks as he joins the group. He pushes me out of the way to stand by Lily. Another one touches her hair. Lily giggles, relishing the attention.

A shiver runs down my spine. A premonition. A warning.

"Lily," I whisper. "Maybe it's time to go."

"N.O.Y.L.," she hisses in Lilyspeak. I mentally translate: Not On Your Life. I shoot her a look of annoyance. This is not what I want to be doing right now.

Connor claims Lily with an arm around her shoulders. One of the football players takes Connor's baseball cap. They toss it around. Then they start trying to tackle one another. Before I know it, someone is pulling Connor toward the pool. He drags Lily with him, holding onto her for safety. They are at the edge of the pool. Lily is enjoying the game, and she pretends to protect Connor. Her arms are wrapped around him. She is still laughing.

"Lily, I want to go. I have the show tomorrow," I remind her.

But she ignores me. Like she can't hear me.

I want to escape, to leave this place. But I can't. Not now. Because in one instant, everything changes.

"Hottie needs a cool down." Five words alter everything.

One of the football players picks up Lily and pretends to throw her in the pool. Lily plays along, flailing her arms and legs, but she is giggling. At the last second, he pulls her back. He hands her off to another player like a football. The guys line up so they can pass her around.

"*Lily, I need to go,*" I call out, trying to get closer. Desperate to leave this party, to go home. And there's something else—this inexplicable foreboding I cannot shake. The crowd moves closer to watch, and I am pushed to the side. Hemmed in by nameless faces laughing at—and with—my friend.

Hollering mixes with the drumbeat, cocooning the party in discordant sound. I duck under arms and around shoulders, finally emerging near the edge of the pool. I am just in time to see two things: Lily lands in Connor's arms, and Connor tosses her into the pool.

Everyone starts clapping. Everyone except me. Lily surfaces and swims toward the edge. I reach out a hand, help her out of the water.

"Can we please go now?" I whisper. Lily has curls plastered to her face, eyes dripping mascara tears. But she is smiling.

"G.M.A.B.," she hisses. Translation: Give Me A Break.

It's a standoff. I want to leave; Lily wants to stay.

Connor moves toward Lily, arms open for a hug. "Forgive me?"

"Not quite," Lily slides around him, rejecting his embrace. She stifles a giggle as she shakes her wet curls at Connor. "How do you like it?" Then she pushes him toward the pool.

I can't watch anymore. "Then I'm leaving without you," I tell her. I know it's a violation of the Best Friend Code to abandon a BFF at a party, but Lily has left me no choice.

Lily shrugs. "Nada importante."

I don't know if this means I am not important, or that my leaving is not important. It stings either way. And either way, it's my signal to go.

Connor wrestles Lily back, easily swinging out of her grasp.

"You'll have to do better than that," he teases. "Maybe you want to go in again."

Lily laughs and runs around Connor. She pushes him from the other side.

I am still standing here. Why am I still standing here?

I turn to go. I'll have to call my mom to pick me up.

Then Connor spins around. Pulling away from Lily, he collides with me.

The force hits me sideways. I can't catch myself. I am falling.

The music is blaring. But I hear one voice.

"St-st-el-la . . ."

My head strikes concrete. The blow reverberates through me like a prelude to something ominous. And I know, but it's too late. I scream. The sound is muffled. It comes out wrong.

Water engulfs me.

I'm drifting. Down, down, down.

Weightless. And then there is blackness.

Just blackness.

Blond curls float like a halo around his head. His arms encircle me, lifting me as though I'm a feather. It's so quiet here. I feel safe. Peaceful. Free.

I let go and just be.

One moment is all it takes

HAYDEN

"St-st-el-la!" I call out to her, try to warn her, but it's too late. When I see her fall into the water, I don't even think. I just dive in after her without waiting for anyone else. I expect to help her out, but she isn't swimming. She is floating.

Drifting. Motionless.

Something is wrong. I sense it immediately. The water is murky, lit only from the lights above. Her hair spreads out like a dark cape around her shoulders. I reach for her and hold her in my arms. She is so light, so beautiful.

I bring her up through the water. Out of the darkness to the light.

I hear a buzzing sound like the humming of bees. When I break the surface, I realize.

It's not bees.

It's chaos. All eyes are fixed on me. Someone is shrieking. I recognize the voice of Stella's friend, Lily.

I gently carry Stella out of the pool, holding her tight against my wet shirt. Wishing I had a warm blanket to wrap her in.

"St-st-el-la, breathe," I whisper. I don't know if anyone else tries to get close, to help. I don't give them a chance. I learned CPR a long time ago, because in my life, emergencies are an everyday occurrence. I never imagined that one day I would use the skill at a high-school party.

Her lips are blue. I lean over her still body and listen for her breath.

Nothing. I fit my mouth over hers. And I breathe for Stella.

I will her to live. To come back to me.

"Breathe," I plead.

Live.

And then, as if she can hear me, she breathes. Water sputters in her throat. I turn her to the side to let the water spill out of her mouth. Someone cheers. Then I hear sirens. They silence us all.

Someone hands me a towel. I lay it over Stella to tuck the warmth into her.

That's when I see blood seeping through her hair on the side of her head.

"I need another towel," I call out. It's worse than I thought, but I know better than to panic. Staying calm in an emergency has saved my life more than once.

So I stay in control and focus on what I need to do. Someone hands me another towel. I place one hand on her cheek. With the other I press the towel against her head and try to stop the bleeding.

Then there is one moment—one silent moment—when she opens her eyes. They are deep and full. And she sees me. The past, the present, and a future that hasn't even been written are there in her eyes. I am in her eyes. Then she closes them. Slips away from me.

The paramedics arrive, and I have to back up. They thank me for my help, and then they take over. I don't take my gaze off of Stella. Behind me, I can hear Lily crying and making a big scene about calling Stella's parents.

I just watch her. I want her to wake up again. To see me.

But she doesn't.

The paramedics move her to a stretcher. They wrap her in a blanket and head toward the back gate. I move with them, not wanting to let Stella out of my sight.

"I'd like to ride in the ambulance," I tell one of them. The friendlier looking one. "So she isn't alone."

"Only family's allowed." He raises an eyebrow, challenging me to say I am her brother, or her cousin. To lie. But I don't lie. Ever. My mother lies with every single breath she takes, and I have vowed never to be like her. Even now, even when it matters.

So I try for the truth instead. "Can you make an exception?" I plead. "Just this once?"

He looks over at the other paramedic. "The kid did save her life," he offers.

The other paramedic finally nods.

They let me ride in the ambulance with her. They give me a blanket, which surprises me, because I forgot I was wet. I sit beside her and hold her small, cold hand in mine. Her eyes are still closed. She hasn't opened them. I don't know if she can hear me, but I talk to her anyway.

"St-st-el-la, it's me, Hayden. You're go-going to be o-okay. You g-got pushed into th-the pool and h-hit your head. B-but you're o-okay. We're go-going to the hospital. They'll t-take care of y-you there." Then, "I'm here."

I don't speak after that; I just hold her hand. A mask covers her nose and mouth. Her skin is pale against the blue blanket tucked around her. Like moonlight against a midnight sky. Her lashes fan delicately across her cheeks. Everything about her is so still.

They have bandaged her head. Bruises are already forming in patterns on her forehead. This is not how I imagined being with Stella. But here I am.

Why am I doing this, letting myself get so close? It's better if I keep to myself. It's better not to let anyone in. Trust is synonymous with pain. And love is nothing more than a shiny, wrapped present that turns out to be empty inside.

But from the first moment I saw her in the school hallway, I knew. Something was different. I was drawn to her. Not just because of her beauty—her long, dark hair, and her golden eyes. Not just because of her voice, which is so natural and pure it is like nature's song. It's something more. It's as if an invisible chain binds us together. So even though I know I shouldn't be reaching out to her, I can't help myself.

I may not believe in love, but I do believe in destiny. I was meant to be at the party tonight. I was meant to save her life. I knew it the moment she looked at me. I just don't know why.

NOT ME

STELLA

I open my eyes. Everything's blurry. I'm in a room I don't recognize. Green walls, blinking machines. And I realize—this is a hospital.

Dreams drape around the edges of my consciousness like sheer curtains. Confusing me. What am I doing here? I can't remember.

My mother sleeps in a chair next to my bed. She looks like she needs a shower.

My mouth feels gummy. Dry. My head throbs. I smell like blood. Disgusting. My stomach rises to my mouth. I can taste the vomit. My eyelids are weighted down and achy. I lift my fingers and reach out for Mom's hand. I brush it lightly. Her eyes flutter open. She sees me. Starts to cry.

That's when I remember. The party. The pool. Drifting into nothingness.

Mom is saying something. Kissing my face.

It's only then I realize.

The silence.

I can't hear her. I can't hear anything.

What's happening? Why can't I hear her? My mother's mouth is moving, but it's like someone pressed mute on the remote.

I open my mouth to speak. "What happened?" I still can't hear anything, so I say it louder. "What happened?!"

Still nothing.

I feel my voice rising in the back of my throat, gliding across my vocal chords, exploding out of me.

"I can't hear anything!"

My mother stands. Her eyes wide, she reaches out for me and holds me tight. All I hear is silence.

I squeeze her hand and close my eyes. Maybe it's just a dream. A nightmare. If I can just wake up . . .

When I open my eyes again, a nurse is here. My mother grips my hand. My father is speaking to the nurse. I see his lips moving, but I still hear nothing.

Weird to see my parents in the same room.

I float in and out. I can't tell if I'm asleep or awake. Maybe I'm dead. Maybe this is heaven. It's peaceful. Simple. Quiet.

I see him again. Blond curls float like a halo around his head. His arms encircle me. Lift me and hold me close. I feel safe.

I want to stay here forever.

Walking an unfamiliar road

HAYDEN

I've been at the hospital for hours. Waiting. Here, there are no exceptions for me. Only family is allowed in the room. But I know she is going to be okay. I heard the doctor tell her parents. She is sleeping now.

Her mother has been really kind to me. She thanked me for saving Stella. Hugged me, even. Her dad thanked me too, shaking my hand over and over like he didn't know what else to do. Her little sister just looks at me like she can't quite figure me out. But that's okay, I can't figure myself out either. Like why I am still sitting here, waiting for her to wake up.

I sip the hot chocolate that one of the nurses brought me. I've read every magazine on the table, and I've watched the news on the television in the corner.

Time passes slowly when you are waiting. I try not to think about other times I've been in the hospital. Those thoughts only make my chest hurt, like it's in a vise being tightened and tightened until I can no longer breathe. Instead, I think of Stella. It's way past midnight, almost morning, which means that tonight is the musical—her musical—but she won't be on stage. After all her hard work, someone else will be Maria tonight. That will break her heart.

I stand to throw out the paper cup, and that's when I see her mother coming down the hallway toward me.

"She's still resting," she tells me. Tears are in her eyes. "But I thought you might like to see her."

"But I thou-ought it w-was only f-family," I manage. I hate my voice. It's such a traitor. It betrays me over and over again.

Stella's mom doesn't react to the sound of my stammering; she just nods. "I know they said that. But you've been here all night. Maybe if you could see her, you could go home and get some rest."

I nod and follow her back to Stella's room. I stand in the doorway and see her in the giant hospital bed. Her beautiful eyes are closed, but she doesn't look peaceful. There are tubes in her arm, a mask over her face. Beeping machines monitoring her every breath, every heartbeat. It is cold in here. Stark.

Suddenly, I am hit with a barrage of memories coming so quickly, I cannot sort through them; I can only feel their impact as they hit me. That familiar pain shoots through me like an arrow, leaving me alive but wounded. Damaged.

For a split second, I do not see Stella in the hospital bed—I see myself. And I am all alone with my broken limbs and bruised face. Grandfather would say time is the great healer. But after all these years, I am still a battered ten-year-old boy lying in a hospital bed. All alone.

I am startled by a touch on my arm. I turn my head to see Stella's mom beside me.

"P-Please don't le-leave her a-alone," I plead.

"I won't," she promises. "Hayden, thank you for everything you did for Stella." Her voice catches, and she begins to tear up. "I am so grateful to you. If you hadn't been there . . ." Her voice trails off. She doesn't need to finish. We can both imagine what might have happened.

Stella is lucky to have a mother who loves her so much. For a split second, I wish she was my mother. Standing in a hospital room, crying because she might have lost me. And grateful because I am still here.

I blink away the thought before it takes hold. Because if I have learned anything, it's that there is no sense wishing for things that can never be.

"Th-thank you for let-letting me s-see h-her," I say.

"Please go home and get some rest. You can come back in a little while and see her again. Maybe she will be awake by then."

"Okay," I answer. I don't want to leave, but I am still in the same clothes, and I stink of chlorine.

"Is there someone who can come get you? I can have Stella's father drive you home," she offers.

"My gr-grand-father," I say. My grandfather will come and get me. He already knows I am here.

I take one last look at Stella. I will her silently to wake up, to open her eyes, to see me.

She doesn't.

I turn and walk away.

HER

STELLA

Next time I open my eyes, I know.

I'm not dead.

This is not a dream.

This is happening to me. I don't need a doctor to tell me. I already know.

I can't hear anything.

Only silence.

I have no concept of time. It's like I've gone into a bubble, like in Miss America when the contestants go into that plastic room so they can't hear the questions. I'm in a bubble. Only I'm not sure I'll ever get out.

My face is swollen and bruised all over. My legs are achy. And my skin is raw from the stiff sheets that bind me to this bed. I hate the hospital gown, which smells like chlorine. The sleeves ride up on my shoulders and bunch up, irritating me. The florescent lights burn my eyes, so it's easier to keep them closed. I flex my feet back and forth. Counting from one to one million backward to one.

I go through a bunch of tests. They stick things on my forehead and watch me expectantly. They give me hearing test after hearing test. As though if they keep testing, the results will change.

When I do open my eyes, this is what I see. My mother is devastated, even though she tries to hide it from me. Her face is weepy every second. Emerson can't make eye contact. Her eyes dart around the room, looking for a way to escape. And my dad just stares at me, expressionless, like a rag doll without features. Between the three of them, I'm getting a pretty clear picture of what's going on. That what has happened to me is really serious. Maybe permanent.

A mixture of smells leaves me constantly nauseated. My dad's sandalwood cologne. The antiseptic soap the nurses use. The chicken soup they left on the tray next to my bed. Flowers from the bouquets that keep arriving. One of the nurses smokes on her breaks. Another one takes garlic vitamins. A third wears cherry Chapstick. I wonder if I have turned bloodhound. Every once in a while, when my sister is close by, I breathe in her clean-scented lotion. It makes me feel normal.

My mom never leaves. She is either sitting next to my bed or just outside the glass door. I stare at her. Notice how many lines she has around her eyes. When she smiles, her face crinkles. The lines used to make her look friendly. Now they just make her look old, like her face is cracking into pieces in front of my eyes.

I play a game with myself. When my dad is here, I try to find a wrinkle in his shirt. Just one little crease. I can't.

I try to read their lips. They move too fast. I can catch only bits and pieces.

They write me notes to explain things.

The injury to your head caused sensorineural hearing loss. That's why you can't hear anything.

When you're better, you can have surgery. You can get cochlear implants to help you hear again. Bionic ears. You'll be just like before.

Just like before.

I really have no idea what any of this means except that I don't want to deal with it. Any of it. I just want to disappear.

I close my eyes. Go back to that place in the blackness. Where I don't know anything.

The next time I open my eyes, Lily is here. Her gray eyes brim with tears, and she reaches for my hand. I test the feeling as her smooth, manicured hand touches my cold, clammy hand.

Everything around me instantly becomes clear. The fog lifts and reality comes into focus. This is my life. I can't disappear. This is real.

I wonder, am I angry with her? Do I blame her?

But there is nothing inside me except the feeling that this is Lily. She is my best friend.

I can't blame her; this wasn't her fault. It wasn't anybody's fault. It was an accident. A terrible accident. It could have been her instead of me. Or Connor. Or any of them.

I don't want Lily to wish it were her instead of me. But I know she does. I can tell from the look on her face. I close my eyes to hold back the tears that threaten to melt my mask. I refuse to let her see how scared I am. I don't want her to feel worse than she already feels. I know she would do the same for me.

So I force a smile. It feels fake, like it has been painted on my face.

That reminds me of something. Something my conscious mind has not allowed me to process, even if my unconscious mind has remembered. I think of Quinn. Her lipstick clown smile. Waiting for my failure so she could succeed. So she could play my part.

That's the moment the clouds move from my mind. Because while I am lying in this bed in silence, the school musical is going on without me. My chance is over.

My throat closes, and I can't breathe. I am gasping like I am underwater again. Pain and grief press in. Paralyzing me.

Lily touches the side of my face. I am numb. As though I am no longer myself. In these short moments, I have ceased to be me. Stella Layne is dead. Someone else is in her place.

Lily moves her mouth. I can't hear what she is saying. I try to make sense of it. To imagine what she might be saying to me.

"I am so sorry, Stella. How can you ever forgive me? You wanted to go home, and I stayed. It's all my fault."

Her words only make it harder for me to pretend. Because I realize just how alone I am. Lily presses a white teddy bear with a red T-shirt reading "Get Well" into the bed next to me. I wish it were that simple.

Lily's vanilla perfume and gardenia shampoo surround her in a pretty cloud. When she reaches out and hugs me, the cloud wraps around me. I want to feel comforted. I really do.

But I don't. I feel nothing.

HIM

STELLA

They leave me alone. All of them. Even the nurses. I stare up at the white ceiling. One thought drifts into another, like waves on the sand. Connecting and not connecting. Meaning something and meaning nothing all at the same time. I close my eyes.

And then I feel something. And I know. I don't see him enter the room. And I certainly don't hear him. But I know he is here. My skin tingles, and my body is warm all over. The aches and pains and tears are forgotten.

I smell meadows and sunshine. And then I open my eyes. I have to—I can't help myself. Our eyes connect.

The world that has been spinning around me comes to an immediate stop. And it freezes.

I see the moment from that night again like a movie on fast-forward.

The edge of the water. My fall. Floating. And Hayden.

"St-st-el-la. Breathe."

It was him.

Hayden saved my life.

I realize now that I have always known. He has been floating in and out of my dreams. Hayden.

He's holding a bouquet of daisies. For me. I don't know what to do. I feel the pressure of the bandage on my head. The ache of the bruises beneath my eyes. The grit on teeth I haven't bothered to brush. I smell the bloody, sweaty scent of myself. I want to yank the covers over my head. To hide. Anything to escape feeling this disgusting.

I cover my face with my hands. Humiliation sears every pore in my body. I want to disappear, to fade away. I close my eyes, waiting for him to walk away. To leave.

I wait for what seems like forever. But I can still feel him in the room. Even with my eyes covered. I know. So I peek through my fingers. He is still here. Watching me. I let my hands fall. I dare to look at him. Escape into his eyes.

And at that moment, I find my voice. I know exactly what to do.

"Thank you," I say. It isn't enough. I should say more. Only I don't know how my voice sounds. For the first time in my life, I can't rely on my voice. The awareness of it feels like a punch to my bruised face. I flinch from the knowledge.

Surprisingly, he smiles back. He moves his lips slowly. So slowly that I can read them. "You're welcome."

I can understand him.

I don't know how, but somehow I do. I understand.

I'm not alone. *I'm not alone.*

That's when tears fill my eyes and overflow onto my cheeks. The tears I have been holding back, bravely hiding from everyone. Everyone except for Hayden.

"Quinn?" I ask the question I haven't been able to ask anyone else.

I know the answer. Of course I do. She got her wish. While I lie on this bed, she is singing my songs.

What I don't expect is to see his eyes fill with tears. As if he understands just how much this means to me. And he isn't afraid to show it.

When I have run out of tears and my sobbing slows, Hayden leans close. He runs his warm fingers across my skin. Wiping away my sorrow.

Rays of sunshine splash across my face.

I want to fall into him. To lose myself there.

I bask in the sunshine for a moment. It is wonderful. Wonderful to have a moment of pure happiness.

Behind Hayden, I see my mother come through the door. She greets him as though she already knows him.

And I realize he's been here before. Maybe while I was drifting in the space between reality and memories of him. He was here. I just didn't know it. The idea feels like a feather of hope, floating pure and white, untouched, through the darkness of my thoughts.

I watch as he hands my mother the flowers, glancing toward me. I can see her saying something to him. Gesturing toward me. I look back at him. Hayden dips his head, letting his curls shade his eyes. As he watches me with hesitation. He gives me a half-smile. My stomach does a flip-flop. I smile back gently, no longer embarrassed. Hayden nods at my mother.

He smiles at me again. And then he is gone.

Hayden.

Understanding without words

HAYDEN

I didn't expect her to open her eyes. I didn't expect her to know it was me. But she did. I have been willing her to wake up—to see me. And when she finally did, she was so beautiful, all I could do was stare.

She looked so small and fragile in that big hospital bed. So lost, alone, silent.

I know about her injury. I know she may never hear again, may never sing again. But she's alive and that's all that matters. Life is precious. I should know.

My life has always been like scattered puzzle pieces, never fitting together, so I can't see the picture it's supposed to be. But there, in that hospital room with Stella, I could see a picture for the first time. And Stella is in it.

I walk slowly through the parking lot, wondering when I will see her again. Her mother says she will go home in a few days, and maybe I can see her then. It doesn't matter if she can't talk to me, can't hear me. She *understands* me. I saw that flash of realization in her eyes when she read my lips. Ironic that my speech problem would actually be good for something.

I wish I had brought her something better than daisies. My grandmother always said that daisies are happy flowers. I want to make Stella happy. To see her smile. But there are so many other flowers in the room already, fancy ones with teddy bears and balloons. Mine will be forgotten, overlooked.

She means something to me. It started before the accident, but I didn't want to admit it, didn't want to accept it. Now I know for sure. What I don't know is what Stella thinks. She seemed so unhappy to see me at first—covering her eyes and hiding from me. But then she let all that go, and we connected. She seemed peaceful, happy even. She has friends, family. So many people who love her. She doesn't know what it feels like to be alone, to have no one.

I pull my keychain out of my pocket. The sun glints off the silver knot, reminding me of my grandfather and of the day he made this for me. I was ten. He and my grandmother had taken me in. I wasn't alone anymore, but it took me many years to understand that. I will never forget his words to me that day.

"This knot binds us as family. We are stronger when we are woven together. We are unbreakable."

I think of his words as I drive home. Grandfather was wrong. Nothing is truly unbreakable.

DAYS

STELLA

Days flow one into another. I have no idea when one ends and the next one begins. I'm a bystander in my own life. Things happen around me, but I am oblivious to all of it. The daisies are my only happiness. My only reminder of something outside the endless silence.

I feel the softness of the white petals. They remind me of my feather of hope. Of him. And of the peace I felt when I was drifting through the water, held tight in his arms. I smell the scent of sunshine and meadows. And life. And it keeps me breathing.

As each day passes by.

In silence.

On the day the daisies begin to wither and turn brown, Connor Williams walks into my hospital room. He stands there looking like a character from a teen werewolf movie. All movie-star gorgeous—and completely out of place here. Here, with the antiseptic scent that floats through the room like a pungent cloud. The blinking machines that will hypnotize you if you look at them too long. And the broken girl in the bed clutching withered daisies.

His dark brown eyes widen at the sight of me. He glances behind him, looking for his mother or father, no doubt. Whoever forced him to come today. He takes a step toward me. I can smell his spicy cologne. It reminds me of my dad's. Connor wears a Richmond High Football shirt. I wonder if he has any clothing that doesn't advertise his status at school. His mouth moves, but I can't understand him. This is nothing new. I don't understand anyone. Anyone except Hayden.

Connor offers me a box of designer cupcakes and a single red rose. He is trying to make amends. To ask for my forgiveness. But there is nothing to forgive. It was an accident. It could have been any one of us who fell that night.

Only it wasn't. It was me.

And I didn't get to sing because of it.

I may never sing again.

I don't tell Connor any of this. I just force a smile to crease my face. I lift my arms and take the cupcakes from his hands. The scent of sugary frosting leaks through the cardboard box. It reminds me of my last birthday when I turned fifteen. The first birthday my parents celebrated separately.

My dad took me to his new house with his new family. And his new wife served me fancy cupcakes. I remember watching as she licked frosting off of my dad's fingers. Right in front of us. It made me want to vomit. Happy birthday to me.

I realize that Connor is staring at me. And that I am staring at the cupcakes. He is still holding out the rose. I take it from him. I hold it awkwardly.

"Thanks," I try to say. My throat is dry, and my tongue feels really thick.

Connor stands there shifting his weight from foot to foot. A muscle in his cheek tenses. And he keeps clenching his hands into fists and then stretching them out. I can almost hear the awkward silence in the room. I would have struggled to fill it before. When I could hear. It doesn't matter anymore.

After a few moments, the door opens, and thankfully, my mother enters with another woman. She has the same coloring as Connor and looks like she is my mom's age. So I guess this is his mom.

As she sees me in the bed, she tears up. Her eyes shift to her son and narrow. She is disappointed in him. Maybe disappointment will go away as soon as he throws the next winning touchdown.

"I'll be okay." I move my mouth to say the words. I want Connor and his mother to go away, to stop staring at me as if their feeling bad about me being here will make me better. It won't. I force my mouth into a smile again. I look at my mother. Beg her with my eyes.

End my misery. Make them go away.

Mercifully, she understands. She lifts the cupcake box from my arms. Takes the rose and sets it next to the bed. Then ushers them out of the room.

Connor doesn't even look back. I am sure I am forgotten the moment he steps across the threshold. Maybe even before.

The daisies are dead now. I can't keep them anymore. My mother brings me wax paper and shows me how to press one of the flowers. I choose my favorite daisy. We fold the wax paper around it. I press it between the pages of one of the books people have sent to me—a book of poetry. I think it is symbolic. My mother hands the rest of the flowers to the nurse. I watch as she carries them out the door. Away from me.

The sunlight is gone now. Darkness sets in.

I am in the shadows when the cast comes to visit. Mr. Preston leads them in. Like a final bow, they stand shoulder to shoulder around the bed. Kace and Quinn and all the rest of them. They have brought me a poster of the show, signed by everyone. The poster is a photo of me dressed as Maria, standing with Kace dressed as Tony. We hold hands and look at the camera. A sharp pain pierces my stomach. I use one hand and hold it there to keep the pain from spreading, from infecting the rest of me with its poison.

Mr. Preston takes one look at me and his eyes fill with tears. He reaches for my hand. Holds it gently and says something very moving to me—I am sure of it. If I could hear him, I would be touched.

I smile back, say my standard line. "I'll be okay."

Kace steps closer and gives me a half-hearted smile. His eyes look at me but there's no sparkling today. Ribbons of gray run through the green. Like snow melting in the mountains. I think he feels bad for me. I manage a small smile for him. He touches the top of my head softly, like a blessing. "You can do it," he seems to be telling me. Then he steps back to join the others.

Quinn looks in my direction but not actually at me. She wrings the sides of her dress in her hands, twisting the fabric tightly. Her shoulders are hunched. A sheen of sweat covers her forehead. She is the one who feels my loss most profoundly. Of course she would. My tragedy was her triumph.

They hand me gifts: candy and stuffed animals, books and magazines. I wish I could be happy to get them, wish I could feel grateful for their caring. But seeing these people around me is like ripping a fresh scab off a wound. I am bleeding again. And the pain is searing. Blinding. Tears burn my eyes, making the room swim in front of me. The faces blur and blend together.

I close my eyes for an instant as I struggle to gain control. I breathe deep, tasting the colognes and perfumes in my mouth. Tasting sympathy. I hate it. I hate being the center of attention for something that happened to me. If I had earned something, I'd be happy to receive accolades, applause.

This feels like being a caged eagle at the zoo. Chained at the leg. Restrained from flying. Watching with resignation as people stare. Gawk. Point. Knowing they will all talk about you later. Behind your back. This isn't the me I want people to notice.

But this is the me I am.

When I open my eyes again, they are all gone. But the poster remains to remind me of who I used to be.

Fading into the shadows

HAYDEN

I have visited her twice, but she didn't see me. The first time, I waited for two hours, but she didn't wake up. Didn't open her eyes.

She looked like a painting of Ophelia floating on water. For a moment, I thought she might never wake up. I wanted to kiss her to see if she would wake for me. But I didn't. I didn't leave a note or anything either, so she will never even know I was there. But I will know.

The second time, Connor Williams was walking down the hallway with his mother, carrying a box of cupcakes. I wanted to grab the box and throw it away. Tell him he has no right to see her, let alone speak to her. He caused her accident. I know it, he knows it, and she knows it. I blame him. Anger welled up in me, so strong I had to walk away. Or say something I would regret. Or do something I might regret. I have to remain in control—always. I can never let anger take over. Not like my mother—she can't control it. I can.

So I walked away. I didn't see Stella that time. I went for a run instead. Pushed myself to sprint harder and faster. Ran until each breath burned my lungs—and the anger had drained away.

My days are tedious, long. It's like someone has closed the shutters. I can see the sunlight streaking through the slats, reminding me of what is outside, but I can't touch it. I am closed inside the shadows until I can see her again.

DARKNESS

STELLA

It may be hours or minutes that go by. I don't know. Mom comes to my room with a pair of sweats and a tank top. She helps me out of bed. I get dressed. I slip my feet into flip-flops. Sit down in the gray-blue wheelchair. And Emerson wheels me out of the hospital. The nurses wave good-bye, as if leaving this place is a good thing. As if I am healed.

It takes forever for my dad to load all of the flowers and balloons and stuffed animals into the trunk. I know it should make me feel good that so many people care.

It doesn't.

I sit in the car and stare out the window. For once, I am glad I can't hear. It's weird to be in a car with Dad driving and Mom riding shotgun, with Emerson and me in the backseat. It's like we are a family again. Something we haven't been for two years.

The conversation will be about all the things we can do

when I get home. How I will be back to normal in no time. Only it's all a lie. In my silent world, I don't have to pretend otherwise. I can just shut them all out. And no one can blame me for ignoring them.

When we get home, I walk right into the house and straight to my bedroom. I close the door and turn to the mirror. It's not the first time I have looked in a mirror; there was a little one in the bathroom at the hospital. But it's different looking in my full-length mirror. Last time I looked at myself like this, I was on my way to a party. I was thinking about dress rehearsal. About Hayden.

Today is a new day. A different me. I study my reflection.

A white bandage clings to the side of my head, a white flag to remind me. As if I could forget. My hair has been shaved on one side. That doesn't even matter. The rest of my dark-brown hair looks greasy and tangled. My usually rosy cheeks are pale, which makes the purple and green bruises look even worse than they are. Amber eyes peer over gray circles, like a lamp that has been turned off. Dark and empty.

After all the sleeping I've done lately, it seems strange that I look so tired. I'm only fifteen but look forty. The aged remnant of the girl who used to be.

I don't look like myself. I look like someone else.

I *am* someone else.

I climb under my blue and white comforter. It feels soft compared to the sandpaper sheets at the hospital. I breathe in the smell of our detergent. And I pull the covers up over my head. Fresh lavender surrounds me.

Someday Broadway. The thought flutters in the darkness.

A golden butterfly seeking escape. It frees itself. Flies away. I watch *Someday Broadway* disappear.

And I close my eyes.

I wake in darkness. Still fully clothed, wearing my flip-flops in bed. I have no idea how long I've been sleeping or even what day it is. I sit up and feel the emptiness in my stomach. I need to eat something.

I climb out of bed and open my door. The house is dark and quiet. Then I remember, the world will always be quiet for me now. I head for the kitchen, flip on the light, and open the fridge. A wrapped turkey sandwich sits on a plate. Mom surely left it for me. It makes me feel bad, in a way. She is still trying to take care of me, and I have shut her out. But the truth is, I have no choice. I have no idea how to communicate now. And I have no interest in learning. I think about that movie about Helen Keller I saw years ago. It all seemed so inspiring then. When I wasn't her.

I sit at the table to eat my sandwich. For a split second, I think about turning on the small television in the corner. Then I remember. So I eat in silence.

The thing about not hearing is that it gives you a lot of time to think. Too much time to think. My brain keeps reliving the accident, over and over again.

I see myself standing near the edge of the pool. Falling. The water coming closer and closer. Then blackness. Silence.

NORMAL

STELLA

I wake up to see bright sunlight streaming through my shutters. It illuminates the posters on my wall. *Wicked, West Side Story, The Phantom of the Opera, Les Misérables, Chicago.*

Someday Broadway.

There is no Someday Broadway now. Without singing, I am invisible. A nobody. The girl with the voice is dead. Nothing can fix that. I lie there looking at the posters. Not moving, barely breathing.

Mom comes into my room. Her eyes fill with sympathy when she sees me staring at the posters. She comes to the bed and sits on the edge, wrapping me in her arms. She holds me tight. She's trying to tell me it will all be okay. When I was little and hurt myself on the swings at the park or by falling down at school, her embrace worked.

It doesn't anymore.

Because I'm not that girl anymore.

Mom hands me a small box wrapped in pink and white paper.

I tear off the paper, open the box, and there it is—the phone I have been coveting for three years. It is finally mine. I take it carefully out of the box. Run my fingers gently over the touch screen. It lights up. I glance at Mom. She is smiling. I can see tears glistening in her eyes.

Then she pushes the button for texting. And I realize. I can text. A message is waiting. I open it.

Your surgery is scheduled for Monday. It will only take a couple of hours, and then you can come right home. After a few weeks, they will program your implant, and you will be able to hear again. You can even go back to school.

"Thank you, Mom," I say. I don't know how loud or soft my voice is. I don't know what it sounds like at all. "This was a really good idea." I mean it. About the phone. It will make things seem almost normal. Almost.

I don't want her to know that the idea of returning to school terrifies me. That I am afraid I will never want to climb out of this bed. Afraid that the shadows of grief will suck me into blackness and never let me go.

So I pretend. I am a better actor than I thought. I force a smile and say, "Everything will be okay. I know it will" to make her feel better. I don't want pity or sympathy. I want to be treated just like before. So I do the only thing I can think of: pretend I am fine.

Even though I'm not.

I'm empty inside.

Locked in this cell of silence, time passes slowly for me. I am stuck with myself and my own mind.

Which can't think of anything good to say.

Turns out, the phone can hear for me. Mom has downloaded an app that turns speech into words I can read. She says something to me, and I can read it on the screen. Much better than writing things on paper. Much faster too. Sometimes the phone gets the words wrong, though.

Mom comes into my room and asks me about lunch. The phone transcribes the words. According to the phone, she wants to know if I want "grilled seas and tomato shoes for lunch."

I smile and say, "Yes. I would love grilled seas and tomato shoes." Mom doesn't get it. It's an inside joke between me and my new best friend, my phone.

Emerson resets the televisions for closed captioning. Now we can watch our favorite reality shows together because I can read what is happening in the white words on the bottom of the screen. It's like reading subtitles in a foreign film. Reading reality TV isn't nearly as much fun as hearing it. You can't exactly read the level of emotion in someone's voice. But it's better than not watching at all.

Dad tries to help by dropping off a stack of books from the library—mysteries and science fiction. Too bad he has absolutely no idea what kinds of stories I like. As Emerson and I look through them, we play a game. She holds up each book, making a pretend serious face as she does. We read the title together. And then we burst out laughing. Each one makes us laugh a little bit harder. The truth is, there is nothing funny about the titles. Or about the fact that Dad tried to do something thoughtful by bringing the books. We just need to laugh, and this is the first thing that has seemed amusing. So we laugh until our stomachs ache. We lie on the floor of the living room, side by side. And then Em reaches out and takes my hand in hers. She holds it tight. We stay like that. For once, my little sister is trying to take care of me. And for once, I let her.

Three days later, as promised, Mom takes me to the hospital. When she pulls into the parking lot, I shiver. The last thing I want is to be back here again. Mom parks and gets out of the car to open my door for me. She takes me by the elbow, like I am blind instead of deaf. We walk slowly through the parking lot. She leads me through the automatic doors. The smell hits me instantly. My reaction to it is so strong that I stagger. Stumble. Only Mom's grip keeps me from tumbling to the ground into the fetal position. She holds me tighter and nods at me.

We will get through this, I tell myself. And I move forward. Breathing through my mouth.

We take the elevator to a different floor. I am an outpatient this time. When we get to the waiting room, we sit on a small blue sofa with gray dots. Mom reaches for her purse and turns off her cell phone. I just look around the room.

We are not alone. A woman and a man sit across the room on a matching sofa—blue with gray dots. They have a little girl with them. She is tiny and frail. Maybe five years old. And completely bald. Her heart-shaped face houses two giant green eyes. So bright and large, they are like spotlights turned on me. She smiles. A beautiful, wide, happy smile. A smile of hope.

I return the smile, sending her good wishes with my eyes. Because in that split second—the amount of time it takes to receive and give a smile—a rainbow of emotions spreads through me. Guilt, regret, and embarrassment take on shades of green, purple and blue. Resolve is orange. Hope is pink. And love is red. I have been spending so much time feeling sorry for myself. With bitterness coloring my world gray.

This little girl is ringed in golden light. I remember Lily telling me about auras. This little girl's aura is one of faith. I wonder what my aura looks like. I imagine it is quite the opposite. This shames me. Causes me to break contact, study my fingernails.

I have been cloaking myself in misery. Wearing it. My situation is nothing like hers. I bite my lip as I think about my pity parties. In that moment, I make a silent promise to myself and to her. I will find my happiness again. I will make myself whole.

With my hearing.

Or without it.

I stand and move toward the little girl. She smiles as though she knows what I am going to do. As though she has been waiting for it. I smile at her parents. And then I sit next to her. I wait with her.

My mother watches me from across the room. A soft

expression of wonder plays across her features. Smoothing them. Making her look younger somehow.

When the nurse comes to get the little girl, she leans over and wraps her arms around me. She hugs me tight, resting her tiny head against my chest. She is so slight, but the weight of her hug is tremendous. It takes my breath away.

And then she is gone.

For the first time since my parents' split, I find myself praying. I close my eyes and pray for her.

When it is my turn, my mother touches my shoulder. I open my eyes to see a nurse waiting for us. We follow her to a small room. There I change into a gown decorated with a swirly blue and green pattern. The touch of the scratchy fabric on my skin triggers my nerves again. By the time the nurse gives me medicine to relax me, my heart is beating so fast that I can almost hear it. My hands and neck are sweating even though it's freezing cold in here.

I climb into the bed. Mom in the brown plastic chair next to me. She has brushed her hair today, pulled it off her face. Dark circles are around her eyes. Has she slept since the accident? Probably not.

Mom doesn't read a magazine or play with her phone. She just fixes a pleasant expression on her face. And watches me. While I watch her.

We wait. I think of the little girl. So brave and hopeful. Then I think of Hayden. Of his white daisies of hope. The touch of his fingers on my face. I start to get drowsy—the medicine is working after all.

The doctor comes in to see me. He writes everything down on a piece of paper. He uses really simple sentences. Here's how I interpret what he tells me:

I will go to sleep. He will cut into my skull and implant a transmitter in there. Then I will wake up dizzy. After a few weeks, I will get programmed. And I will hear again.

It sounds so simple. So easy.

The doctor is suntanned, as if he spends his afternoons on a boat in the middle of the Pacific Ocean. He has that confident look all doctors seem to have, like everything is going to be alright because they say so. For a split second, his confidence touches me. So when he gives me a thumbs-up and then waits for my response, I hold up my own thumb.

This is going to work. I am going to hear again.

When I open my eyes a few hours later, I'm not so sure.

I can't hear anything. And now my eyes don't work either. The room is spinning, and I feel seasick. My throat feels like someone has scraped it with a fork. I can barely swallow. I taste something bitter, like metal. All I can smell is antiseptic. I remember being wheeled into the operating room and counting backwards. I remember seeing Hayden's face in the blackness. That's the last thing I remember. I try to remember more, but I can't.

A nurse comes in and smiles when she sees I'm awake. She brings my mother into the room. Another smiling face. She writes me a note.

I can't read it. I shake my head, but that just makes me dizzier.

I close my eyes and go back to sleep. Back to the same dream I keep having over and over.

A dream of him.

When I open my eyes again, I have no idea if I've been sleeping for ten minutes or ten hours. But I do feel better. My stomach isn't churning anymore. And I can see clearly. Now I can read the note.

You did great. In a few weeks, you'll meet with an audiologist, and she'll help you with the next step. Soon you'll be able to hear again.

I wish I could say that I believe her. I wish I could say I am excited about it.

But I'm not. All I am is tired. And I want to go home.

Mom helps me into my clothes because I am still dizzy. The floor moves up and down like a fun house at the carnival.

Somehow, Mom gets me home.

I just want to sleep.

HIDE

STELLA

I feel the morning sun snake through my shutters, slithering across my pale blue walls, tempting me to join the living. I'm still dizzy, but I climb out of bed anyway. I stumble to the mirror to see how I look. A new bandage is attached to the side of my head, behind my ear. Otherwise, I look the same—like a train wreck.

I look at the calendar hanging on my wall. I flip the page to April and use my marker to circle April tenth, the day I meet with the audiologist. The day she programs my ears. The day I can maybe, possibly, hear again. Twenty days to go. I let the page drop back to March. That date seems as faraway as if it were a year.

I swallow a lump that is about to overflow into tears. As if pushing it into the rest of my body will somehow camouflage the feeling.

It doesn't.

I take a deep breath. My throat is still raw, but my stomach feels better. And I'm hungry. Really hungry. I manage to creep down the hall to the kitchen. Every step or two, I have to grab the wall to steady myself. Sweat runs down the back of my neck, and by the time I reach the end of the hallway, I am panting.

Emerson sits at the kitchen table, finishing last night's homework and munching on a bagel. She grins at me and scribbles a note on the side of her folder.

You look good. How are you feeling?

My sister has apparently adopted the party line: Stella is going to be fine. Em matches my mother in Positive Attitude 101. They are twin Pollyannas. It's like a bad dream. Everywhere I look are little yellow happy faces smiling at me and telling me to look on the bright side. I want to run from the room screaming. Instead, I grimace at her.

"Liar. How do I look like I'm feeling?"

At least you don't have to go to school, she writes. *Lucky you.*

That's looking on the bright side, I guess. Lucky me.

My younger sister has always wanted whatever I have. It's a given, ever since we were little. If I have it, she wants it. She has masses of auburn curls and melting brown eyes, a gorgeous combination, but she'd trade them in a second for my long, dark hair and tawny eyes. She's an amazing dancer, but she'd rather have my voice.

Just thinking about my voice makes me want to weep giant, bloodred tears.

I swallow them and force a smile at Emerson.

"I'm going back to school. As soon as I can stand up without toppling over."

Emerson's almond eyes widen at my words. Her mouth drops open, and I can see chewed bagel on her tongue. She writes in giant letters. *WHAT?*

"I'm going back to school," I say, as if repeating it will make the idea more palatable.

Because the truth is, the thought makes me sick to my stomach. But I know that going back will make me feel like it's all going to be okay. Staying home will make me feel like I have lost everything—even my academic success. No, I will just have to figure out how to get better in a day or two so I can get back to class.

Emerson frowns at me. Her slender face scrunches up, and she looks like a pug. I laugh. She writes another note.

This is your chance to stay home every day. That's what homeschooling is for! I'd do it if I could. Spend all day at dance class. No homework . . .

I laugh. "You wish." It feels good to talk to Emerson. It feels normal.

She writes again.

You should check your texts. Some people have been asking for your number. A certain person, actually, which my friends thought was really cool. This whole thing has been really good for my social status, you know. :)

She's teasing, of course. That's Emerson—always trying to make me laugh. I smile at her. "I'm really happy it's worked out so well for you," I retort.

She throws her head back. I can tell she is laughing even if I can't hear it. I imagine the sound, like tiny fairy bells. Emerson gets out of her chair and puts her arms around me—and almost knocks me over. But I steady myself and lean into her. It feels good to let her hold me. Tears prick the backs of my eyes. I blink them away quickly. Breathe deep.

When Emerson lets go, she helps me into a chair. Then she makes me a toasted bagel with butter, my favorite. I try to eat it. I take one bite. Chew slowly, willing the nausea to calm down. I try to swallow, but the bread claws at my throat. Almost chokes me. I grab the glass of milk Emerson has just poured. And I drink the entire glass. I look up to see Emerson watching me. She stands and heads to the fridge. Comes back with vanilla yogurt instead. I take the spoon she offers, dip it into the shiny, whitish mass in the cup. The yogurt slides down my throat. Soothing it. Cooling it. I nod. Then I smile. "Much better."

Emerson grins and munches her bagel. We eat together. It feels peaceful. Normal.

After breakfast, I make my way back to my room. I am less nauseated now but still gripping the wall. But better, definitely better. I lie down on my bed. Close my eyes. Breathe.

I can get through this, I tell myself. I know I can.

Mom comes in to check on me. She writes a note to say that she has to take Emerson to school and then she is working at home so she can keep an eye on me. I nod and smile, pretending to feel much better than I really do. Mom kisses the top of my head.

I close my eyes, will my body to rest. To heal. So I can get back to normal. This time, I don't dream of Hayden. I dream of bees flying into my ears, blocking them. I try to swat them away, but they keep coming until I can no longer hear anything but their buzzing. Then the bees swarm my throat, choking me. Stinging me. They make my throat swell up. I can no longer speak. Or sing. My head is filled with buzzing. I try to scream, but nothing comes out.

When I wake up, it's afternoon. The clock on my bedside table reads 3:30. I can still hear the bees in my ears. Feel them in my throat. I am disoriented. Confused. My head aches. The phone glows in the shadowed room, daring me to touch it. I am treading water in this sea of darkness, but a teeny tiny part of me fights for survival. For the light of hope. That part reaches for the phone. For a connection to the world outside.

I click to read the text messages. The first one is from my mom.

Just wanted to tell you how much I love you. I am so proud of you.

Not much to be proud of. But I save it anyway. The next is from Lily.

Stella, I'm so sorry. I would do anything to change what happened. If you need anything, please let me know. You're my BFF.

Another is from Kace.

I hope you get better soon. Drama isn't the same without you.

Then there are messages from people I don't even know. They say *Feel better soon!* and *We miss you!* They're like Hallmark texts. Lots of happy faces and exclamation points. I wonder if Emerson passed out my phone number on flyers.

My dad has sent me one as well.

Hope the surgery went well. See you later today. Love you.

A couple more from Mom checking on me from the car when she's gone dropping Emerson off and then later, picking her up from school.

I come to the last one.

How are you?

It's from Hayden.

I don't know how long I sit staring at the message.

Then I answer. *Better. I'm going to be ok.* I don't hit SEND though. To anyone else—to Lily, Kace, Emerson, even to my mom—this is my response. But for some reason I can't begin to understand, I don't want to pretend with Hayden.

I erase the message. I type a different answer. An honest one.

Afraid.

Afraid of not being brave enough. Afraid of losing hope. Afraid of never hearing again. Afraid of life without Someday Broadway. Just afraid.

SEND.

I stare at the phone. As though anyone would actually respond to that message. I want to call it back, erase it.

But it's too late.

I sigh and leave the phone on my bedside table.

In the bathroom, I leave the light off while I brush my teeth. Better not to see myself in the mirror. If I don't remind myself of what happened, I can keep living inside this bubble of silence.

I climb back into bed. The warmth of the tears on my cheeks comforts me in an odd way. I hide my face in the neck of my T-shirt and wrap my arms over my head. I bury myself there as though I can block it all out. As though this time will be different, and I won't dream about it.

I do anyway.

Hours, or even days, later, for all I care, my door opens. It's Dad. Strange to see him here in my room like this. He stretches his face into what might pass for some as a smile. He hands me a large frozen yogurt. Then he sits on the edge of my bed. His brown eyes take it all in. His hair is perfectly combed. His blue dress shirt hasn't got a crease in it. I smirk.

The cold yogurt tastes good on my throat, soothing the bee stings. I feel it hit my empty stomach like a heavy weight. It settles in. Peach and vanilla. Emerson's favorite. I wonder if he realizes, if he knows that I would choose chocolate.

Dad has a yellow pad in his hands. He writes a note.

How are you doing?

I answer, "Peachy." Just like the yogurt.

Does anything hurt?

"My head." *And my heart.* But I don't add that part.

You'll be back to normal before you know it.

He wants that to be true; I can tell. Not just for me. I understand that now. Because I've noticed that he isn't looking at me at all. Not really. Not at my scarred head and bruised face. Not my defective ears. He can't deal with the damaged me. I'm not a problem he can fix. Suddenly, I don't want to talk to him anymore.

"I'm really tired," I say. "Thanks for coming."

A look of relief passes over his face. And then, just as

quickly, he covers it with another stiff smile. He leans over and gives me a kiss on the cheek.

I watch him leave. Seeing my dad leave always makes me sad. I used to think he was my hero. But after what he did to my mom—to us—it can never be like that again. Now he's a hero to his new kid, I guess. I think he visits out of obligation, to prove to himself that he's not such a bad guy. That just because he divorced my mom, he didn't divorce us.

He might be able to lie to himself like that, but I know better now.

I turn onto my side and face the window. I wonder if I will ever be happy again. I think of the little rainbow girl in the hospital. Happiness danced in the air around her. Surrounding her with a joy for life. I want to be like her. Instead, I am treading water, trying desperately to stay above the depths of despair threatening to pull me under. Threatening to drown me in sorrow and self-pity forever.

I am struggling so hard. And I know, even if I don't want to admit it, that right now, I am losing the battle.

A lone tear slips down my cheek. Lodges itself between my skin and the pillow. I feel the dampness soak into the pale blue cotton. I keep the other tears inside, not letting them fall. One tear is enough. If I let them out one at a time, maybe I won't drown.

The freedom in honesty

HAYDEN

I know the instant she sends the text. I look at my phone and wait for it. I can almost hear her clear deep voice speaking the single word to me: "Afraid."

I waited to hear back from her, second-guessing my text. Maybe I didn't say enough. I wondered why she hadn't responded.

But now she has. I stare at her message, thinking of the subtext beneath the single word. *Afraid.* I think of her sitting alone in silence. Feeling lonely, lost.

I want to tell her that she isn't alone, that I am here for her. But I don't want to scare her away, not when she is already afraid. Not when she is brave enough to be honest with me. So I write back, carefully. As if she is the tawny cat basking in the sun on our porch.

For weeks, the cat watched me, and I watched her, knowing that one day, she would learn to trust me. Every day, I sat on the porch. I played my guitar, pretending not to notice her. And every day, the cat moved closer and closer. Until one day, I found her lying in a sliver of sunlight right next to me. Since that day, she has waited for my truck to pull into the driveway after school. As soon as I step onto the porch, she takes her spot. The streak of faded sunlight across the dusty porch calls to her. Just as Stella calls to me.

We are all afraid, I text back. *Some more than others. It takes courage to admit it.*

I hit SEND before I change my mind. I am far more eloquent in writing than in person. I feel more like myself—somehow—when no one can hear my voice.

I pick up my guitar, strum softly. The cat stretches, moves closer. Her litter of kittens settles around her, lulled by the music. Like the cat, I bask in sunlight once again.

Stella will write me back, and then I will ask how soon I can see her again.

DAYS

STELLA

When I wake up in the morning, I am still tired. My eyes are swollen and achy. My head pounds. I roll onto my side. But just before I close my eyes once more, I see it.

A new text message.

We are all afraid. Some more than others. It takes courage to admit it.

A current of excitement runs through me. He isn't trying to make me feel better—he isn't pretending. It feels so good to talk to someone. Through the shadowed aches and deep pain inside me it feels like a river flowing through a forbidden forest. Daring to enter the darkness.

I heard you call my name. Why? Did he know I would fall into the water? Hit my head? I send it. And I wait.

I had a feeling, like when you know it's going to rain. You can smell it in the air, feel the weight of the clouds press down. It was like that. I just knew.

A feeling. A premonition.

Does that happen often?

I don't wait long for his answer.

Sometimes. With you, it happens a lot.

A tingle runs through my stomach. What else does he have premonitions about? I want to ask, but I resist.

I stare at the phone, deciding whether to write back. Then, this:

Are you coming back to school?

Good question. I answer honestly.

Maybe next week.

SEND.

His answer comes so fast, I feel like he's sitting next to me. *Are you ready to go back?*

I just want to feel normal. Something about talking like this is freeing. I can be myself because he can't see me.

I don't know how I expect Hayden to respond. Maybe it doesn't even matter. This is all like a game. A game that doesn't mean anything, except that while I'm playing, I don't want to disappear.

What is that? Normal?

I try to explain. *The way I was before.*

Before the accident. Before everything changed. Before.

A long moment goes by without a response. He doesn't write back. We both know I'm not the way I was. That girl is dead.

Looks like I have to save you again.

I remember his arms around me. Holding me close. Saving me. I write back. *Save me? From what?*

I wait for his answer.

From yourself.

That's the last message he sends. I keep checking. It breaks up the monotony of my geometry and history homework.

Doing homework is a better torture than sleeping. It makes me feel normal. I can still read chapters and take notes. Still make flash cards. Still research online. Normal.

I am reading about the Industrial Revolution when I glance at my phone again. I have a message.

Still pretending?

Pretending? I write back. *I'm not pretending.*

I'm not.

He responds immediately. *Ok. If you say so.*

What is that supposed to mean? I respond with a question mark.

His reply comes quickly. *I bet nothing bad has ever happened to you before.*

He is so wrong.

You don't know anything, I type.

Tears burn my eyes. This time, I can't hold them back. He thinks I am some Princess of Perfection. He has no idea what my life has been like.

How my family shattered into pieces, slicing all of us, leaving wounds that will never truly heal. Hayden doesn't know a thing about that. He doesn't know me. If I have been pretending, it has been that he is some hero on a white horse, riding in to save me from my fate.

But no one can save me. I see that now. Even through the haze of tears.

I leave my homework and find Emerson. We watch subtitled reality television. We sit on the sofa and share a bowl of sliced bananas. I know Emerson would rather be having our usual—popcorn doused with salt, but the salt and the popcorn would hurt my throat. So we both have bananas instead. I feel better when I am with Emerson. She treats me as she always has. No different.

Later I get another text from Hayden.

I think I know what your problem is.

I angrily reply. *You don't know me at all.*

What if I do? Let's make a bet—and if I'm right, you have to say yes.

A bet for what?

If you lose, you'll go somewhere with me.

Do I want to go somewhere with him? Like this? Probably not. But I can't resist the idea of learning what he thinks is wrong with me. I want to see if he's right. Somehow, he has tapped into my competitive streak—the one thing that can overcome my pity party. And that's what makes me answer. *Ok.*

You can't imagine how to be a different you.

I read it over three times to be sure. It's not a very nice thing to say to someone. *What makes you say that?* I write it as a defense, and I know it. He's onto me. Someone I barely know. He knows my secret.

And I don't like that. Another text comes in.

I see you.

And another.

Am I right? Be honest.
He is. He is right.
I hate to admit it. But he does see me.
And I felt that right away the first time I saw him.
Maybe, I say.
See you tomorrow at 2.

Seeing the unseen

HAYDEN

I like working in the nursery, watering plants and helping them grow. I think about Stella. Maybe I can help her too.

I took a big chance calling her out. It was risky, and I might have lost her right then. She might never have wanted to see me again. But she is depressed. I can sense it. I want to help her, help her to be happy.

Maybe that is the reason I was at the party that night. Maybe that is the reason we are connected. Because I can help her. Because I can see what no one else can. Being silent for so long left me as an observer of life rather than a participant. So I see things, know things. Sometimes before they happen.

I see Stella, and I know what is happening to her. The silence is closing her in, and she is giving in to it—drifting into the darkness. I can help her. I can bring her out of the darkness. But to do that, I have to be honest with her—and she has to be honest with herself.

She may never hear again.

She needs to learn that there is more to life than what she has always thought. There is a world without sound. I want to show her all of the things she can still do. All of the things that make life worth living.

I turn off the hose and coil it back into its holder. I turn the gardenias so their blooms face out. I line up the containers of basil, oregano, and thyme. Another thing I like about working at the nursery: you don't have to talk to plants. You just have to water them and give them sun.

"Hayden, give me a hand with those empty flats, will you?" my boss, Jeremiah, calls from the counter.

"N-n-o pro-blem." I cringe at my voice. I hate it. The stutter and stammer. It sounds like it doesn't want to come out—and for eight years, it didn't.

From seven to fifteen, I was silent. After eight years, my voice forgot how to work. Now, every time I hear myself speak, I am reminded of the silence, and the reason for the silence. It takes me right back there, to the place I want to forget. I call back the words as they come out, pulling and pushing them at the same time.

That is why my voice sounds like a train chugging up a hill, pulling and pushing. Never knowing if it will ever reach its destination.

I collect the empty flats. Stack them neatly, fitting each one into another. I enjoy the mindless work. I carry the pile to Jeremiah. He points to a spot near the door.

"That's great. Just leave 'em there."

I set the flats down.

"Can you give the indoor plants a drink before you go?" Jeremiah asks.

"Sure th-ing," I tell him. I step into the shaded part of the nursery. The indoor plants are neatly arranged in circles on a large table. In the middle is a giant fern. I smile at my display, which is much better than the one Jeremiah had before—the plants in complete disarray. Now they look like they belong.

I fill a giant blue watering can from the nearby faucet. Then I give each of the plants a long drink. I watch as the clear stream pours out of the neck of the can, disappearing into the shiny green leaves.

If I'd had a friend when I needed help, if I hadn't been so alone, maybe things would have been different. Maybe.

I think of Stella's last text message. *Maybe.*

I move around the circle, watering each of the plants. A ray of golden sunshine trickles through the awning. I watch as it showers light on the leaves of the giant fern, and I add water to it. I can almost see the leaves stretching before me, reaching to the sky.

I think of Stella again. Maybe she needs a little sun and water. Maybe that will help her reach out.

And that's when I know exactly what we will do tomorrow.

SIGNS

STELLA

It's 1:45. I'm standing in front of my bathroom mirror.

Half of my head is shaved. A bandage is on one side of my head. My eyes are still sunken, the bruises faded to a pale green. Add that to my inability to stand without getting dizzy, and I'm not exactly looking my best.

But I made a bargain, and I am going to keep my word.

So, looking in the mirror, I make a decision. I won't worry about how I look. There's absolutely nothing I can do about it anyway. The decision is surprisingly freeing. I'm letting go of what is on the outside. Letting go of what is out of my control.

I pull on a white T-shirt and a pair of jeans. I push my feet into my sneakers, lean over to tie them, but the room begins to swim, and my stomach churns. I leave them unlaced.

I open the front door and sit on the front step. Mom is at work. Emerson is at a friend's house. I am the only one here.

I have no idea why Hayden is coming here. Maybe he's the

type who likes charity cases. Like the people who bring home stray kittens and injured baby birds. Maybe he thinks he's responsible for me because he saved my life. Or maybe (and this is the worst possibility of all), he likes me. The thought is so scary that my throat closes up. I gasp for air.

No boys has been my mantra for two years. It has anchored me to my other mantra, *Someday Broadway.*

That mantra is gone now. I'm set adrift without an anchor. I don't like being tossed about on the currents of the unknown. It makes me feel even more unbalanced. Confused. Through the haze, one thought becomes clear—I am going back inside.

Just at that moment, his blue truck pulls up. I close my eyes and will myself to normalcy. When I open them again, he is walking up the sidewalk to my front door.

Taller than I remembered, blonder than I remembered. And definitely handsomer than I remembered.

But his eyes are just as I remembered. Piercing.

He's wearing faded jeans and a blue T-shirt with a plaid shirt tied around his waist. No clue from his clothes where we're going. But I do know that I have dressed appropriately.

He's smiling at me, and before I realize it, I am smiling back. The haze has disappeared. I can see clearly now. I see Hayden.

I stand, a little shaky. I wobble slightly as he towers over me.

"Hi," he mouths slowly.

I smile back.

"Ready to go?" he asks, again slowly enough for me to read his lips.

I nod. He notices my laces and looks at me, a question in his eyes.

I shake my head. "Dizzy."

"May I?" he asks.

I lower my eyes. "Thank you."

Butterflies crash around in my stomach as I watch Hayden tie my shoes for me. I'm not sure I even breathe as he stands up again and grins.

I walk beside him to the truck. Wait while he opens the door for me. I climb in, and he shuts the door.

While he walks around to the driver's side, I have a moment to collect myself. I've never really been out on a date before. Not a real one, anyway. Just those group outings with Lily to hang out with boys she had crushes on. And I've never had a boyfriend. I don't know whether this is even a real date, but suddenly, I am overwhelmingly shy.

I look around. The truck is clean inside. Mint gum sits on a shelf in the dashboard. His cell phone lies on the seat. No other clues as to who this magical person may be.

Hayden gets in and smiles at me again before he starts the car. The keys in the ignition dangle back and forth on his keychain—a knot woven of silver. I've seen it before. That night.

I shiver slightly, remembering when he said my name. How it sounded like music. I may never hear Hayden speak my name again. My chest is tight with the loss. I watch the knot swing back and forth. Better than staring at him.

I turn to look out the window, watching the streets we pass. I think about why I am here. Try to imagine myself in a new way. And that means letting go.

I am here with Hayden. That's all that matters. I glance at him. As if he knows I am thinking about him, he looks at me. The tightness in my chest begins to loosen like a rosebud beginning to bloom in the sun. Petals slowly open.

I'm still a prisoner in my Miss America bubble of silence, but I notice something new. The silence isn't as lonely as it was before. Somehow, it feels . . . peaceful.

After about fifteen minutes, Hayden turns onto Pacific Coast Highway, which runs along the beach. Sapphire waters melt onto the shore. Hayden leans across me to roll down my window. He's so close that for a moment, I can feel his warmth. His hair brushes softly against my cheek, leaving the scent of coconut shampoo in its wake. Heat rises in my cheeks, and I resist the urge to cover them with my hands. Before I know it, the moment is over. The rush of fresh air from the open window cools my flaming skin.

I breathe deeply. Taste the salty air on my tongue. Then I lean forward to let the wind blow on my face. I close my eyes and let myself be.

When I open them again, we are pulling into a parking lot. Hayden turns off the truck and comes around to my side to help me out. He grabs a backpack from the bed of the truck and slings it over his shoulder.

Then he turns to smile at me. "Let's go," he says.

As I walk beside him, he slows his pace to keep time with mine. His stride is smooth, effortless. He glides.

At the edge of the sand, he leans over to pull off his sneakers. I try to do the same, but as soon as my head drops below my waist, I stagger. I give up. I can't even take my own shoes off.

This is not how I pictured my first date.

I step into the sand, and my shoes sink into the softness. Hayden walks closer to the water. Then he stops and pulls a blanket out of the backpack. Together we lay it across the sand. Gingerly, I sit down. Hayden sits next to me.

Being so close to him makes my heart race. I imagine he can hear it pounding in my chest. I dare to look at him. He gestures to my sneakers.

"Can I help you?" he asks slowly.

I nod.

Hayden unties my sneakers. From there, I can push the shoes off my feet. I dig my toes into the sand. Touch the coolness beneath the surface.

The ocean sparkles in the bright sunlight. Seagulls swoop into the water, making U shapes in the sky as they rise and fall. The waves roll and wash on the shore, sending foam splashing into the air. The spray drifts across my cheeks. Sprinkles me. The beach is almost empty, save for a couple of joggers and the occasional surfer. I sense my breathing slow. My heart rate calm.

"You remembered," I say. He remembered that the beach is my dream vacation. I don't say that I remember it is *his* favorite, too. I don't have to.

"I remember everything about you," he says. I imagine how his voice sounds as he forms the syllables—slow and staggered. But when I read his lips, the words are smooth and easy. Slow.

The meaning of his words dawns on me, and a delicious joy curves my lips into a smile.

I marvel again at how easily I understand him, when I cannot understand anyone else. Even Emerson.

I pull my eyes away from him and look out at the rolling water. A whole world is out there. A world that knows nothing about Stella Layne. The thought makes me feel free. Hopeful. Grateful.

We sit there, side by side. After a time, I steal a glance at Hayden. He looks out at the waves. His skin shines like gold, and his lion's mane is tousled by the ocean breeze. He is smiling the half-smile that makes him look shy and approachable. I want to know everything about him. Where he got the scar along his chin. If anyone else in his family has eyes the color of jewels. And more than anything, I want to know why he is helping me like this.

Suddenly, Hayden turns his head and looks at me. And that's when I see it—something in his eyes. Something so painful. It's like I can see into his soul. And what I see there is so tragic that I forget about my own problems and reach out to him. I don't think. Just touch him.

It is a simple gesture; my hand rests on his arm just above the woven bracelet. But in that movement, in that touch, something happens. Something so profound that it extends beyond this moment. Beyond this day. The moment passes as quickly as one breath, but the world has shifted. And I understand something I have only partially grasped until now. That somehow, Hayden and I are linked. I can tell from the look in his eyes that he feels it too. Words aren't necessary. Hearing isn't necessary.

Suddenly, a mischievous smile flits across Hayden's face. He stands and runs toward the waves. I push myself to my feet and follow. Hayden is knee deep, waiting for me. The water is so cold it stings my toes, makes them feel numb.

Instantly, memories collide in my mind. The water of the pool, me drifting down, not breathing. I stumble backwards, away from the pain. Hayden moves toward me, his expression etched with understanding. Looking at him brings me back to the present. Hayden stands with me. On the edge of the water.

I let the waves lap my toes. I get used to the temperature, used to the feeling. Then Hayden kicks some water toward me. I smile and splash him back. Within moments, we are playing like little kids. Splashing in the ocean. And for those moments, I completely forget about everything.

When we come out of the water, Hayden tosses me a towel. I dry off. Then he offers me a peanut butter and jelly sandwich and an apple. Surprisingly, I am starving.

"Is this you saving me?" I ask. I am trying to tease him, but I don't know if my voice has the right inflection. I imagine that it does. I watch for his reaction, suddenly wishing I hadn't tried to say something that needed inflection to make sense.

But Hayden grins. He seems to understand that it is a joke. His hair curls at the ends where it is wet. I resist the urge to touch it. "It's a beginning."

He winks at me, and my stomach does another flip-flop. I should be getting used to them by now. I find myself studying the skin of the red apple in my hand. Where the red fades to pink. I touch the stem. Think of the game Emerson and I used to play: Twirl the stem and recite the letters of the alphabet. On the letter the stem releases, that will be the letter of your true love. I spin the stem around and around and think the letters to myself. A-B-C-D-E-F-G. On the eighth twist, the stem comes off. H.

Hayden touches my shoulder briefly, and I turn sheepishly to meet his eyes. "Tell me," he says. When he speaks to me, I can read his lips as clearly as if I could hear.

And that's when it pours out of me. All of it. I tell Hayden everything. What's wrong with me, and how I don't know if I will ever hear again. How I pretended with Lily so she wouldn't feel guilty. My dad not even looking at me. Losing the starring role to Quinn after all that work. My fear that I will never sing again. And the surgery that promises to make me whole again, the promise that feels like a giant question mark hanging in the air over my head.

I don't know how my voice sounds. If I am using too much volume—am I screaming at him? Or if I am speaking too softly—maybe he can't hear me at all. But then I realize that it doesn't matter, because I am saying these words aloud. My fears are revealed. My loss is revealed. I don't have to pretend. Not with him. Suddenly, the way my voice sounds doesn't matter at all.

He listens without responding. He just watches me with his mesmerizing eyes and his calm spirit. And I am present. Here and now. Then he reaches out and gently places his hand over my eyes. Closing them. He lifts my hand. Turns it over.

Then, grains of sand. Cool. Smooth. Pooling in my palm.

I open my eyes. Look at Hayden, curious.

"What did you feel?" he asks.

"Sand. Cool as a shadow. Soft and heavy at the same time. Like time was passing and standing still. Both at once."

Hayden nods. "Close your eyes again. Breathe."

I close my eyes. Breathe.

Smell the salt in the air. Freedom.

Hayden's coconut shampoo. Excitement.

The scent of the peanut butter, tangy and sweet. Comfort.

I open my eyes again. This time, beaming at him. I'm beginning to understand.

Now I can feel the wind blowing my hair, lifting it off my neck. Making me warm and cold at the same time. The same feeling I have being close to Hayden.

"Look," he tells me as he gestures to the sea.

I see sparkles of light dancing on the water. The waves moving, like life always moving. An ocean of possibilities stretches out in front of me, leading to worlds beyond.

Then I notice something else. Dolphins. Three of them. Their backs arch out of the water, shiny and silver. Gliding through the waves. I am blessed to be here. Blessed to experience this day.

I turn to look at Hayden. He is watching me.

"What day do you see the doctor?" he asks.

"April tenth."

He says nothing else, just turns his eyes to the horizon once more. As if all of the answers are out there somewhere, waiting to be found. We sit side by side without another word. Until the sun sets like a ball of fire melting into the water.

And then he drives me home.

That night, I lie in bed, reliving every single moment of the day. For those hours, I could breathe. I was present, alive. And I could communicate. Even without telling him things, he seemed to know, to understand. I could hear his voice in my mind.

I know only one thing.

He is the white feather of hope drifting through the darkness of my days.

And if I can hold on, I just might be able to fly.

A pledge of time

HAYDEN

I can't stop thinking about her. The way she looked sitting on the front step, her shoes untied and her face set with determination. How her eyes lit up like a little kid's at Christmas when she saw the dolphins. Listening to her talk, seeing her smile, just being with her.

Stella sees me—the real me, not the stuttering, stammering me. Even before her accident, she saw me. She didn't turn away when she heard my voice in the theater. She didn't ignore me and walk away. Stella wants to be with me; I can tell from the look in her eyes. And I want to be with her—she makes me forget everything that came before.

She has seventeen more days to wait—seventeen days of silence. After that, she will know if her life will return to the way it was before, or if it will be silent forever.

I can help her. I saw how she responded to the sand in her hand, to the ocean breeze in her hair. She's open to life in a way that makes me feel something I have never felt before. Hopeful.

Hope is like stepping out of a prison cell into a grassy meadow on a spring day. The darkness becomes a distant memory, and it seems anything is possible.

I finish my calculus homework, and then I write to her.

I have a challenge for you. You have 17 days to wait. Until then, I can show you all the things you can do without hearing. At the end of 17 days, 1 of 3 things will happen: 1. You will hear again. 2. You can give up. 3. You will be able to imagine yourself differently. Will you let me help you?

I don't know how she will respond. Will she say yes?

She doesn't say yes or no. She sends this:

Why would you want to do that for me?

My answer is simple.

Because I had to figure things out on my own, and I wish someone had helped me.

There's more, of course. Like the way I felt when she touched me. How everything disappeared—the past, the memories. It was like the earth stood still for a split second, and we were the only two people in the world. No one has ever made me feel like that before. I want to feel it again. I want to be with her again.

I don't wait long for her response. It shines with promise. Hope.

Yes.

17

STELLA

My first thought when I read Hayden's challenge is that I am depressing scenario number one—a charity case. But my second thought is that I don't care. Not if it means more time with Hayden.

When I receive his response to my question—that he wishes someone had helped him—I answer him in the only way I ever would answer him. It seems that we are bound together by circumstance, by pain, and maybe by something more.

Yes.

It's 3:20. Hayden will be here at 3:30. I pull on my favorite jeans and a blue tank top, wrap a sweatshirt around my waist, and head for the front door. I plan to wait outside again. I sit on the step, reach over to tie my shoes. This time I can do it. Baby steps, I tell myself.

When Hayden's truck pulls up, I am suddenly nervous. I twist a strand of hair around my finger as I wonder why I agreed to this. But the second Hayden comes walking toward me, I am calm. And happy. Really happy.

He's wearing a blue baseball cap and a navy T-shirt with tattered jeans. His smile is wide and welcoming. I stand before he reaches me.

"Hi," he says. His eyes sparkle like the waves in the ocean.

"Hi," I return shyly.

He is looking at me in that way again, like he can see into my soul. It's unnerving and exciting at the same time. I have to look away.

"Tied my own shoes today," I say, looking at my sneakers. The bows are lopsided, but I did manage to do it myself, which is an improvement. I sneak a look at him to see his response.

"I guess you don't need me anymore," he teases.

I grin. "Guess not."

We stand there smiling at each other. But it isn't awkward. I'm warm inside. Giddy, even.

Hayden offers me his arm. "Ready?"

"Just one thing."

Hayden waits, studies me. My stomach flips over once. Twice. I take a breath.

"My mom wants to talk to you."

I don't know what I expect his reaction to be. Annoyed, frustrated, even maybe self-conscious? But Hayden is none of these things. He smiles and nods. "No problem."

I turn and open the front door. I step into the foyer, and Hayden follows.

"Mom," I call.

She comes out of the kitchen, smiling. I see her mouth move. Then she surprises me by hugging Hayden. She gestures toward me, touches me gently on the arm. Her mouth is moving too quickly for me to decipher anything. I look at Hayden instead. I watch his mouth.

"Don't worry. I'll take good care of her. She'll be completely safe."

I turn to look at my mother. She nods, giving me permission to go with a smile that reaches all the way to her eyes. I can tell she is happy that I am out of bed and actually wanting to do something outside the darkness of my bedroom.

I hug her and whisper in her ear, "Thank you."

She kisses me on the forehead.

"I'll have her back before dinner," Hayden promises.

Hayden opens the front door, and I follow him outside. I breathe in the air. I suddenly feel like I could fly.

I float to the truck, where Hayden opens the door for me. I climb in and wait for him to get in and start the car. I am smiling in a way I can't remember doing for so long. Hayden glances at me and then he smiles, too, like it's catching.

"Where are you taking me today?" I ask.

Hayden laughs. I can't hear it, but he throws his head back a little. "You'll just have to wait."

I sigh and settle into the seat. Again I notice the silver knot keychain dangling back and forth. I look out the window. Hayden pulls into the mall parking lot. Then he parks.

"Ready?" Again, it strikes me that he is the only person I can understand. I meet his eyes and nod.

Before I can open my door, Hayden is helping me out of the truck. We walk side by side into the shopping center. Once, his hand brushes against mine. I resist the urge to look at him. I'm always doing that—resisting the pull toward him.

The mall is different without sound. I feel like an alien from another planet, like I have never been here before. I am almost dizzy from the blending of colors and smells. The scents of vanilla and gardenia assault me from the Candle Shop, and my eyes can barely take in all of the colors in the windows of the clothing stores.

A warm breeze blows across my cheek before Hayden pulls me out of the way of a whirling helicopter toy from a kiosk. My mouth waters with the smell of buttery popcorn from the movie theaters. People bump and jostle me as they hurry by. I never realized how much people rush. They don't take in the moment.

Then Hayden stops in front of Paint It, one of those paint-your-own-pottery places. I've never been inside; I'm not much of an artist. My talents are all musical. Correction, I remind myself. *Were* all musical. But before even a drop of sadness can flow through me, Hayden is pulling me inside the store.

Small round tables covered with white paper are scattered around the space. Shelves are filled with white pottery pieces—vases and bowls, plates and different shapes and sizes of piggy banks. The place is almost empty, except for a mother and two young girls painting princesses at the back table. Hayden leads me to the wall of pottery.

"Which one do you want to paint?"

"Really?" I say. Then, "I'm not much of an artist."

He grins. "We'll see about that."

Together we look at all of the choices. I like the vases. One is shaped like a treble clef, with the top part opening to hold flowers. I pick it up to look at it. I am too shy to tell Hayden that this is the one I like. But I don't need to tell him, because he already knows. He gently removes the vase from my hands and carries it to a table. He sets the vase in the center then waves at me to follow him. At the back of the studio is a shelf with containers of paint, a rainbow of colors. Next to it are bowls of brushes in all shapes and sizes. Hayden picks up a large, flat, white tile and looks at me.

"Choose your colors," he says.

I pick up a pale blue that reminds me of the sky over the ocean. I hold up the bottle for Hayden to see. He takes it and pours some on the tile. Then I choose another like ivory sand. I pour this one onto the same tile next to the blue, but not touching. Last I choose sapphire, which reminds me of Hayden's eyes and the sea. I don't tell him this, of course. And for a second, I am too shy to look up at him. I set the bottle back on the shelf.

When I do finally look at Hayden, he seems to be studying me rather than the paint color. I feel my cheeks burn hot with his gaze. Then he tilts his head to the side as though considering something. I want to ask what it is, but before I can figure out how to ask the question, the moment has passed.

"Any more?" he asks, holding up the tile for me to look.

I shake my head no. "That's good," I answer.

"Choose some brushes," he tells me.

I select one small thin brush, one wedge-shaped wide brush, and another in the middle with a long point at the end.

I follow Hayden back to the table. He sets the tile next to my vase. Then he leaves to select a piece for himself. I sit down, suddenly excited to paint. I choose the widest brush and dip it into the light blue paint. I like the way the brush bends and swirls as the color saturates the bristles. I carefully smooth the brush down the side of the vase. Watch as the white clay turns the color of the sky. Up and down I run the brush. Revel in the power of creating something the way I see it. In the possibility of mistakes.

I am so absorbed that I don't even notice when Hayden returns. So I am surprised when I look up and see him painting across from me. He is working on an oval-shaped box. He feels my gaze and looks up.

There is the connection again. For a split second, he understands everything. How peaceful and happy I am in this moment. I don't have to tell him. I can see it reflected in his eyes.

Once again, Hayden has taken me to a place I have never been before. A place inside myself that needs no words, no outward communication. I can express myself with a paintbrush. Through my emotions painted across a vase. In blue.

"Thank you," I say simply.

He doesn't answer. He doesn't need to.

From time to time, as I paint, I glance over to see what Hayden is doing. He is a very talented artist, I realize. On top of the box, he is painting a detailed ocean scene. The bottom is the same blue I am using for the vase—the color of his eyes.

I use the sand-color paint to line the inside lip of the vase.

The sand touching the edge of the sky. My work is almost complete. I have left the best part for last. I choose the smallest, finest brush and dip it into the sapphire paint. Then I line the treble clef. And the whole time, I feel as though I am painting the memory of this day, of Hayden, into this vase.

When I am finished, I sit back and look at my work. It isn't perfect, to be sure. But that's what makes me feel so good about it. I am not an artist. But it doesn't matter. I still created something beautiful. And I didn't need to hear a single sound to do it.

Hayden has also finished. I stand and walk around the table to look over his shoulder. He has painted a miniature version of the beach we visited together—the sand dunes, the waves, and the birds in perfect detail.

"It's beautiful," I tell him.

"It's a beautiful world," he responds. When he looks at me, I feel for a moment that I am lost in time. Suspended, as if nothing else exists. The burning in his gaze is so intense, I don't even breathe.

"It's for you," he says. "So you will always remember."

I feel the smile reach my eyes before it touches my lips. "I could never forget. Any of this."

"Neither could I," he says.

Hayden stands and looks at me for another long moment. Then he turns to the counter to pay.

I take the next few breaths to calm myself. What is happening to me? I have been through so much. I am not myself anymore. I know this. I like to think the old me would have known exactly what to do. What to say. But I know that is a lie.

I wish I could ask Lily for advice. She would know what to do. She knows everything about talking to boys. Thinking about Lily pinches my heart as if to remind me of what I've lost.

Hayden returns, holding a little green receipt. "They will be ready next week," he tells me. "Are you hungry?"

"Starving," I tell him.

Outside the store, Hayden turns in the direction of the food court. I walk beside him, happy to feel normal for a few minutes. I glance into windows, smile when he points something out.

His hand lightly brushes mine. An almost imperceptible touch, except it's not because I feel a hundred electrical impulses run up my arm. When he brushes me again, his hand gently reaches out. An offering that I can accept or refuse. If I weren't so completely aware of every breath he takes, I might not even notice. But I do notice. And I accept.

I fit my palm into his. Hayden's fingers interweave with mine. The jolts go all the way through my body. I expect to feel nervous. Shy. Even afraid. But I don't. I feel only one thing—

Safe.

Hayden's hand is slender but strong. His fingers press tightly against mine, but he doesn't grip my hand. I am connected and free at the same time.

Hayden's holding my hand gives me a message. It is as loud

as if he were singing a song I could hear. That's all I need to know.

I don't know what we see after that. I don't know what we smile and laugh about. Because I am gliding on a tide of euphoria.

Hayden buys us junk food. Pretzels, frozen lemonade, pizza slices. The smells make my mouth water. We're laughing, trying to juggle all of it when it happens.

We run right into them—Lily and Connor. Arms wrapped around each other. Some other kids from school with them I don't know. Seniors, I think. I feel like an anchor has dragged me to the bottom of the sea. My lungs collapse, and I can't breathe.

I just freeze. Lily doesn't. She smiles at me and says something I can't understand. It's too fast, too jumbled. Connor looks me up and down. There is something in his expression. Narrowed eyes. Pretended indifference. Something else too. It sends shivers up my arms. Then he says something to me, but I can't understand him either. My skin burns with the heat of their stares. I want to claw at my face, make it go away, but my hands are full of pretzel bites. The heat of the bag seeps into my skin. I do nothing. Say nothing. I am like a statue.

I watch Lily's expression turn from happiness to pity to frustration. She doesn't know. Doesn't understand. Can never understand.

And that's when I unfreeze. I force a timid wave at Lily. A half-smile that feels like it is cracking my face in two. Lily half-smiles back. But behind it, I can see the truth. The green monster is still there even now. A fleeting thought touches down, stings me before it flies away. She is embarrassed by me. And it is that thought that makes my throat grow thick. I look at Hayden. He's watching them. Only I can't read his expression. I can't tell if he's uncomfortable or annoyed. Or maybe something else. But he feels my gaze and turns to meet my eyes. A silent moment of understanding passes between us. I watch as he turns back to them.

"See you later," he says, and then he hands me one of the drinks so he can take my arm. He leads me away from them and away from the humiliation. And it is over. Just like that.

I think he's going to stop at the tables in the food court, but he doesn't. His hand is strong on my arm as he guides me all the way back to his truck.

Then, and only then, does he let go of me. He sets the food on the hood of the car then takes the pretzels and drink out of my hands. One hand is cold from the drink. The other warm from the pretzels. Both are shaking. *I* am shaking. My eyes start to blur, and I feel nausea well up inside of me. I am gasping for breath. Hayden takes my hands in his and holds them tight. Standing so close to me, he smells like chocolate and the ocean, the wind and the sun. I don't know how long we stand like that. I only know that I feel like I am drawing strength from his body. I am breathing him in.

His expression is serious. Concerned. And something else. Something that lingers like the last bit of starlight in a new morning sky.

"I'm sorry."

I shake my head. "Not your fault."

He insists. "It's too soon. I shouldn't have brought you here."

I shake my head again. "I'm glad you did."

"I'm going to take you home now."

His words hurt. I know he doesn't mean them to, but they do. I feel like he wants to get rid of me, like I have been imagining our connection. The moments. And I am once again the stray puppy on the side of the road.

I can't speak. I feel one traitorous tear run down my cheek. I reach up to brush it away. Hayden opens the door for me. He gathers up the junk food and crosses to his side, where he puts the food on the floor.

We drive home in silence.

Silence is my life.

BEST FRIENDS FOREVER

STELLA

I was so happy 2 c u 2day. U look amazing. Über amazing. I am so sorry u had to c me with Connor like that. I wanted to tell u in person. We're sort of seeing each other. I wanted to talk to u more, but SC pulled u away so fast. He was très rude. Is he your BF now? Maybe I can come over 2morrow so we can talk. BFF, Lily.

I wish I could say I want to talk to her. That I think her words are genuine. Or that seeing her with Connor didn't bother me, but it did. More than I realized. I can't pinpoint why Connor is angry with me. Except that maybe I am a reminder of that night. He wasn't a hero that night. Probably for the first time ever. Even though I don't blame him. Maybe he blames himself. Which makes him angry with me.

I wanted to go back to school on Monday. Now I'm not so sure.

I don't write back to Lily.

I have nothing to say.

Reflection in a mirror

HAYDEN

I made a mistake.

A colossal mistake.

I didn't think it through. I didn't think about people she might see. How she would feel. I was only thinking about myself. Impressing her and being the hero.

Saying good-bye to her just now, I felt like it might be the last time. Maybe Stella won't want to see me again.

I didn't know what to say except sorry, and that didn't seem like enough. She looked so broken, so sad. Today erased all of yesterday's progress, and set her back. She had to see her friends like that, and with me.

I promised Stella's mother that I would take good care of her, and I broke that promise. That's all I could think about on the drive home. Every time I glanced at Stella, her eyes were staring out the windshield as if she couldn't get home fast enough—couldn't get away from me fast enough.

All I could do was walk her to the front door, make sure she got inside, and leave.

I turn left at the corner and pull into an empty parking lot at a park. It is almost sunset. The park is empty, but I know the bench where the homeless man sleeps every night. I have seen him here before when I have come here to think, to get away.

I meant to share this food with Stella. Instead, I am giving it to a stranger.

He is sleeping when I approach, so I set down the drink and snacks near his shopping cart. He will find it later, after I am gone.

I walk back to my truck, listening to the birds call their good nights to one another. A squirrel scurries in front of me, dashing away to climb up the nearest tree. A little boy walks home hand in hand with his mother. I watch them, imagining what their life must be like. How lucky they are to have each other.

My mother never held my hand, never smiled at me like that.

When I think of her hands, they are clenched into fists. Breaking things, causing pain, hurting me.

Stella makes me forget about all of that. About everything that came before her—all of it. I get lost in her, in the moments.

And so at the mall, I wasn't paying attention. Seeing her best friend like that, with him, seemed to knock the wind out of her. And I did nothing. I froze, like I always do when someone talks to me. I don't see them anymore. Instead, I see my mother, yelling at me, demanding that I speak.

Stop ruining my life, she would say. *Speak.*

But I didn't speak, because even after everything she did to me, I still loved her. I knew my silence would protect her. And me. People didn't notice anything wrong. They didn't see the cuts and bruises—or they didn't want to see them.

Until I stopped speaking, until I was silent. It was silence that saved my life.

Speak! The voice screams in my ears. Yet I can't say a word.

But today, when Stella looked at me, something happened. Pleading, begging me to save her. She was counting on me. Her need was greater than my own, and I had to protect her. So I did what I had to do—I found my voice, and I took her away from them.

But it was too late; the damage was done. I could see it in the tears swimming in her eyes. All I knew was that I made her cry. Her tears pierced my heart.

Holding her hands, standing so close, I never wanted to let go.

I only hope she can forgive me.

ME AGAIN

STELLA

If I am going back to school on Monday, I need to be caught up. That's what I tell Mom and Emerson, anyway. I don't want to tell them about my afternoon. I avoid them with homework. I plow through Spanish and health. Then I escape with Hamlet. Somehow, I can identify with him. His frustration. His disillusionment with the world around him. I find comfort in his words.

O, that this too, too solid flesh would melt,
Thaw, and resolve itself into a dew!
Or that the Everlasting had not fix'd
His canon 'gainst self-slaughter! O God! God!
How weary, stale, flat and unprofitable
Seem to me all the uses of this world!
Fie on't, ah fie! 'tis an unweeded garden

That grows to seed; things rank and gross in nature
Possess it merely.

I lie on my bed, reread the passage over and over. Let the language seep into me like rain seeping into parched summer grass.

Seeing Lily and Connor was a neon sign reminding me of what I have lost. I've lost everything. They have lost nothing. The accident that cost me my dream has made Lily's dream come true. It gave her popularity. A boyfriend on the football team. A spot on the varsity cheerleading squad.

I imagine how I must have looked to them—to Hayden—in my silent bubble.

He wanted to get rid of me after that. I really am some kind of charity case.

That last thought bothers me the most. Hayden. More than Connor. More than Lily.

I want to disappear.

I close my eyes, seeking the blackness where I am free.

Suddenly, I am floating. Drifting down, down, down. In a sea of words and confusion, I don't know who I am. I don't exist. I am nothing.

The darkness surrounds me. Blankets me. Erases me. Then a hand reaches out. Touches mine. Grasps for me. I take hold. Know this is my chance at survival. My chance to breathe again.

The hand pulls me upward, to the light. I want the light. The hope. I want to breathe again. To be me.

I burst from the water, gasping for air. I am enveloped in strong arms. I am safe. I am me.

I look up and see only blue.

I wake up confused. Disoriented. Sweaty.

I remember everything. My body trembles. I wrap myself in a blanket and reach for the glass beside my bed. Take a long drink, letting the cool water glide down my throat. Calming me. I am here. I know that now.

I cannot disappear. I cannot give up.

This happened for a reason. Someday I will understand why. For now, I have to keep going.

I have to believe in myself.

I have to trust in me.

I reach for my phone to connect with him somehow. To ground me in this reality.

I find a message from him.

I'm so sorry about what happened. I promise I'll be more careful with you, if you'll let me.

He wants to spend more time with me? I don't understand it. Not when I embarrassed him. I text him back, even though it's the middle of the night.

It wasn't your fault. I'm ok.

Liar, I accuse myself after writing the last part. But I don't want to be his charity case anymore.

I don't expect him to respond, but within seconds, he has texted back. A shiver runs through me as I realize that he, too, is awake right now. It makes me feel close to him.

I know you aren't ok. You don't have to pretend with me. I want to be the one person you never have to pretend with. Just be yourself.

I read his message over and over. Let the words wash over me to wash the humiliation away. They leave me fresh. Ready to begin again.

His words and my own determination give me the courage to reply.

I won't pretend. But u can't pretend either. B honest. Why r u really doing this? Because u feel sorry for me? Cause u don't have 2 anymore.

My heart races. I have never been so honest. With myself or anyone else. The prospect is exciting and terrifying at the same time. Both turn my stomach upside down and make the back of my neck suddenly damp.

Minutes tick by. He doesn't answer. Moments of my life are spent staring at a cell phone. I won't stare at it any longer. I'm going back to bed. Back to my dreams. Or nightmares.

That's when he answers.

I don't feel sorry for you. I thought I was helping. I want to help you, but the truth is that you are helping me. Like no one ever has.

His words fill me with joy. Pure joy. I want to jump up and dance around my room. I breathe in and taste hope. Then I write back.

U r helping me 2.

I press SEND then type: *I am going back to school on Monday. After today, I know how hard it will be, but I need to go.*

He answers right away, like he is sitting beside me.

I know.

See you tomorrow at 2:30?

16

STELLA

It's a typical Saturday morning. Saturdays used to be family days, full of forced activities no one really wanted to do, but we all felt obligated to pretend to enjoy. But ever since Dad moved out and we became a split family, the pretense is gone, and we can be ourselves. On Saturdays, we are free to do whatever makes us happy, which, for Mom, is planting flowers. For Emerson, it is dancing. She is already dressed in her leotard and tights, hair pulled back into a tight bun. Mom is decked out in army pants and clogs, but she has to work before she can dig in the dirt.

Mom's an accountant. She mostly works from home, so her schedule is pretty flexible except in March and April—tax season. With everything going on with me, Mom has taken entire days off. She must be behind schedule. She has been working really late the past few nights; I can tell by the circles underneath her eyes. She surely has work to finish before she can go outside.

"I can help with your work," I tell her.

Her eyes widen in surprise. She smiles, happy to have my help. Mom shows me which office tasks I can do. I get started while she drives Emerson to the dance studio. I begin by assembling packages for Mom's clients. I make copies of tax returns and stamp them COPY. Each tax return and copy go into a special navy blue folder with extra envelopes that hold federal and state tax returns. Then I put everything into a giant mailing envelope. I like the mechanical nature of the task; it is relaxing. I don't have to think too much, so I can let my mind drift.

I think about Hayden.

He's an unknown to me. Maybe that's why I like him so much. Maybe, if I'm being honest, I also like that he seems to understand me even though he hasn't known me for long. He was right when he said I couldn't imagine myself differently. I couldn't. I only thought about Someday Broadway. It was my everything. I was so focused that I lost track of everything else. I used to like other things.

Now I can't really remember what those things were.

I thought I knew who I was. But I was limiting myself to being one thing. Defining myself by my talent. There's more to me than that. More I can give. More I can share. The truth is, I'm starting to like this new Stella better than the old Stella.

My mind turns again to Hayden. I think of the day he walked into the theater. When he stepped onto the stage. How nervous I was to sing in front of him. Until he began playing.

Then I remember something else. That day was also the first time I heard him speak.

And I was disappointed in the sound of his voice. That it wasn't smooth and commanding. Or accented. How much importance I placed on sounds then. Sounds I can't hear now. I remember the first time he said my name. It sounded beautiful the way he drew out each letter like music. And it hits me. The reason I can understand Hayden.

It's his speech.

His words are slowed down. Stretched out. That's why they're easier to read on his lips.

The thought shames me and causes an ache deep in the pit of my stomach. That the thing which causes him so much pain would be the key to our connection. To my understanding. Does he know? How does it make him feel?

Mom calls a stop to our work at lunchtime, and we eat peanut butter and jelly at the table in the garden. It is a beautiful day, and I'm happy to have this time with my mom. It occurs to me that we don't usually have much time alone together. With Emerson and me only a year apart, I can't remember a time when I didn't have to share my mom.

"I like this day," I tell her.

She smiles and says something. I imagine it's, "Me, too."

When we finish lunch, Mom decides to work in her vegetable garden. Emerson is still at dance class. I check my phone messages. Another one from Lily.

Can I come by tomorrow? 2 talk 2 u? I am très bereft without u. Please.

I debate whether to respond. I think about the past year we've been friends. How knowing her made being at a new school bearable. How I let her drama and excitement spice up my own quiet life. I thought she would be my best friend forever. That nothing could come between us. Would she feel the same about me if I'd hurt her? Even if our friendship will never ever be the same again, I can at least try. I owe her that.

Maybe tomorrow after church. Text me first.

I send it. I breathe. And I realize that a weight has been lifted from my shoulders. Maybe letting Lily back into my life is something I need to do. Something that I need to heal.

Tomorrow, I am going to church with my mom in the morning. After that, if Lily wants to come over and be friends, well, I will let her. The sooner I get back to my old life, the better.

That decided, I look at the rest of my messages. One from my dad wanting to know how I am and reminding me about his firm's annual picnic next Saturday. I write back.

I'm better. Thanks for checking. See u Saturday. XO

And then a message from Hayden.

I'll be there at 2:30. Wear jeans and sneakers. H

I check the time—1:00. For the next hour, I read *Hamlet* then go to my room to exchange my sweats and T-shirt for jeans and a plaid shirt. Then I take out my ponytail and brush what is left of my hair smooth. I grab my sneakers and head for the front step. Mom has already left to pick up Emerson. She knows I am going out with Hayden and that I will be home by dinner.

At 2:30, I watch the indigo truck pull up in front of my

house. I stand and meet Hayden at the bottom of the front steps. My earlier thoughts still run through me, causing me to twist my fingers around one another like knots.

Hayden wears a baseball cap, a T-shirt, and khaki shorts. He said I am helping him, but I have no idea how. So I don't know exactly what to do and am a little shy today. I duck my head when he looks at me and only catch a glimpse of his smile.

When I raise my eyes to his face, he is waiting for me. He tilts his head to the side, regarding me with a serious expression. As though he wants to tell me something. Something really important. I hold my breath.

And then the moment passes. He must have changed his mind. I can see it in his change of expression, as if he drew the blinds closed. I can no longer see inside.

"Ready for some fun?" he says instead.

"Sounds good," I answer.

Then he takes off his cap and puts it on my head. He nods. "*Now* you're ready."

Hayden opens the passenger door, and I climb into the truck.

As soon as he is in the driver's seat, I ask, "What do you have planned for today?" I don't expect him to answer, but I have to ask anyway.

He turns to me and gives me a lopsided grin. "Helping others. How does that sound?"

"I think it sounds perfect," I tell him.

The drive is really short. At the corner, Hayden pulls into the parking lot for the elementary school. The lot is full of cars and people. The parents and students have made an assembly line to soap up people's cars—a car wash. Hayden parks on the side, and we get out.

"What is this for?" I ask.

"A student here who has leukemia. The family needs funds for her treatment. The car wash is to raise money to help them."

I think of my rainbow girl at the hospital. Her courage. This student's courage. They inspire me. And I want to help. I tell Hayden.

He nods. "I thought you would. Let's go."

Together, Hayden and I join the assembly line. He helps with the drying. I help with soaping the cars. I hold a giant wet sponge in my hands. When cars come by, I dip the sponge into my bucket and scrub away.

Before long, I am soaking wet, but I don't care. I'm here to help—and I'm happy to do it. Hayden waves at me. I wave back and notice wryly that he doesn't have a drop of water anywhere. So when he comes by to see how I am doing, I let him know with a quick splash of some soapy water.

"Much better," I say. He laughs and splashes me back. We are both drenched—and laughing.

I reach out to squeeze the sponge onto his shirt, but Hayden stops me with a touch on my wrist. He moves closer to try to turn the sponge around. His arm is around me. His eyes are the exact color of the sapphire paint. So deep. There is a whole world to see in his eyes. Suddenly, we aren't laughing. He is so close. If I lean forward, I will meet his mouth with mine. But I don't. I am dizzy with the nearness of him. I want him to kiss me.

He doesn't. He smiles tightly and takes a step back. Releases my hand. Releasing me. Cool air tingles my wet skin. Or is it the coolness of rejection?

Hayden gestures to a bin of sodas. I force myself to breathe in and out. I follow him. I choose a lemon-lime; Hayden takes a bottle of water. We sit side by side on the swings in the playground.

"How much money do they need to raise?" I ask. I can't stop thinking about the little rainbow girl.

"Thousands," he tells me. "There's a walk next week to raise more."

"I can walk," I say. "Will you take me?"

Suddenly, Hayden's eyes fill with a light so bright I almost have to look away. Then, just as quickly, it is gone—he looks away, embarrassed. "Of course," he says.

I use my feet to push myself slowly back and forth while I sip my soda. "You never talk about yourself," I say. Watching him.

Hayden shrugs as if he isn't important. But he is. To me.

"What do you want to know?"

Everything, I want to say. *I want to have a book about you that I can read over and over. Memorize.*

But instead, I shrug, too. "Do you live with your parents?"

"My grandfather," he answers. There is something in that moment. A flicker of something. So quick, like a flash of lightning—there and gone. But the impression is left in his eyes. A jagged streak of pain.

I pry further. "No brothers or sisters?"

He shakes his head, mouth tight as if he has to keep it from saying more. About things he doesn't want to share.

I am sorry for him then. I can't imagine life without Emerson. Even when she drives me crazy, frustrates me or embarrasses me, she is still so much a part of me, like my right arm.

"It is lonely," he responds. As though he can read my thoughts. It is disconcerting—having him read my mind. I wonder if he has been able to tell what I am thinking about him. The thought brings heat to my cheeks. I imagine they are flaming red.

"Are you and Emerson close?" he asks.

My answer is immediate. I nod. "We've been through a lot together."

He looks surprised. I am reminded of his initial criticism of me. That nothing bad had ever happened to me, so I couldn't imagine myself in a different way.

"My parents are divorced. My mom moved us here last year." I think of my first day at Richmond. "We didn't know anyone." And we didn't want to move here. I don't tell him that part.

Hayden's expression changes; he didn't know. "That must have been hard for you," he says. "I thought—you just looked like everything came so easy for you. I'm sorry."

"It's okay." It doesn't matter anymore.

Then he broaches a difficult subject. "Do you see your dad?"

I shrug. "When he schedules us in. Emerson sees him more

than I do." I take a deep breath. "He really doesn't know me at all." It hurts to say it. Even though I can't hear the words, I know they are out there.

Hayden shakes his head. A muscle tenses in his cheek. "I don't understand how parents can just walk away like that. If I were your dad, I would want to spend as much time with you as I could. Nothing would be more important than being with you."

His eyes blaze with passion. I can almost hear the intensity of his tone. My heart beats faster under the heat of his gaze.

And I know he means it as a criticism of my father, but also as a compliment of me.

"Thanks," I tell him. He meets my smile with one of his own. Then he shares something with me.

"My grandmother passed away two years ago. It's just me and my grandfather now."

I picture him at a table, eating dinner with his grandfather. It does seem lonely. I catch Hayden watching me. And again, I have the sense that he is reading my mind.

"I'd like to meet him," I say.

"He wants to meet you, too." He is teasing me, of course. His grandfather can't possibly want to meet me. But the thought gives me courage. Enough to say the words I have wanted to say all day.

"Hayden?"

He looks over and waits for me to speak.

"These days with you—they've meant everything to me."

Hayden's gaze takes me in. Holds me. Then he smiles. And

it's the way it always is when he smiles at me like that—like the sun is shining on me.

"I'll never forget one moment," he says.

We sit like that for a while. Just being together. And then we go back to help.

Postcards from the past

HAYDEN

"About time you showed up," my grandfather calls the moment I open the screen door. "I'm all ready for you."

"G-good, 'cause I'm-m st-starv-ing," I say.

My grandfather is standing at the kitchen counter, pizza fixings neatly laid out in front of him. He never reacts to my stutter. He just waits for me to finish like he has all the time in the world. It must be the artist in him. He sees the world in terms of moments. Always reminds me that life is a journey, not a race. His gray hair is neatly combed back from his lined face, and his blue eyes watch me, sharp as ever. Practicing yoga three times a week and eating vegetarian has made him look fifty instead of sixty-five.

"How was Stella today?" he asks.

"B-better, I th-think." I have shared details about Stella's accident, her injury and her recovery. I have not shared my feelings about her, but I think he knows. I can see it in his eyes, and I can hear it in the lilt in his voice when he asks about Stella. As though he is happy about me seeing her. Happy that I have a friend.

I drop my backpack on the kitchen floor. Wash my hands at the sink.

Gramps has already made fresh dough. He is pressing a ball into a flat circle. I watch his fingers work. Deft fingers that can sculpt a lump of clay into an animal bursting with life. Within moments, he has made a perfectly shaped pizza crust.

"You're up," he announces, as though I am seven and up to bat.

I take over and gently brush the dough with olive oil. Then add a spoonful of tomato sauce. I use the spoon to spread the sauce across the surface of the dough, swirling it in a circular motion. The dough turns from ivory to red. Next, I sprinkle cheese across the sauce. Then I decorate it with olives, peppers, mushrooms, and artichoke hearts. I create a pattern so that the entire pizza is symmetrical.

"G-good to g-go," I say.

Gramps lifts the pizza stone and carries it to the hot oven while I pour myself a glass of cold milk.

"This one's a beauty," Gramps gushes. He always praises. Never criticizes. "Wish Bessie could be here to see this one."

Even though my grandmother passed away two years ago, Gramps still refers to her as though she has just stepped out to run an errand and will be right back. He even talks to her in his sleep. I hear him sometimes. Having full conversations. They were married for forty-two years. Only cancer separated them.

She was so different from my mother, their daughter. We never talk about my mother. Not a word. It's like an unspoken agreement between us. My grandmother used to speak about her, though. She wanted me to forgive my mother for her mistakes. She didn't want me to carry anger and resentment. She said it would make me bitter, full of rage. Grandma said my mother was flawed and that she wasn't meant to be a parent. But she loved me.

If that's love, then I want none of it. Love brings you nothing but pain. And a feeling of emptiness when you get left behind. Because when my grandparents brought me here, that's exactly what she did. Left me behind. Traveled the world. She came and visited a few times. Brought me T-shirts from exotic destinations. They were always in the wrong size, like she didn't remember her own son's age.

The last time I saw her was just after my twelfth birthday. She showed up with a wooden flute and a boyfriend she'd picked up in Thailand. I haven't seen her since. She stopped sending postcards about two years ago. I don't know if my grandfather hears from her, or if he even knows where she is.

I haven't forgiven her. And I never will.

15

STELLA

Sunday morning.

I pull on shorts and a T-shirt and head to the kitchen. I am ravenous. I take out eggs and flour and milk. By the time Emerson comes into the kitchen, I am already flipping pancakes. Emerson finds chocolate chips, and we make little faces on each one. Then Mom comes into the kitchen and adds whipped cream. We sit down to eat our little clown pancakes. Emerson makes funny faces, and we all laugh together. And it feels like it used to—maybe even better than it used to.

Mom writes me a note. *Church?* I haven't been to church in a long time. Not since the divorce. It was something we did as a family. I went alone once, but it felt lonely. I haven't gone since. I smile and nod. I want to go today.

An hour later, Mom, Emerson, and I are walking into church. It's crowded. Mom finds seats on one of the back rows. We slide in. I won't be able to hear the service or sing along with the hymns, but I can pray. I close my eyes and talk to God.

I pray for my family. I pray for healing in my ears. I pray for my rainbow girl. I thank Him for my life. I thank Him for Hayden.

I feel the vibrations of song and organ filling the air around me. I open my eyes. My mother and sister are singing. I look around the church. Everyone is singing and praying. And then I see him.

On the stage. Playing the organ. Singing.

For a second I wonder if I am imagining it. Maybe that's not him. But then his blue eyes meet mine.

Golden sun shines on me, filling my day with color and light. I sense my mother's eyes on me, and I turn to look at her. She has seen Hayden too. She raises an eyebrow. She thinks I knew he would be here and that this was the reason I agreed to join her today. I shake my head.

"I didn't know," I say.

She slips an arm around my shoulder. I turn back to watch Hayden. Even though I can't hear the music, I can feel the power in it. A heat begins in the center of my chest and moves outward until my whole body is warm. Everyone is clapping along with the song. I can watch the rhythm and clap in time. I find myself smiling—no, beaming—right at Hayden. And when he looks up from the keys and smiles back at me, I am flying again.

After the service, Emerson finds two of her friends. I stand with Mom while she talks to someone. I search for Hayden in the crowd. But I don't see him. I swallow a lump of disappointment and don't even bother trying to read Mom's lips to participate in the conversation. For the moment, I am content in my bubble of silence.

And then I know he is here. I don't see him; I feel him. His presence like fire racing up my veins. I turn around slowly. Hayden and I are face to face. Words are no longer necessary between us. Our eyes speak instead. His expression is almost proud, like I have passed some kind of test.

We stand there like that, staring at one another, until my mom turns around and sees us. She steps across me to hug Hayden. She must compliment him on his playing, because he thanks her. He says he doesn't always play here, but he was asked to fill in for someone. Mom glances from me to him. Back to me. Then she points to the door and holds up five fingers.

"Outside in five minutes," I confirm. So she waves goodbye to Hayden and leaves.

I stand there for a moment. Saying nothing. Just breathing in happiness. Then I say, "You don't seem surprised to see me."

Hayden's eyes are filled with little lights like wishing stars. "I had a feeling you would be here." He holds out his hand. Palm up. Closed. "This is for you."

He opens it slowly.

A perfect pink seashell.

I reach out to lift it gently from his hand. His fingers slowly close over mine, holding my hand for a brief moment, keeping us together.

When he releases my fingers, I am holding the shell. I turn

it over in my hand. Marvel at the color and shape. It is still warm.

"It's beautiful. Thank you." My eyes drop to the floor. "I wish I could have heard you play."

His fingers gently tilt my chin. I meet his azure gaze. "You *see* me, Stella."

Tingles run up and down my legs. His expression is so intense, I can't breathe.

I see him. It doesn't matter if I can hear him. I see him.

And he sees me. The real me.

I understand. I watch him watch me.

Then he turns his head to look away. When he looks back, he grins sideways, narrowing his eyes. "Ready to meet the family?"

I don't have time to answer. A tall, handsome gentleman with gray hair joins us. I know who he is instantly because he has Hayden's eyes.

He takes my hand in both of his and holds it tightly. I can't understand what he is saying, so I look from his mouth to Hayden's.

"This is my grandfather, John Rivers."

"I'm so happy to meet you, Mr. Rivers."

He says something, and Hayden translates again. "He says you can call him Gramps. Mr. Rivers is too formal and reminds him of his teaching days."

He was a teacher. I wonder what subject he taught. I want to ask. I want to know everything about Hayden's family.

"Your grandson is very brave," I tell him. His eyes twinkle at my compliment of Hayden.

He says something, but again, I can't understand. I crinkle my forehead as I try to read his lips. I want so much to impress him. My forehead is damp, and my hand clenches the seashell so hard, it is digging into my palm. But I cannot make out his words. I turn to Hayden. Shake my head. "I don't understand."

Hayden nods slowly, wearing an expression I cannot read. He translates once again. "My grandfather thinks you are brave."

Oh.

My eyes flicker back to Hayden's grandfather. He nods, eyes still twinkling.

"Thank you," I say, ducking my head. When I look up again, they are both watching me. Twin eyes.

I grin at them. And then I remember that my mother is waiting for me, and it has been more than five minutes. "I have to meet my mom outside," I explain. "I'm so sorry."

I want to stay. I want to have one more minute with Hayden, but I have to go.

"Maybe later?" Hayden asks.

I hesitate; I have agreed to see Lily. And tomorrow is my first day back at school. I need to finish my homework.

"Tomorrow?" I suggest instead.

If Hayden is disappointed, he covers it. He nods. "After school."

I walk away slowly, resisting the urge to look back. In my hand, I still grip the pink seashell. And Hayden's touch.

Lily will be here any minute. Emerson is in her room. Mom in the kitchen. And I am waiting in the living room. I'm more nervous than I was auditioning for the musical. In fact, I'm pretty sure I'm going to vomit.

When I see Lily's blonde hair out the window, I start to breathe heavier. I'm almost panting. I tell myself that this is Lily. My best friend. Nothing has changed. It will be just like it has always been.

I stand and open the door. And there she is. Her blonde hair is pulled into a ponytail. She's wearing a lot of eye makeup, but her cheeks are pale under the blush. She's nervous. The realization makes me relax.

"Hi," I say. I step back. "Come in."

She comes into the house and hugs me. She smells of cigarettes. The scent clings to her clothes, surrounds her like a gray cloud. It makes my stomach flip.

I head into the living room. Normally, Lily and I would go straight into my room and close the door. Not today. Today, I want to stay out here.

I sit on the blue and white sofa. Lily stands for a second, unsure of where to sit. Then she takes a seat in the chair opposite the sofa. She looks at me. Her eyes dart back and forth, looking from my scar and my partially shaved head to my ears and back again. She chews on her lip, and I can tell she has no idea what to do, now that she is actually here. I have brought paper and pens to make this easier.

I hand her a pad with a pen. "I can't read lips very well, so if you want to tell me something, write it down."

Lily nods but doesn't use the pen. She just stares at me. I decide to speak again.

"I'm going back to school tomorrow."

Her gray eyes widen. She begins talking. I shake my head, point to the pen.

"You have to write it down for me. In a couple of weeks, I will be able to hear you. But for now . . ." I trail off. I don't want to go into a full explanation.

Lily nods and starts writing. Then she hands me the paper.

Stella, I am so, so sorry for what happened. It should have been me. Not you. You didn't even want to be there. Connor is really sorry too. He didn't mean for things to get out of control.

I know everything's going to be fine. It has to be. You are going to hear again. And it will be like this never even happened.

It's très fabulous that you are coming back to school. We'll have the BTE. We both have boyfriends and we're popular. How cool is that!?

I read her note over twice to give myself time to process it.

She doesn't get it. Not one bit. But then, how could she? She isn't living it. I am.

I consider telling her. Explaining that I don't care if I'm popular. It doesn't matter to me. Not anymore. I consider explaining that nothing will be like it was. Ever again. But I don't. It wouldn't change anything. Instead, I force a smile at my best friend, who may as well be a stranger. And I say, "Hayden isn't my boyfriend."

There it is. Hayden is not my boyfriend.

A smirk crosses her face before she douses it with a pout. So she does reign supreme after all. Lily has the first boyfriend. Now she can be benevolent.

She takes the pen.

Well, SC wasn't right for you anyway. And Connor has lots of friends.

Yes. I've met some of his friends, and I have zero interest in meeting any more. But I don't tell her that.

"Don't call him SC," I say. Maybe in a stronger tone than I intended. But I can't hear it. "His name is Hayden."

There. He may not be my boyfriend, but he's my friend. And I won't let Lily or anyone else make fun of him. Not in front of me.

Lily shrugs and crosses out the last two sentences. She writes something else.

No problemo. There's a whole football team. And we're almost juniors.

Instead of being disappointed or hurt, I find I am relieved. I can finally see what I only glimpsed through a haze before, what I couldn't quite grasp. Not using my ears has made me use my eyes.

I see Lily now. The real Lily.

"I know you're sorry—and I know you didn't mean for me to get hurt. I forgive you. Of course I forgive you. But I'm not the person I used to be. I'm different now. So I think I just need some time to see how this all goes."

Lily has always been about Lily. I didn't see it before. Or if I did, it didn't bother me like it does now. I was just happy to have a friend. In my heart, I know that we'll never be best friends again. Not like before. There's no point in telling her that, either. I can tell she feels really guilty. That's enough pain for her to deal with right now.

Lily nods. She stands and comes over to give me a hug. I

hug her back. Tears start to sting my eyes. I blink them back and walk her to the door. When I pull it open, I see that the clouds have moved in and it has started to drizzle outside.

"Do you have an umbrella?" I ask.

Lily lives a block away, so I know she walked here. She shakes her head.

I go to the coat closet and pull out a red umbrella. I hand it to her. "You can drop it off next week."

Lily hugs me again and takes the umbrella. At the doorway, she turns to look at me once more. Raises her hand in a small wave. And then she leaves.

I close the door. Then I sit down right there on the floor.

And I cry.

STEPS

STELLA

Monday morning at Richmond High School. Only I don't hear the melody of the school anymore. I can't hear the thunder of feet moving across concrete floors. Lockers clanging. Cell phones ringing. Flirtatious laughter. Hollered greetings. Books dropping. Doors slamming.

I can no longer hear the soundtrack of high school. It *looks* the same. But now it is silent.

Emerson walks beside me, one arm looped through mine. Chewing on her lower lip. She is worried that this will be too much for me. And the truth is, she may be right. It may be too much for me. But I need to try. I need to be normal.

I glance around for Hayden. Seeing him would make me happy, like getting a present when it isn't your birthday or Christmas. But I don't see him anywhere.

Students wave to me. People I've never even met. Girls come up and hug me. Saying things I can't understand. I put on a happy mask. Move through the bodies. Now seeking Hayden like a life jacket to keep me afloat in the current. Lily waits for me in front of my locker.

She smiles and says something I can't understand.

I open my locker, put my books inside. Pull out my notebook for history. I can go right to class. My mom has already spoken with my teachers and the principal. They know I have an app that lets me see their words translated onto my phone's screen so I can read their lectures in real time. I should be able to fit seamlessly back into school.

Should is the operative word, because it's hard. Really hard. I am locked in my cell of silence. The day is happening around me. Not to me.

Classes are okay. I can get a pretty good idea of what I am supposed to do. Most of my teachers write a lot on the boards and screens. We use remotes in math to transmit our answers. Technology is definitely my friend.

It's just that everything is so different. I am removed from it all. I feel like I am on the outside of a store, looking through the glass windows. I can see everything, but I am not part of it.

The amount of schoolwork is overwhelming. It's block schedule today, so I only have three classes, but each one is ninety minutes long. I get a headache in first period. By the time I reach third—English—my skull is throbbing. We spend most of class reading *Hamlet.* I stare at the page, but I don't comprehend anything at all. I just want to go home. This is so much harder than I thought it would be. Being here forces me to acknowledge the truth. The fact is that I am changed. And I am completely alone.

When the class is over, I slide my book into my backpack. I move into the hallway and go with the flow toward my locker. The irony is that now I am more popular than ever. But I can't enjoy it. And popularity no longer matters to me.

On the way to my locker, Kace stops me. Gives me a hug. The drama crowd is very touchy feely. He tries to tell me something; I can't understand him. I shrug and shake my head. He writes it down instead.

So happy to see you back. I missed your smile.

I am warmed by his compliment. And it makes me smile. Big and wide. For the first time all day. Kace grins back. For a split second, we are back on stage in the spotlight. Tony and Maria. In love.

Then I remember. And the color in the hallways dims. Fades. My headache pounds once again.

He writes something else down and hands me the note.

Want to eat in the drama room?

"Maybe tomorrow," I answer. I'm self-conscious of my voice. Its volume. Sound. Quality.

But Kace nods. He winks, and then moves away into the crowd of students. I have just rejected lunch with the King of Drama. A few weeks ago, that would have been a dream come true—to be a sophomore invited into the senior lunch crowd by the King himself. But it no longer matters.

I would rather stumble through lunchtime with Emerson and her friends than pretend with Lily or Kace. And that is exactly what I plan to do.

Another reminder of how much I have changed.

When I reach my locker, Hayden is leaning against it.

Wearing jeans and a white long-sleeved shirt he has left untucked. His hair is brushed back off his face. His eyes have never looked so dark. Like the sky just before the stars come out. Suddenly, I can breathe.

"You inspire me." His words are as clear as if I heard them.

I take them in. Place them in a special place where I can remember them over and over again. His gaze holds me.

"Would you like to eat lunch with me?" he asks. Formally. Politely.

I smile. No words are necessary.

I am pulling my lunch bag out of my locker when Lily arrives with a full posse in tow—three cheerleaders and one sophomore. She takes one look at Hayden and then turns to me. Eyebrows raised. Waiting.

This is Lily giving me time? She doesn't understand waiting. Delayed gratification isn't her thing. She's a here-and-now girl. I know she expected me to eat lunch with her and that everything would go back to the way it was. I would be added to the posse, another member of her entourage. The silent girl. Seen, not heard.

Before, I would have gone along, but now, I take a deep breath. I must speak in front of all these people without knowing how I sound. I let the air out slowly.

"I'm eating lunch with Hayden."

Lily's eyes widen. Then narrow. A brief hint of sadness crosses her face before vanishing. She tosses her blonde curls.

She says something I can't understand, then she turns and walks away. The entourage follows closely behind her pink heels.

I am left standing in front of my locker, grounded in my red Converse sneakers. I seek Hayden's eyes; I swim in them for a moment, soaking up the appreciation I see there. For choosing him.

Hayden and I walk together to the far side of campus to a large grassy area with trees. On the way, I see Emerson sitting with her friends on the ground near the front entrance of school—the area reserved for freshmen. Before I can tell her I am eating with Hayden, she jumps up to meet me. She grabs my hand and squeezes.

Since the accident, Emerson and I have grown as close as when we were little. Now we, too, can communicate without words. She is happy for me. She understands. I squeeze her hand back to thank her. She lopes back to her friends. Her stride is graceful, musical. Emerson turns back to look once more. Waves at Hayden.

We sit underneath the largest tree. All alone. I sink to the ground, suddenly exhausted. I am no longer hungry.

Hayden pulls a sandwich and apple out of his backpack and begins eating right away.

His face is more angular with his hair pulled back. His scar more noticeable. I watch him twist the apple stem. I think of my name game.

I finally ask the question I have been wanting to ask. "Don't your friends mind you eating with me?"

Hayden twists his lips. "They might. If I had any."

I don't understand. "You have friends." Of course he does.

He shakes his head. "Only you. You are my friend, aren't

you?" His eyes sparkle. He's teasing me, I think, but without hearing the inflection of his voice, I can't be sure.

"I'm your friend," I say. *Friend.* A word laden with so much meaning, but it's missing something. I ache for that something—something I never wanted before.

This bittersweet pain is an unfamiliar feeling.

Hayden's eyes drop to the ground. He studies the laces on his sneakers. "This is the first time I haven't eaten lunch alone."

I read the words on his lips without seeing the expression in his eyes. When he finally raises his gaze to mine, there is the vulnerability again. I understand.

Without thinking, I reach out and touch his cheek. My fingers brush his skin. He is warm and cold at the same time, like fire and ice. Sun and moon. Day and night. Love and loss.

I catch my breath. His hand reaches up and wraps around mine. I am spinning, like a leaf in the wind at the mercy of a force greater than myself. Falling. Only suddenly, I'm no longer afraid. Because I know that when I land, Hayden will be there to catch me.

We stay like that. Hand in hand. Connected.

"Close your eyes," he tells me.

Like at the beach. Hayden wants me to use my senses. To open my mind to possibilities. The difficulties of today have left me locked inside my bubble of silence. Hayden is opening the door. Letting in the fresh air. Coaxing me outside.

I close my eyes. Open my mind. Free myself.

The spring air teases my hair, lifting it off my shoulders. I can smell orange blossoms and new grass. Hayden's hand is warm, secure. I open my eyes. Hayden offers me a handful of trail mix. I bite into the raisins and nuts. Crunchy and chewy. Sweetness bursts in my mouth.

I see Hayden watching me. Waiting.

I am so grateful to him for bringing me back to myself. We sit there quietly. Touching. Being.

Then Hayden speaks. "There we two, content, happy in being together, speaking little, perhaps not a word."

He watches me as the words sink in. Touch me. Move me.

"It's Whitman." He shrugs. "Speech therapists love poetry."

It's not the first time he has talked about his speech. Hayden reveals himself in bits and pieces. I have to put them together to understand him. I want to ask about speech therapy, gather more of the pieces, but there isn't time. Behind Hayden, students are gathering their things. Lunch must be over.

That means it's time for drama. My stomach churns at the thought of passing through the red doors. I'm not sure I can do it. I pick up my uneaten lunch. Open my backpack. Put the lunch inside. Stalling for time.

I am planning escapes instead of facing this challenge. Maybe I should go home early. Maybe I should change electives. Maybe it was too soon to come back. Something warm brushes against my shoulder. I look up. See Hayden. Like a soft summer breeze coaxing me into the sun, he reaches out to me. Without words or movements. I know he understands. Somehow, he knows. And just like that, the doubts fade. I am left with a clear, conscious focus. To move forward. And to have the courage to face my fears.

He leaves me at my locker. "See you later," he promises.

I want to call him back before he disappears into the crowd. To ask him to shepherd me through the red doors. To be with me.

But I don't, really. Because this is something I must do myself. I breathe in deep. Put one foot in front of the other. And move down the hallway toward drama.

When I arrive at the crimson doors, I stop. There, right in front of me, is my poster. I have made the wall. And there, I am Maria. Forever.

The poster doesn't make me cry like the last time I saw it. Seeing it here, like this, I am proud. Proud of my work, my talent. It is with that burst of strength that I open the doors and walk through. Because I belong here. I have earned my place here.

The class is seated in the mini-theater, a small stage used for plays and other more intimate productions. This is the area where we perform pieces and suffer critiques, first by Mr. Preston, and then from the class. When I enter the back of the room, I look around for an empty seat near the back. Kace sees me and motions from the back row. He has saved me a seat next to him. Quinn is seated on the other side, playing with her cell phone. I slide next to Kace.

"Thanks," I say.

He nods. Quinn looks up, and her expression is one I have never seen on her—an actual real smile. Directed at me.

"Hi," I tell her.

Class begins. I can read the words Mr. Preston speaks on my smart phone. There are mistakes in the translation, like

"Blonde will be the first ringer pup" instead of "John will be the first singer up." But I get a good idea of what is happening.

That is, until the students each stand and begin singing. Then the app goes crazy. It can't follow the rhythm of the music. I give up and watch their body language to see if I can understand the emotions they are conveying. It's a new way of watching performances. I try to learn from what I see. I imagine using more body language and facial expressions in my performances. Kace writes me a note.

Mr. Preston probably sounds better on mute.

I write back. *Especially when the app gets his words wrong.*

I show him my phone. Kace slaps his hand over his mouth to keep from laughing out loud. He writes back. *That's priceless.*

I watch Quinn on stage. Her arms open wide, face upturned. Mouth filled with a song I cannot hear. I am useless here. Unable to perform, I can't use my talent. I can't even comment on others' performances.

Someday Broadway, I think wistfully.

What is she singing? I write to Kace.

"Defying Gravity" from Wicked.

Oh, I love that song. I look back at Quinn. A deep ache courses through me. I want to be up there filling my lungs with air, breathing out emotion. Song.

I remember the power flowing through me. Bursting out like fireworks. Lighting up the stage, the theater. With color.

Now I sit.

Silent.

I don't write any more notes to Kace. I just stare at the

other performers. Pretending to watch. But I see nothing. Hear nothing. I am invisible.

My loss has never been as painful as in these moments. In this class, which was once the center of my world. The center of me. Can one grieve the death of a dream? Is that what I am doing now?

When the clock finally reaches three o'clock, I am free. I stand and reach for my backpack, happy to escape.

"See you tomorrow," I tell Kace.

He stops me with a hand on my arm. Then gives me a leading man smile, sparkling eyes. He seems like he wants to tell me something. I pause for a moment, out of politeness. Sometimes being polite is a negative trait. It makes you do things you would rather not do. Like stay when I want to leave. Kace scribbles something on a slip of paper.

He hands it to me with a wink. *Lunch tomorrow. You promised.*

Speaking the unspeakable

HAYDEN

School has always been a prison, a place where people judged me, laughed at me, and asked questions I didn't want to answer. Until today.

Because today, for the first time in my life, I belonged. I belonged with her. Stella forces me to come out of the shadows—to be seen, to connect.

Speaking to her, I am free. I am free to be myself. Reciting poetry in a tone so smooth it would make my speech therapist proud—envious, even. Stella's silence has given me a voice. A way to communicate with words but without sound. Who would have thought it was possible?

Today, I saw how strong Stella is—willing to attend classes where everyone else can hear what she can't, willing to walk hallways with people pointing and talking about her, willing to walk away from her best friend because she isn't the same person anymore.

Stella inspires me with her courage. As though by being near her, some of her fearlessness might touch me and make me more like her.

I haven't admired many people in my life. Only my grandfather, President Lincoln, and Stella. I never knew my dad. My mother couldn't even remember his name, let alone where to find him, and there was nothing admirable about her. To my grandmother, I was grateful. But there was something about her—maybe in the way she spoke or in her mannerisms—that reminded me of my mother. It wasn't until she died that it was safe for me to speak. And then only to my grandfather. I admire him—his gentle ways and his optimism, his faith, and, of course, his many talents. For seeing the unseen and speaking the unspeakable. We don't speak of love, my grandfather and I.

My mother said she loved me. Right before she split open my chin.

I have the memory engraved in my skin. A reminder in case I ever forget.

At the end of the day, I look for Stella. The hallways are crowded, but I can always tell if she is near. My senses become heightened in those moments. Sounds are defined, smells more distinct, my sight acute. She has this effect on me.

I see her near the far doorway, and her sister Emerson is with her. Students wave at Stella. She waves back. She makes it look so easy, making friends. I meant it when I told Stella she was my only friend.

When I was young, I was afraid to make friends because they might find out my secret. Later, when I stopped speaking, I repelled other students. I was the freaky kid no one wanted to stand next to or sit near in class. I ate lunch alone every single day. Lunch I had usually made myself. Lunch was the worst time of the day for me because that was when everyone else had someone. Everyone except me. Eating lunch alone wouldn't be so bad if you weren't the only one. Then it's worse. Then it's like a banner over your head reading LOSER. Once you have that moniker, you can pretty much guarantee the rest. My journey hasn't been a meandering path, but a climb out of the mouth of a volcano. Someday, I will understand why.

Gramps likes to say that it is the way we overcome obstacles that defines us. But what happens if we don't overcome the obstacles? What if we become the obstacle itself?

Stella and Emerson exit through the door together, and I watch them go before I turn toward the parking lot. I am expected at the nursery for a couple of hours after school. Then I will stop by Stella's house. I have a surprise for her.

14

STELLA

After dinner, I help my mom wash the dishes. Emerson finishes her homework on the computer. The kitchen is my favorite room. It's peaceful in here. Mom rinses while I put the dishes in the dishwasher and tell her about my day.

I still can't understand my mom, but I have learned how to read her face. So when I say, "I didn't eat lunch with Lily today," her eyes widen with understanding.

"It's not the same," I explain. Mom nods. She writes something on the pad on the counter.

Give yourself time.

"Okay," I tell her. "I will."

But she doesn't know. Time has already driven me and Lily apart. I have been replaced by a posse of populars. Time is my enemy. Each moment that ticks by takes me farther from the life I had. Moves me into a future I don't recognize. The unknown scares me. I resist it even as I know I have no choice. I must learn to see myself differently.

Just like Hayden said.

Emerson brings Hayden into the kitchen. He looks taller in our house. More golden. As if the room has been lit by his presence.

He's holding a bag of groceries in his arms. I smile and cross the room to greet him.

"Hi," I say. It seems inadequate. Too small for all the things he makes me feel.

His eyes rest on me, and for a long moment, we just gaze at each other. Silent. Like we are the only two people in the room.

Then my mom reaches over and hugs Hayden. It is how she always greets him. He gestures to the bag. "Would you mind if we used the kitchen?"

She answers him with wide open arms. I imagine she is saying, "It's all yours. Just clean it up when you finish." Then she leaves.

"We're cooking?" I am surprised. This is the last thing I expected.

He tilts his head to the side. "Baking, actually."

"Is chocolate involved?" I ask as I take the bag from him and set it on the counter.

Hayden reaches into it and begins unloading. Flour, sugar, brown sugar, eggs, chocolate chips, and butter.

"Let me guess," I offer, considering the ingredients. "Chocolate chip cookies?"

"You must be an expert."

I take a couple of mixing bowls out of the cabinet, then preheat the oven. I show Hayden the drawer with the measuring cups and spoons. Hayden hands me the bag of chips and points to the recipe on the back. I laugh; I know this one by heart.

I've made chocolate chip cookies dozens of times before, but it's never been this fun. We work together silently, in unison, as though we hear each other's thoughts.

Hayden deftly cracks the eggs with one hand, like chefs on television. I am impressed. I measure the flour and baking soda. He adds the salt. I pack the brown sugar. He measures the cane sugar. I pour the vanilla, and he mixes in the butter. He holds the measuring cup while I shake out a cupful of chocolate chips.

Our movements are harmonious, almost like a dance. I notice things I never have before. The smooth, powdery texture of the cool flour against my fingers. The sweet aroma of soft, brown sugar. The cocoa tang of the semi-sweet chocolate chips I steal. The deep sunflower shade of melted butter, which reminds me of the center of the daisies Hayden gave me.

We use tablespoons to drop balls of dough onto the cookie sheets. I'm not surprised when Emerson barges into the kitchen. She grabs a spoonful of dough and dashes away before we can stop her. I know she will be back when she smells the scent of baked cookies. Hayden seems to find it amusing.

"Life with a little sister," I say as I roll my eyes.

Hayden picks up the cookie sheet dotted with clumps of dough. Puts it into the oven. I set the timer for 10 minutes. We sit at the kitchen table with glasses of orange juice to wait.

"This was a good idea," I say.

Hayden fixes me with his sapphire stare. I see a scattering of freckles across the bridge of his nose. I've never noticed them. What else haven't I noticed?

He grins and tilts his head to the side. "You don't need to hear to cook."

It's not a question. It's a simple statement. A reminder of his challenge. He is showing me all of the things I can do whether I can hear or not. He is showing me that life is beautiful.

"Thank you," I say.

He nods. Once again, words are not necessary.

For a long moment, neither of us moves. We just watch each other. I feel bonded to him. Sealed, as though this moment was decided long before I ever fell into the pool. Before I ever auditioned for Maria. Before everything.

Hayden breaks eye contact first. The sweet smell of sugar, butter and chocolate fills the kitchen. Tells me the cookies are done. I am not surprised when Hayden moves toward the oven. I know the timer is beeping even though I can't hear it.

I bring over oven mitts and remove the trays. The cookies are golden brown, the chocolate chips slightly melted. They look delicious—soft and chewy.

Bringing back memories of baking with my mother.

"My mom and I used to make chocolate chip cookies together," I say. "Whenever I had a bad day at school."

Hayden has a faraway expression in his eyes. "I don't think I have any good memories of my mother."

I imagine the emptiness in his voice from the expression on

his face. He doesn't envy me. He just grieves for something he never had. I ache for him, for his loss.

"She hurt you, didn't she?" I don't think about it. I just say it.

And bam. It's like I've slapped him. He reels back. Wariness crosses his face. I sense he is about to change the subject. He has done it before. Every time I start to get close to the truth. So before it's too late, I blurt out, "I'm so sorry, Hayden."

This time he doesn't speak for so long, I am sure he won't answer. Then he says, "It was a long time ago. It doesn't matter now."

But I can see from the look on his face that the wounds are still raw. Hayden hasn't healed. I want to hear his story. To listen to him. But his expression has shifted. It's closed off. He won't let me in.

That's when Emerson saves me by sneaking into the kitchen and making a big fuss over the cookies. Stuffing them into her mouth. If she notices the tension in the room, she doesn't show it.

I'm grateful for the distraction. I busy myself with making her and my mother a plate of cookies and glasses of milk on a tray. Not until she leaves the kitchen with the tray can I face him. I am sure he will leave, offended by my imposition. I am prepared to apologize. To tell him that I have no right to pry into his past.

But he doesn't leave. He waits while I make a plate of cookies for us. When I dare to raise my eyes to his, he is still here. Not running away. Still with me.

I reach for something to say. Anything.

"Do you play backgammon?" I ask.

His smile is all the answer I need. I hurry to the cabinet in the hallway to retrieve the game. I hope he won't disappear while I am gone.

When I return to the kitchen, he is still at the table. He has waited for me before eating any cookies.

I grin at him. "I have an unfair advantage, you know." I set up the backgammon board on the kitchen table. "I'm the family champ." I can beat everyone in my family, including my father. I expect to beat Hayden as well. He just doesn't know it.

"Not so fast, Layne. I may be better than you think," he teases me.

The cookies are delicious. Warm and sweet, they taste of happiness and comfort. I will never bake them again without remembering the sweetness of this day.

Within a short time, I am not surprised to find myself the winner of our game.

I sit back and tell him, "I did warn you."

"Fair enough. Do you have a chess board? That's a game I can win."

"I'm pretty good at chess, too," I say. "You'd better bring your A game."

I love chess. Not because I am so good at it—at least, not as good as I am at backgammon—but because I love the idea of it. Chess takes thought and strategy. There's no luck to it—winning is all about the talent of the player.

We don't speak while we play. I can't read lips and watch the board at the same time. Hayden seems to understand, so we play in silence. I open my thoughts to hearing Hayden—not with my ears, but with my mind. I try to anticipate his moves by watching him. I study the expressions on his face, watch his body language. I move my pieces accordingly. I've never played chess like this before. Truthfully, I've never played this well before.

I move my queen, putting his king in check. I glance at Hayden's face. His expression is one I haven't seen on him before, sort of a half-smile with a raised eyebrow. I have surprised him and impressed him. He is seeing a new side of me. I can tell all of this without words. I grin at him, and then watch in dismay as, with only two moves, he escapes my queen, and puts me into checkmate. Hayden has won.

He stands and bows. A really formal bow. "That was the best chess game I have ever played," he tells me. With anyone else, I would think they were lying. But I see nothing but truth in Hayden's eyes. So I smile and thank him.

Then I add, "Me, too."

Mom comes into the kitchen. Taps her watch. It's getting late. Hayden stands. His grandfather will be waiting for him. I walk him to the door. He has shown me yet again how to enjoy my life without hearing. And I am grateful to him.

"Thanks for today," I tell him. I hand him a baggie with four of the cookies we baked. "For your grandfather."

He grins. "See you tomorrow."

"Tomorrow," I echo. And then, to my surprise, he reaches over and trails his fingers across my cheek. His touch is as soft as a daisy petal brushing across my skin. But it leaves an imprint that I can feel tingling even after his hand drops back to his side.

"Sleep well, Stella."

And then he is gone.

Pieces of a puzzle

HAYDEN

I almost told her. I almost told her everything.

I drive home slowly, thinking of her. The way she looks at me, as if I mean something to her—something real. Stella is the first person outside my family who knows something bad happened to me. I can tell by the emotion in her eyes, the expression on her face.

What makes her different from everyone else is that I sensed no pity in her. It was more like an embrace. In her reaching for me, I was comforted for one split second. And in that second, I was understood.

I can't allow that to happen again. I can't let her get so close. I have fit the pieces of myself back together. Pieces that were tossed around by my mother. Some were destroyed, but I glued myself together. If I let Stella in, she could pull some of those pieces loose. I don't think I could put myself back together again—not after Stella. She could destroy me.

If I were smart, I would pull away now, before it's too late. But I made her a promise—seventeen days to show her that she can imagine herself differently, without sound. I am showing her what she can do without hearing. I am opening her mind to possibilities. I can't walk away now.

I will just have to be stronger.

Love brings pain. Don't let yourself fall in love.

Anything but that.

13

STELLA

The second day of school is better than the first. I know what to expect now. And time seems to move faster at school. In less than two weeks, I will know if I can hear again.

Lily is waiting for me at my locker. Looking prettier than ever, she smiles and hands me a note.

Would you come to my cheerleading tryouts after school today? It would mean a lot to me to have my BFF there.

Before I even finish reading the note, I know what my answer will be.

It's hard for me to say no to Lily. Even now.

I nod. "I'll be there."

I text my mom and ask her to pick me up an hour later. Then I hurry to class. I can't hear the bell ring, but I can read the clock. And I am about to be tardy.

We watch a film in health. It isn't captioned, so I can only watch the images. Time for my mind to wander. I think about yesterday. About Hayden.

Because of him, I have started to see the world differently. I see myself differently. Walking through the halls this morning, I couldn't hear the melody of school. But it didn't matter. And people stared at me. Before, I would have cared, worried about what people thought of me. How they viewed me.

But I am changing. I'm stronger somehow. Less afraid. I am more myself without a part of me than I ever was with it.

So I open my senses and use them. I may not be able to hear the melody of Richmond High, but I can smell the paper on the hallway floors and the markers used to make the posters announcing the school dance. I can smell mints in the backpack next to mine. The guy in front of me uses the same shampoo as my mom. And I can see the giggles on the face of the girl to my right. I play a game with myself.

I look around the room at each face. I try to see if I can tell what they are thinking, feeling, doing, just by watching their expressions.

Some are enjoying the film. Others are lost in their thoughts. Daydreaming. Sneaking bites of breakfast from under their desks or texting. A few are sleeping. I never noticed how much was going on around me. I never looked around to see. Not like this.

My mind drifts back to Hayden, although he is never far from my thoughts. Yesterday, I tried to draw him out, get him to trust me. I asked him a question about his mother. And

I got my answer. She did hurt him. I saw it on his face. As clearly as if he had spoken the words. She broke his heart.

He told me it was a long time ago and didn't matter anymore, but it isn't until this moment that I register the importance of what he said.

His disillusionment. What that means for me. He is broken. Damaged. It isn't his speech; it's his heart. It's been silenced. I sit nestled in the quiet of my world. Allowing me to look deep inside him.

I have vowed for years never to make the mistakes my mother made. Never to trust my heart to another. But it happened. Even when I didn't want it or ask for it. It just happened.

And Hayden needs my help.

So I ask myself the question: Am I willing to risk my own heart to save his?

When lunchtime arrives, I still have no answer. It seems like a stroke of luck that I have already promised to eat with Kace in the drama room. I'm not ready to be with Hayden. Not until I have resolved my own feelings.

He is waiting in front of my locker just like yesterday. Today, his hair is loose, almost covering his eyes. But it can't hide his smile. It is just for me. I meet it with one of my own. The now-familiar butterflies fluttering in response.

"I'm eating in the drama room today," I tell him. I don't know why I say it. As soon as the words are out of my mouth, I want to call them back, but it is too late. His smile fades instantly. He is expressionless, like his face is carved in ice.

"No problem." He forces a grin. His eyes are frozen.

Nothing could melt them. Then he walks away, disappearing into the crowd.

I watch him go, wondering why I have made this choice. Even though I already know the answer.

I am afraid. Afraid of my feelings for Hayden. And I am pushing him away. Just when I need him most.

Lunch in the drama room is an honor reserved for only the top echelon. Kace and Quinn preside. You attend only by invitation. I've dreamed about this moment for over a year. Only now that I'm here, it doesn't matter to me anymore.

The drama crowd eats in the mini-theater's green room, which we use for running lines before shows or waiting for class. It has big old, plaid sofas and coffee tables. Mr. Preston's office door is on the right side. The backstage entrance is on the left. It's like a coffee lounge minus the coffee.

Kace is sprawled in the big armchair. He has saved a seat for me on the sofa next to him. Quinn sits opposite on her own throne, a faded blue director's chair left over from Mr. Preston's acting days. Someone has ordered a pizza. Someone else passes a box of donuts. There is camaraderie and friendship here. No one stares. I am treated like one of the group, like I belong. Kace writes notes to me, explaining the conversation.

Preston is thinking about having one last play at the end of this semester. He's never done it before. We're tossing around possibilities. Some say it'll be a play like The Crucible *or* Our Town. *I'm casting my vote for Shakespeare. Quinn is hoping for* Pirates of Penzance *or* Singin' in the Rain.

I glance across at Quinn. She would make a wonderful Mabel.

Kace hands me another note. *I think it has something to do with you. I think he wants you to have your moment in the spotlight.*

I look up at him. His smirk tells me he can read the surprise on my face. "Seriously?" I say.

Kace winks. Nods. His expression reminds me of something. My memory searches for it, then seizes on it. The moment on stage after the kiss. That fleeting moment of sensing something more, something unsaid.

It is gone almost as quickly as I grasp it. But it warms me just the same—a compliment. Even if I don't feel that way about Kace in return, it is flattering to know he sees me that way.

I watch as he scribbles.

(Quinn thinks he's doing it for her, since it's her last semester and all, so don't say anything!)

I mock locking my mouth with a key and throwing it away. Then I crumple the note and shove it into the front pocket of my jeans.

I pass the donut box. Take a bite of my apple. I think about Kace's note. Another chance in the spotlight. For me.

Could it be true?

I watch Quinn laughing and throwing a pillow at Kace. The idea of performing again sends tingles up and down my arms. In my first days of silence, I let go of my dream for Someday Broadway. I was sure it could never ever happen. Not with my hearing damaged forever. But I am different now. I am hopeful. Because of Hayden. I can see possibilities for myself. Chances.

Maybe it won't be the same as before. And it might be a whole lot harder to do things that came so easily to me before, but that doesn't make it impossible. Excitement bubbles inside of me. I want to tell Hayden. Right now. On impulse, I pull out my phone to text him. And then I remember how I treated him today. How I acted like he isn't important to me, when he's exactly the opposite.

I put my phone away. I don't share the news with him because I am ashamed of myself. Of my fears.

In this moment, sitting with the drama crowd, I know. Here, in my moment of triumph, of belonging, I know that the only place I want to be is with Hayden.

And I have the answer to my question. I *am* willing to risk my own heart to save his because I have already given him my heart, whether I wanted to or not. I must have always known, ever since the first moment I saw him. I just didn't want to admit it to myself.

I have fallen in love with Hayden. Even knowing that he might not love me back. Might never be able to love me back. It doesn't matter. I love him.

After school, I make my way to the football field. I know where the cheerleading tryouts will be—in the same place Lily and I watched the tryouts last year. I take a seat on the bleachers and scan the crowd of girls in shorts and miniskirts, looking for Lily.

There. There she is. Her blonde hair is pulled into a high

ponytail. She came in the Richmond colors: red shorts and a white polo shirt. Smart.

The girls have to learn a routine and then perform it one by one. Lily stands in the front line. She's marking the moves. When she looks up and spots me, I wave. She waves back, beaming.

Lily is in the first group; I won't have to wait long. Just before the girls take their turns, the football team arrives. They are conditioning now that the season is over. Today they are running around the track. A bunch of the girls turn to watch them. They point and giggle. Some wave. The guys don't wave back. But they do start to run faster. I roll my eyes and shake my head at the Neanderthal display. That is, until Connor Williams runs to the front of the pack. Sprinting off of the track, he catches Lily around the waist. Swings her right off the ground like one of those commercials for perfume.

Wear this scent and you, too, can have the romance you've always dreamed of.

He kisses her. Right in front of everybody. It's such a display that I can't look away. I have to watch.

There is one split second, though, right before Connor runs off—it's shorter than the time it takes to breathe in and out—when he looks toward the bleachers. At me. He tilts his head slightly, as though challenging me. I freeze, not daring to take a breath. Not until he moves off. And then I can't be sure any of it happened at all.

Lily tosses her hair. Grins like the Cheshire Cat. She'll make the team now no matter what. Even if she forgets the entire routine (which she won't) or doesn't do a perfect split jump (which she will). I may as well go home.

But I can't move. The blood in my veins is on fire. I want to scratch my arms. Tear them to pieces. Shred my skin to stop the burning. A scream chokes me, longing to be freed. I swallow it. Taste the bitterness. Hold it in. Holding it all in.

I thought I was prepared to see Lily with Connor. After the mall, I thought I could handle it. I knew they were together. She told me herself.

I just didn't know I would react this way.

Even though I want to run as far away as I can, I don't. I can't move. I stay and watch the routine. Over and over again. Lily performs it well. Brimming with confidence, her smile is bright as neon. Her moves crisp and sure.

I breathe in and out. To calm myself. To bring myself back to the present. I think of Hayden. My white feather of hope. And the thought gives me strength. Thinking of him reminds me that this is just one moment. And I have many other moments to live. To enjoy. I can do this. I can get through this.

Second by second, I talk myself through it. So much so that by the time Lily finishes her routine and does a perfect split jump, I can clap for her. I wave. Give her a thumbs-up. I move down the bleachers to the side gate. And I am free. I don't look back.

Thinking about not thinking

HAYDEN

The afternoon sun beats on my back, and sweat runs down my face. I brush it away with the back of my hand, the only part of my arms not covered in mud. I lift pieces of sod one by one, stacking them on wooden risers. It is physical work—demanding, exhausting.

Just what I need right now. My work at the nursery is an escape from the rest of the world. An oasis of calm where I am surrounded by life, color, quiet.

Usually I can find a meditative peace here. Whether the work is physical like today or monotonous like lining up flower pots in rows, I can find my center. Not today.

Because today, all I can think about is Stella. The way she looked when she told me she was eating lunch in the drama room. The way she didn't quite meet my eyes, as though she couldn't bear to talk to me. But actions speak louder than words; this I know to be true. Stella was eating with Kace

Maxwell. She didn't say the last part; she didn't have to. It shouldn't bother me—she doesn't belong to me. Stella can eat wherever she wants, and being beautiful and popular, she has many offers, I am sure. Just last night, I was telling myself I needed to pull away to keep myself safe.

She did me a favor today. This is what I wanted.

But if it's what I want, then why does tension have me knotted up so tight that my muscles scream with every movement? Why do I revel in the aching of my biceps, the shooting pain in my back, the throbbing of my hands, the sweat, the exhaustion?

I pull another piece of grass and dirt and heave it into the air to land on top of the waist-high stack.

I push Stella's face from my mind. Her sunflower eyes and petal-soft skin, hair that reflects light like a mirror, lips that tease with the hint of a smile even when she is sad. I force it all from my mind—only to replace it with a memory.

Stella kissing Kace on stage.

I know they were acting, that it wasn't real. But I've seen how he looks at her, even if she hasn't.

I may have promised seventeen days, but I can walk away now. She doesn't need me, and I certainly don't need her.

My thoughts are jumbled, and I can't make sense of the confusion.

"Whoa there, Hayden," Jeremiah calls, walking my way.

"I didn't expect you to finish already. This is a three-day job. How'd you do this all by yourself?"

"I-I don't—know," I stammer sheepishly. "I w-was th-thinking and time fl-ew by."

Jeremiah pushes the beaten cowboy hat back on his head. "Well, you must've been thinking about somethin' pretty important." He nods at the stacks of sod.

I shrug.

"It isn't a lady, is it?" Jeremiah's eyes twinkle, making his craggy face look young and vibrant.

I shrug again.

Jeremiah sits on one of the stacks. "Woman trouble. I been through it all. Me and the wife been together goin' on thirty years. Try me." He waits, like he has all the time in the world instead of a busy nursery to run.

"Th-at's just it. I-I don't k-know."

Jeremiah nods his head. "Confused. Lots going on inside yer head. You don't know whatcha want."

He's summed it up pretty well. I nod.

"Hmmm. Seems to me you gotta know your own heart first. You gotta figure out whatcha want. You like her?"

I do like her. "Y-Yes. May-be t-too much." This is the most I have ever spoken to Jeremiah.

He shakes his head. "Never can like a woman too much. Too much means you're scared of bein' hurt. But there's nothin' to be gained if you don't try." He places a large, heavy hand on my shoulder. "Think of it this way—you'll be hurtin' yourself if you walk away. And she might be hurtin' you if you don't. But maybe, just maybe, it'll work out."

His words make sense, and his point is a good one. I'll be hurting myself and my chances with Stella if I just walk away, but if I give us a chance . . .

"Anything worth havin' is worth fightin' for. My wife 'n'

me, we work hard to stay together because we're better together than apart. Ask yourself—are you better together? If you are, then fight for it, Hayden." He gently taps my shoulder then gestures at the sod.

"Next time don't work so hard. I'll be hearin' from your grandpa about it when you can't get out of bed tomorrow." He laughs low and throaty. It makes me smile.

Jeremiah and Gramps have been friends since high school. That's how I got the job. But to hear Jeremiah tell it, I did him the favor. I never call in sick, and I always show up on time. I do more than he asks me to do. Truth is, I'm grateful for the job and the spending money. But I also like the work. I love the peacefulness of the place, with its running fountains and flats of flowers, blooming trees and nestled houseplants.

So it seems fitting that today, here, I have made a decision about Stella. A decision that has been causing me so much confusion and pain.

It's simple, really. She makes me happy. I am better with her. I don't want to lose that. So I am going to take Jeremiah's advice and fight for her. Even if the one I am fighting against is me.

12

STELLA

I'm sorry about yesterday. I wanted to talk to you last night. To tell you about something.

After I write the text, I delete it. I try again.

Will you have lunch with me today?

It's simple. Direct.

Better.

He may say no. May be angry with me. Still, I hope he will say yes.

There's so much I want to say to Hayden. So much I want to tell him. But I will have to go slow. Take my time. When I was little and saw a butterfly in my mom's garden, I would rush toward it. Scare it away. I remember crying and crying, so sad that the butterfly had disappeared.

As I got older, I learned to wait and observe. And sometimes, if I was very lucky, a butterfly moved closer. Once, an orange and black monarch landed on my shoulder. I stayed very still and watched it closely. It watched me back. My patience showed the butterfly that I was safe. It stayed for a very long time. Long enough for my mother to run and get her camera and then shoot a photo of me and my butterfly friend. I still have it in a frame on my desk. I look at it now. Remember the rewards of patience.

I don't have to wait long for his response. By the time I have finished braiding my hair, Hayden has answered me.

Ok.

That gives no clue to how he feels. But it's the answer I want. Now I have to ask part two. I take a deep breath. Prepare myself for rejection. Even though I know it will hurt whether I am prepared or not.

Would you stay for a little while after school today? I wanted to ask for your help with something.

It's vague, but I am not ready to tell him yet about the possibility of another play. That I want to know if I can still sing. If he agrees, I will tell him today. If not, I will keep it to myself.

Sounds mysterious. And yes. I will always help you. All you have to do is ask.

I expect lunch to be awkward—that things will seem different between us after yesterday. But it's not. Hayden and I sit under our tree. We face one another. Hayden wears a knit cap today, stormy gray. It makes his eyes look like my favorite faded jeans. His hair curls around the edges of the cap, trying to break free. When he catches me staring, I look down at my carrots. After a few moments, I dare to peek again. His eyes rest gently on me.

"I'm sorry," he says.

"I should be the one apologizing."

Hayden shakes his head. "It wasn't fair of me to act like that."

I shake my head now, unwilling to let Hayden bear responsibility for yesterday.

"It was all my fault." I don't shift my eyes from his. If I do, I'll lose my nerve. "I was afraid again," I say, referencing my very first text to him.

He remembers, because he answers with an echo of what he texted back that day. "We're all afraid, Stella. Some more than others." Now I think he's talking about himself. His cheeks color. But he doesn't look away.

"My dad left my mom," I begin. "For someone else."

Hayden's expression caresses my face. I am comforted as though he were touching me.

"And you never want to be left like she was," he finishes for me.

I nod. Unable to speak or breathe now that my greatest fear is revealed. I wait to see how I will react. I gingerly test my emotions. Surprisingly, I am calm.

"I'm not afraid anymore," I tell him. "Not with you."

Hayden's expression softens, and I wonder if he's going to kiss me.

He doesn't. Instead he reaches out and smooths a piece of hair off my face. His touch is light yet weighted with emotion. "I didn't expect this," Hayden says.

"What?" I say, not understanding.

This time, his eyes drop to my lips. Linger there. His eyes slowly move back to meet mine before he speaks. "You."

After lunch, I stop at my locker. Lily is waiting there. Note in hand. *I made the squad!*

"Of course you did," I say. "You were the best one there."

Having a boyfriend on the football team probably didn't hurt either. But I don't say that. It's catty, and I don't want to be like that. I just want to be happy for her.

Lily beams at me, beautiful and perfect. From the curls bouncing below her shoulders to the brand-new pink cowboy boots on her feet. I return the smile. She takes out a pink pencil and writes one more thing on the note.

Thank you for being there. YMMD!

I translate the Lilyspeak: You Made My Day. Even if it isn't true, it's a nice thing to say. I grin again. "What are friends for?" We turn and go our separate ways. We are only going to our fifth period classes, but it seems like a metaphor for our friendship. Because though she will always hold a special place in my heart, Lily and I have gone our separate ways. And we will never be the same again.

After school, Hayden meets me in front of the rehearsal rooms—small, soundproof rooms where students can run lines, sing, or play instruments. Two of them have pianos. I have already reserved one of those.

Hayden grins when he sees me like it's the first time he has seen me all day, even though it's been only two hours. He has taken off his gray sweater and now wears a white shirt with his dark jeans. The gray cap still hides most of his curls, but a few more have escaped.

"So you going to tell me what this is all about?" he asks.

I don't say a word as I push open the door and move inside. I take a seat on the worn piano bench.

Hayden follows me. He closes the door and stands in the middle of the small room, facing me. The space between us suddenly seems really small. And very intimate.

In silence, there are many things unsaid, things I am not ready to say. Responses I dream of hearing with my own ears, not reading with my eyes. So I hurry to fill the space with words.

"Rumor has it Mr. Preston is going to do one last show before the end of the year. He's never done one then, so there is a lot of speculation about what it will be, a play or a musical, and I want to audition for it. Whether I can hear—or not."

I watch him closely for his reaction. He looks at me sideways, a small smile playing at the corner of his lips. He is proud of me. I can tell. But he still doesn't speak.

"Will you help me?"

"Always." His eyes say more. They say words that make me glow. I am a precious gem that has been hidden in a dark cave for centuries, and he has discovered me. Revealed me. Now I can shine the way I am meant to shine. I sparkle under his gaze.

Something is different about him today. I sense it. He's more open, somehow. More present. I have no idea what caused the change, but I like it. Then it occurs to me that maybe the one who is different is me.

Before I get lost in the moment, I bring myself back to the reason we are here. "I want to see if I can sense the rhythm of the music, even when I can't hear it."

Hayden nods his understanding then sits beside me on the piano bench. I slide over to give him space. I smell citrus and sunset, wind and sea. When his bare arm brushes against mine, I tingle. Skin against skin.

His fingers press the piano keys, giving them life. I watch his hands move. Marvel at their grace. His fingers are confident; they know exactly what to do without hesitation.

He speaks to me while he plays. "Close your eyes. Concentrate on the air in the room. See if your body can absorb the rhythm."

I close my eyes. At first, all I can feel is the pounding of my heart, the rush of my adrenaline. The brush of his leg against mine. His nearness. But then I notice something else. Something churning the air. A change. A pulsing.

And I realize.

It's rhythm.

I can feel the music.

I focus on it. Block out everything else. Even Hayden. I reach for the energy with every part of me—embrace it. Let it in.

The sound rolls through me, feeding me a beat. I begin to move my head in time. Then my foot. When I am certain it isn't my imagination, I open my eyes.

I look at Hayden. He knows without my speaking. He can tell from the expression of wonder on my face. Because as much as I wanted it to be possible, I didn't truly believe it could be until this moment. I didn't truly have faith.

A smile breaks out on my face. I am filled with joy and happiness, hope and dreams.

Music is not lost to me. Music is part of me. Even more than when I could hear it. Because now it is inside of me.

"Thank you," I manage as tears fill my eyes. Tears of joy. Tears of gratitude.

Hayden doesn't answer. He rests his forehead against mine. Sharing in my moment. My triumph.

I have a long road ahead of me. There is a big difference between sensing rhythm and being able to sing notes. But just knowing it's possible is all I need right now.

I stand and move to the side of the piano. Place my hands on the instrument itself. "Play something I know," I say.

I close my eyes again and wait for the melody to course through me. Each note Hayden plays breathes life into my soul. Each note pushes through my bubble of silence and leaves a small hole to the world outside, the world I used to know. I am no longer isolated. I am connected.

Hayden plays and plays until his hands must ache. But I am not tired. I am full of song.

Hayden gestures to the keys of the piano. "Do you want to play?"

I shake my head. "Don't know how."

"Want to learn?"

I have always wanted to learn, but the black and white keys are a mystery to me. They hold the power to rhythm and melody.

"Will you teach me?" I say as I sit next to Hayden on the bench.

"What do you think?" His mouth twists into a sideways grin that is both teasing and hypnotic.

Hayden takes my hand in his. Lifts it to the piano keys and sets it down with one finger on each white key.

"Play one at a time," he says.

I press a key. And another. The keys are smooth, responsive. I can't sense the music they make like I could when listening to Hayden play. This is something else. Even though I am playing just one key at a time, I control it. I create the melody. Like when I sing. It's empowering. I am playing the piano. It doesn't matter that I can't hear it. I am making music.

"Can you read notes?" Hayden asks.

"Yes," I say. "I learned in sixth-grade choir."

"This is C." He points to the key under my thumb. Next to it is D. Then E, F, G. Then it goes to A and B before returning to C."

He's teaching me the notes so I can read the sheet music and then play the right key on the piano. That's when I realize that there is no sheet music sitting on the piano. Hayden has been playing all of these songs from memory.

"How did you do it?" I ask. Impressed.

"What?"

"Play all of those songs without sheet music?"

Hayden shrugs, downplaying it. "I have a good memory."

"I think it's called talent. You're really talented."

He seems embarrassed by my compliment. He glances at the floor for a moment before responding to me.

"You're the one with all the talent," he tells me. "I've never heard anyone sing like you. You were like a siren on stage, hypnotizing me with your voice."

His compliment releases fluttering butterflies into my veins, heightening my mood from joy to euphoria.

"As I recall," I say, "sirens led men to ruin with their song. I hope you don't think I'm a danger to you." I hope he can tell I am teasing.

For once, Hayden is all seriousness. And I realize that even if I am teasing, Hayden understands the depth of meaning behind my words. "I do think you're a danger. A very serious danger."

The butterflies circle in a frenzy. Make me short of breath.

I want to touch him. To show him that he is safe with me. Just as I know I am safe with him.

I gingerly lean toward him. Closer. Shortening the distance between us.

Our lips are almost touching.

He leans closer.

Just when he is about to kiss me, he pulls back. Turns away.

My first reaction is confusion. He doesn't want to kiss me.

My second reaction is to follow his eye line. What is Hayden looking at?

That's when I notice that someone has come into the room. A guy who plays in the band. He is saying something to Hayden. And Hayden is responding.

He must be scheduled to use the rehearsal room next.

The moment has passed. I look at my watch: 4:30. It's time to go.

Hayden walks me out. Waves good-bye as I head for my

mom's car. I turn to look at him one last time before we drive away. He is still watching me. Just as I am watching him, with a myriad of emotions churning inside me.

Like a cake mixture of ingredients, some delicious and some tart. Combined, they make something sublime. Right now, I am sublime.

The language of art

HAYDEN

I would go anywhere, do anything. Just to be with Stella.

From the moment I received her text this morning, I knew something would be different today. Just like I have known other things about her before, I knew this. It's the first time she has ever reached out to me, wanting me.

I knew today would be different—and it was.

For the first time, she seemed truly present. Like she wasn't holding back, thinking about something else, hiding.

She was radiant. Her eyes glowed like amber jewels lit by fire. Her lips danced between smiles as though she has never smiled at anyone but me. She smells like honey and wildflowers.

And today, when I touched her hair, it felt like satin. Touching her like that, doing something I have seen her do herself many times—brushing a strand of hair from her face—I was one with her. Moving for her. It was intimate. So small, yet it sent shock waves through me as if I had touched high-watt voltage.

And then, watching her connect with the music, my music. It was one of the most perfect moments of my life.

I wanted to kiss her at lunch, then later in the rehearsal room. I wanted to taste her lips, but I held back.

My first kiss with Stella will be my first kiss with anyone.

The rehearsal room isn't the right place, just like a mall parking lot wasn't the right place. There will be a moment—the right moment—and I will know when it arrives. That's when I will kiss Stella. Until then, it's enough to be near her, to see her. And to know that what I feel for her, I have never felt for anyone before.

I drive home slowly, the melody from her final song in *West Side Story* still throbbing in my fingertips.

Gramps is working in his art studio. I stand in the doorway for a few moments, watching him work. The room is really a converted garage, but you would never know it. Gramps and I worked for two years to turn the garage into his work space. We laid wood floors and installed more windows in the walls to let the light in. Animal sculptures are scattered around on tables and columns, some miniature, others life-sized. The smell of clay permeates the room, bringing with it a sense of comfort. This is my favorite place in the house. Because this is the only room that is entirely Gramps. Sometimes I like to work on homework at one of the benches while he creates. He plays country music on his stereo and sings along—even though he is always completely off pitch.

Today, he is sculpting a wolf. The frame is made of aluminum, which he has bent and worked to form the legs, torso and head. Eventually he'll work layers of clay over the form, turning a stick figure into a living, breathing creature.

"She's a n-new one," I observe.

Gramps talks to me without turning, fingers working the clay into fur. "Your friend Stella inspired me. This one's called *Brave Star.* See how her ears bend down? She can't hear, like all the other wolves, so she's at a disadvantage in the pack. This one has to find her way without one of her most basic senses. She has to learn to survive in a new way."

He still doesn't look at me, but I know he is smiling, as I am. Gramps turns everything into art. That offended me at first, when I discovered how every step in my journey would somehow become a title for a new animal sculpture. My pain is represented in countless bronze pieces. Loss represented by a dying bear. Anger in a panther striking. Silence in a wild, unbroken horse.

I expected that Gramps would eventually carve Stella's journey. What I didn't expect is that she would be depicted as a wolf. My favorite animal is a wolf, and Gramps knows it. I am drawn to their intelligence, their ferocity, and loyalty to the pack.

"I think it's high time you had one of these bookends." He speaks of his art in a deprecating way, as though each piece isn't purchased for thousands of dollars.

Gramps is making this wolf for me as a gift—and as a message. He uses art to speak for him. To say what he could say in words, but can say so much better through art.

“I h-have your art w-with me all th-the t-time,” I tell him, referring to my keychain, the knot that binds us together.

I move to stand behind him and watch him work the wire loop to shape the face of the wolf.

He turns then to look at me. “I’m making one for her, too. This wolf’s mate. He hears for her, and she howls for him. I consider that a perfect match, don’t you?” His way of telling me something without actually saying it.

“I d-do.” Although I don’t really think he was asking the question. It was more of a statement.

Gramps pats me on the shoulder, turns back to his wolf, and I pull out my US history book. The rest of the night is spent in quiet camaraderie—so much said and unsaid at the same time. A sense of peace and understanding floods the room, where there are no secrets and the windows open to the light.

11

STELLA

When I open my locker the next morning, a note is waiting for me.

Nature, the gentlest mother,
Impatient of no child,
The feeblest or the waywardest,—
Her admonition mild

In forest and the hill
By traveller is heard,
Restraining rampant squirrel
Or too impetuous bird.

How fair her conversation,
A summer afternoon,—
Her household, her assembly;
And when the sun goes down

Her voice among the aisles
Incites the timid prayer
Of the minutest cricket,
The most unworthy flower.

When all the children sleep
She turns as long away
As will suffice to light her lamps;
Then, bending from the sky

With infinite affection
And infiniter care,
Her golden finger on her lip,
Wills silence everywhere.

—Emily Dickinson

The handwriting is perfectly scripted. And though I haven't seen his writing before, I know it is Hayden's. He doesn't sign the note. He doesn't need to.

The words move me. Transport me to another place. The last line strikes me the most. *Wills silence everywhere.* Because when I read these words, silence—my silence—becomes beautiful.

It is then I notice a sentence at the very bottom.

Day 11—Shall we visit Mother Nature today?

He hasn't forgotten. He is still counting down the days with me.

I carefully fold the note. Slip it into the pocket of my sweatshirt, where I can touch it all day.

On impulse, I pull out a blank sheet of paper and a pen. I write.

In silence he beckons me
Promises to open my heart

To a world unknown but not unfamiliar
Where I will learn to reimagine

Through his eyes I see
What I have never seen before

The possibilities are endless
Hope is the reward

At the very bottom, I write one word: *Always.*

I fold the note three times, until it is small enough to fit in the palm of my hand. I have an idea where his locker might be—the place I first saw him. So I head in that direction, hoping to find him before my first class.

My reply can wait until lunch, but I don't want to wait. I want Hayden to read it right away.

I round the corner to the far corridor. Some lockers are at the end of the hall. My eyes scan the crowd for a sign of him. I have to hurry, or I will be late for class. There. Just up ahead, I catch a glimpse. I speed up, moving so fast I am almost at a run. He turns just as I reach him. As if he expected me, knew I was there.

Our eyes meet. He waits. Breathless, I reach out my right hand. He touches it with his. Holds it for the merest of seconds. The note slips from my palm to his. We part, though our eyes do not. We are standing in the middle of the crowded hallway, but all I can think of are yellow daffodils and clear blue skies.

"See you at lunch," I manage. Then I turn and hurry to class, leaving my poem and my answer behind.

"I thought I knew every poem ever written," Hayden tells me at lunch. We sit side by side under our tree. Today, we have laid out our lunches on a napkin. We share them like a picnic. I have brought grapes, oatmeal cookies, and a hummus wrap. Hayden has added his peanut butter and jelly sandwich, an orange, and a granola bar.

"You didn't know this one because I wrote it," I say.

Hayden's eyes widen. He really didn't know. "You're a poet." He still looks surprised.

I wrinkle my nose. Shrug. "I don't know. This is the first poem I have ever written."

Hayden pulls the note out of his front pocket. Smooths it open and reads it again to himself. Then he looks at me. Shaking his head. "Stella, I know poetry. I've had to read so much of it in speech therapy. Truly, you have a gift."

A gift. One that doesn't depend on sound. Hearing. Voice. Something that comes from within me, from within the silence. But able to scream out loud.

Words.

Words aren't silent.

Words are happy and sad. Angry and joyous. Bitter and sweet. Full of loss and longing. And love.

Words can be turned into lyrics. Plays. Poems. Stories. They are unlimited.

I feel a blush spread across my face. "I never knew," I tell him, "that I could do this."

"Well, you can." Hayden looks at me through lowered lashes. "I've never had a poem written for me. About me." A beat. "Thank you doesn't seem enough."

I lean closer. "What is enough, then?" My voice feels husky as it leaves my throat. I wonder what it sounds like to him.

His hand touches my cheek. Fingers brush against my skin. I imagine my skin sparkling where he has touched it. Glistening.

"Something more." His lips move just above mine.

"More?" I echo. I want to extend this moment, preserve it somehow. "I meant it, you know. The words in the poem." We are so close that our breathing synchronizes. I'm not sure if I have spoken or whispered my last words.

Then something just behind Hayden catches my eye. In the distance, Emerson is eating with her friends. But Lily and her entourage have joined the group. They're settling in with my little sister and her friends. Lowering themselves to socialize with freshmen.

I hesitate, and Hayden pulls back, a question in his eyes.

"Do you see that?" I ask Hayden, gesturing to Emerson. He turns to look behind him, to see what I see.

My eyes narrow, trying to understand. Why would Lily sit with Emerson?

"Why don't you go see what it's all about?" he suggests. "Might be nothing."

I nod, shooting him a sheepish glance. I have ruined our moment. Maybe interrupted our first kiss. Regret pinches me. Makes me ache as I turn away from him.

I stand and move across the grass. My vision centers on my sister, who is chatting with Lily. Lily, who is smiling and tossing her curls.

And then I stop in my tracks.

Because I have just realized.

I can't hear what they are saying.

How can I possibly listen in on their conversation? Ask questions and receive answers?

I can't.

I turn around, unnoticed, and walk slowly back toward Hayden.

I sit down without saying a word. Hayden gives me a quizzical look, but waits for me to speak.

"I can't hear them," I say. "What's the point of going over there?"

Hayden stands and offers me a hand.

I shake my head, not understanding. Not taking his hand.

"Let me be your ears." He wants to go with me, to help me with my sister.

I take his hand. Stand up. Close enough to look up at him in wonder. "You would do that for me." It's a statement, not a question. The question I want to ask, but won't, is why.

Hayden wraps both of his hands around mine. "This is going to be difficult for you. I'll make it simple. Just remember this one word. *Anything.*"

My heart fills with air. Floating like a red balloon drifting across the sky. Reaching high to the heavens. This is happiness.

My heart carries me across the grass to where my sister sits with Lily. To listen. With Hayden's ears.

We greet one another with hellos. Smiles all around. Lily doesn't quite meet my eyes. Emerson does. She is flushed with excitement. Bursting with news. In that split second, as I look at my little sister, I realize I didn't have to worry about not hearing anyone.

I can understand my sister. Not in the way I understand Hayden. I can't read her lips. But I know her. I can read her body language, her expressions. Her emotions from the color of her cheeks. I am not helpless.

I also forgot to give Emerson credit. She knows I cannot read her lips. Pulling out a piece of notebook paper, she begins to scribble, fast, as though time will run out before she can get her words on paper.

Her smile as she hands me the paper reminds me how she used to look on Christmas morning after coming downstairs and seeing the presents Santa Claus had left. As though she couldn't believe it had really happened. That there were gifts for her.

I take the paper and read it. Sense Hayden's strength beside me. The touch of his hand on my arm. His presence.

Lily wants me to try out for junior varsity cheerleading! She's going to mentor me.

I wish I thought Lily's offer was coming from an honest place. That Lily really wanted to help Emerson. But I don't. Any time my sister used to join us, Lily rolled her eyes and sighed. Tossed a T.T.Y.L. over her shoulder as she walked away. What changed? Nothing. Emerson is still a freshman. Still beneath Lily's social status. The only thing that is different—is me.

I want to say something. To tell Lily to back off. To leave my sister alone.

But I don't.

Because Emerson is glowing. And she deserves a little happiness. Truth is, she would make an incredible cheerleader. With her dance background and outgoing personality, they would be lucky to have her on the squad.

Hayden reads the note over my shoulder. His grip on my arm tenses as though he understands my pain. Even without one look from me. He knows.

I lift my eyes from the note. Kneel by my sister and lean in. I hug her tight. Tears prick, but I blink them back. This is about her. Not about me.

"I'm so happy, Em. I'll come to the tryouts if you want me to."

Emerson hugs me back. I turn to Lily. Paste the widest smile possible on my face. I don't say thank you. I can't. I just stand there with my clown smile. Then lunch ends and everyone walks away. Everyone except Hayden. And then my smile fades.

"You have a heart of gold," he tells me.

I shake my head. "I don't, though. That's the thing. I don't."

And then I walk to class.

Drama class is bustling. No one notices Kace passing a note my way.

Are you busy Saturday night?

I hold the note in my hand. Try to decide what to say.

I'm not busy Saturday night. But my heart is.

Hayden and I have never had "the talk." The one where you tell someone you want to see them and only them. It sort of seems understood that we are spending time only with each other. But it isn't definite. That is, Hayden could see someone else. It's the same for me, I suppose. But I don't want to see anyone else. It wouldn't be fair. To Hayden. Or to Kace.

Because I love Hayden. I would rather be alone Saturday night and be true to my heart than pretend with anyone else. Because I already spend every single day pretending already—pretending I can understand people, pretending Lily is still my friend, pretending this isn't so hard that sometimes I don't want to wake up in the morning.

So much pretending. I can't pretend about this.

I write the truth. The real truth.

Thank you so much for asking. But I'm going out with someone.

I watch Kace as he reads my note. If he is surprised, he covers it well. His expression doesn't change at all. He writes back.

Hayden Rivers.

No need to say anything else. I simply nod.

Seriously? He writes. *You can do better, you know.*

Seeing his words brings back memories. Lily calling Hayden "SC" and making fun of him watching me. Me afraid to speak up and say how I really felt. But I'm not that girl anymore.

I take my pen. *Actually, he can do better. I'm the lucky one.*

And in that moment, a door closes. One that may never open again.

Kace doesn't write anything else for the rest of class.

We just sit there side by side and watch the performers until the bell rings.

Saying nothing and everything

HAYDEN

Kace Maxwell approaches me after school and stops me in the parking lot with these words: "I didn't realize you and Stella were together."

I try not to register my surprise at Kace talking to me as if we are friends. Or at the words he has just said—*together*, *Stella and me*.

"Hey, K-Kace," I say. "H-How are y-you?" Every time I look at him, I can see him kissing Stella on stage. Maria and Tony in love. I shake my head to shatter the image, like glass breaking into tiny pieces. Shards I can cut myself on if I am not careful.

I smile at him, but Kace isn't here to be friendly. He has an agenda. People think he is charming, charismatic, but I see someone else—manipulative, narcissistic, used to getting what he wants. And what he wants right now is Stella.

"Not so good, actually. I just found out that my leading lady is seeing someone else."

Being reluctant to talk gives you one advantage, one very important advantage: you don't rush to speak. Ever. I wait. I listen. I don't jump at the bait. Kace is looking for information, but he won't get what he wants—not from me.

Kace waits for an answer. I shrug, with nothing to say.

He takes a step closer. "She's a star, you know. She belongs with someone like her. Someone who's going places." He pulls out his phone, reads his text messages, glances back at me as an afterthought.

Why am I standing here? Why am I listening to him? With that thought, I walk toward my truck.

Kace continues talking to me even as I walk away. "You're only going to hold her back. You'll see. She'll figure that out one day. And I won't be waiting around."

Kace's words echo over and over in my mind as I walk beside Stella. It is a warm spring afternoon. I should be focusing on the fact that I am with her, but I can't. Stella is talking, pointing out a small red and brown bird in a tree. She takes a book out of my hands—a guide to hiking in Southern California—and she searches for the name of the bird. The book has names of plants and animals commonly found in the canyons.

We walk along a dirt path. Sunlight speckles the ground in patterns. Stella wears denim shorts and a rose-colored T-shirt, and her hair is twisted into a knot on her head. Kace is right—she is a star, and she's meant to shine.

"It's beautiful here. Like another world," Stella says. Her speech is slower than before the accident, her pronunciation more rounded. "It's so magical. I almost expect to see fairies."

I reach out and take her hand. I need to tell her. This seems like as good a moment as any.

"I kn-know I haven't said anything b-before. I didn't w-want you t-to feel pressured or a-anything. And th-things may s-seem different t-to you after . . . after the tenth."

Her eyes deepen in color, from sunrise to sunset. I watch in wonder, way more interested in looking into Stella's eyes than at the scenery.

"I-I'm not s-seeing anyone else."

Stella's eyes drop to my mouth. I watch them as she studies my words without speaking.

"I j-just wanted y-you to know that." *Not seeing anyone else now or ever*, I want to add but don't.

She raises her gaze to meet mine once more. "Me, neither." Her gaze locks with mine. "Only you."

This is the moment, the right moment.

I lean closer, and then, just before I kiss her, I stop. Kace's words echo in my ears.

She belongs with someone like her. Someone who's going places.

It's so loud that for once I am glad Stella can't hear. I can imagine that his voice is on a loudspeaker in the canyon, broadcasting for even the birds to hear.

I pull back, feigning interest in two squirrels chasing each other around a tree trunk. I point them out, giving myself a second while she glances away.

Just then, a sky-blue butterfly floats over us. I tug on Stella's hand—she sees it instantly.

"Mother Nature welcoming us," she says.

We watch together as it curves in its flight, making invisible patterns on the breeze. The butterfly moves closer. Closer still.

It rests on Stella's shoulder as though it belongs with her. She doesn't look surprised; she almost looks as if she expected this. As if butterflies sit on her shoulder every day.

I reach for my cell phone and snap a photo of Stella with the butterfly. Smiling, her cheeks turn the same rose as her shirt.

She's stunning. I catch my breath as I look at her.

And I say a silent thank you to Mother Nature.

10

STELLA

I keep looking at the picture of me and the blue butterfly. It still feels like a dream. But it wasn't. The picture tells me that.

I am bringing Hayden to me. I can sense it. Every day, he comes closer. More open. And like the butterfly, he is beginning to trust me. I can tell by the way he talks to me. The things he shares. But mostly, I can tell by the way he looks at me. It's different. The shade that used to drop over his eyes doesn't close anymore. He is willing to let me see him. Without the need to hide.

I wait for him on our front steps. Today is the cancer walk. It's also Good Friday, so we have the day off school. Perfect day to help others.

Hayden's blue truck pulls up. He is right on time. I walk down the steps to meet him on the sidewalk. He is wearing khaki shorts and running shoes, a gray T-shirt, a baseball cap.

I am wearing white shorts and a gray-and-white striped tank. Red Converse. My hair in two loose braids. "Hi," I say. It is such a small word for the many things I feel when I see him, but it will have to do.

"Hi, yourself." Taking my hand in his, he leads me back to the passenger side of the truck.

He opens the door and waits for me to climb in. Something is sitting on my seat. A red paper bag. White tissue paper peeks out of the top. Begging to be opened.

I lift it and sit down. Turn to look at Hayden, eyebrows raised in question.

Hayden grins. "Open it."

I pull the white tissue out of the bag. Inside the bag is the vase I painted. It is gorgeous. The colors more vibrant after being fired. The sand and sea flow over the vase. While Hayden's sapphire eyes watch me.

I look at him. "I still can't believe I painted this."

"You can do anything. Anything you want." His eyes deepen, reach out to me. I catch my breath. Then, "There's more," he tells me.

Curious, I reach back into the bag. Find something else wrapped in white paper. Inside is the oval box Hayden painted. For me. Holding it in my hands, I marvel at the delicate details. It is so real; just by looking at it, I can see the waves crashing on the shore. The seagulls flying overhead.

"It's beautiful," I say. That's not enough. I want to say more, but I can't. Not here. Not now.

"Look inside," he says.

I lift the top off. A gold chain is nestled in the box. I hold it up and see a pendant—a white daisy with an amber center. There is a note under the necklace. I see the words written in small black handwriting: "Always believe."

The daisy reminds me of the day he came to see me in the hospital and how he gave me hope. Tears blur my eyes. I don't want them to, but they do.

"Hayden," I say. "Thank you." Stepping out of the truck, I hold up the necklace, turn with my back to him so he can put it on me.

After the clasp is secure, I reach up to hold the pendant. Run my fingers over the enameled petals. The raised stone. I turn back around. "How does it look?"

"Beautiful. You are beautiful." Then he crushes me against him as if this is the end of something rather than the beginning. He holds me close. So close I can feel the pulse of his heartbeat through my T-shirt.

Then he releases me.

As I climb back into the front seat, Hayden doesn't meet my eyes.

The keychain knot moves back and forth. I randomly steal glances at the side of his face; his jaw muscles are tight.

Patience will lure the butterfly, I remind myself. I replay his words over and over, like a song in my head. *You are beautiful.*

The charity walk begins at Richmond High and ends at the elementary school. We park and join the crowd. Card tables are set up to accept donations and pledges. I hand Hayden my pledge form. My mom has pledged money, and I have pledged some of my allowance.

Hayden turns in our forms and receives our numbers. He pins mine on my back—242. And I pin a number on his—243.

Then we join the others on the starting line. That's when I see her.

My rainbow girl.

She stands at the front of the line. Dressed all in pink. Her bright jade eyes look over the crowd like beacons.

And then she spots me.

Waves.

I move through the crowd to reach her.

She waits for me, a smile lighting up her tiny face. I reach out to her. She grasps my hands in hers. At her touch, electricity shoots through me. A light brighter than the sun fills me with hope. Strength. Faith.

Her difficult journey humbles me once again. She wears a name tag: Marisol. Now I know her name. Hayden joins me, and warmth spreads through me, glowing embers of possibility.

Marisol stands next to me, ready to begin the walk. She keeps my hand in hers. And so with hope on one side and faith on the other, I walk in support of life. Healing. And love.

I think I knew at the car wash that this was all for her. It had to be. If it hadn't been for Hayden, I wouldn't be here right now, walking beside Marisol. Helping to give her a future.

The hour flies by in a blur of color. Photographers snap their flashes as we cross the finish line. I reach my arms gently around my new friend. Hold her as if she is a china doll. She hugs me back with a strength that surprises me. Marisol is tougher than she looks.

I greet her parents with smiles and introduce Hayden to them. When she walks away, a wave of exhaustion passes over me. Not from the exertion of walking, but from something else. All my emotions, like waves of the sea, are churning inside me. Happiness and joy wash up on shore like seashells. Guilt and pain threaten to pull me down to the depths like anchors. I struggle to stay afloat, to stay balanced.

Hayden's arm comes around my shoulder. Pulls my side against him. I rest there to catch my breath. I've been pulled out of the water by him. Once again.

"You constantly amaze me," he says when I look up at him. And just like that, the anchors break away. And I am left on the shore surrounded by pink seashells.

A shuttle drives the walkers back to Richmond. Hayden and I sit side by side in the small bus. I nestle against his shoulder, lost in thought. One hand holds onto the daisy charm. Hayden weaves his fingers through my other hand. Connecting us.

"Do you think she'll make it?" I finally ask. The question I have been wanting to ask.

I sit up to face Hayden and see that his expression is soft, thoughtful. "She's so full of life. I think she will."

My smile is wistful, hopeful. "I met her at the hospital before my operation," I explain. "I was feeling so sorry for myself, weighed down in shadows. And then I saw her. She's facing so much, yet she's so full of light. She connected with me somehow. Without words. Ever since, she's been in my heart. Like I have to remember to be thankful for all that I have. Like

I owe it to her." I look up to see if he's judging me. He isn't. He's listening, nodding his understanding.

"I pray for her. Every night," I say. "I pray for you, too."

"My grandmother had cancer," he says after a moment. "She died two years ago."

"I'm so sorry." I squeeze his hand.

"Watching her lose the battle was the hardest part. She kept fighting until the very end. My grandfather believed she would beat it. And he wasn't ready to accept it. She was the center of his world. And after she was gone—he collapsed. He wouldn't come out of their room. He sat in the dark, holding on to the memories of her, trying to bring her back through sheer will."

This is the most Hayden has ever told me about his life. I can't hear pain in his voice, but it's etched into his eyes.

"That must have been so hard for you."

His eyes grow cloudy, like the sky before a storm. "I thought I would lose him, too."

"What did you do? To bring him back?" I ask.

His eyes clear, the storm blown away. He looks directly at me. "There was only one thing I could do—I used my voice. After eight years of silence. I talked to him."

Eight years of silence. Almost half his life without a word. And then ending it to save his grandfather. The enormity of Hayden's gift hangs in the air. A testament to the strength of his love for his grandfather. Proof that his heart isn't broken.

His face becomes blurry. Through a haze of tears, I lean forward. Kiss him gently on the cheek. "You're every kind of hero."

He rests his forehead against mine. We stay like that until the shuttle stops.

Games of the mind

HAYDEN

It's selfish, I know. But I have never had happiness like this before. I have never been able to share my story with anyone. It feels so good to have someone to talk to. Someone who can't hear me stammer and stutter. She sees the real me, without the damage. The me I would have been, could have been—and I don't want to let that go.

I park. Grab a cart from the rack outside. As I step inside the grocery store, the lighting jars me, bringing me back to reality. I have a list from Gramps written in his bold printing, but I don't open it. I like to see if I can guess what's on the list, so I toss things into the basket. Then I scan the list before I check out to see if I missed anything. My best score is a three—only three items missed. Tonight I hope to beat that.

The store is quiet tonight. Mostly single people on their way home from work. I see people in suits, scrubs, uniforms.

Lonely people. I smile at an older woman trying to reach a box of rice high on a shelf; I hand the box to her. She thanks me.

I remember another game I used to play in the market. The one where I imagined I belonged to a different family. I'd choose one—maybe the one with the three siblings arguing over which cereal to buy. Or the one with the mother laughing with her son and daughter. Sometimes it would be a couple holding hands. I would pretend just for a moment that I belonged to them and imagine what my life would be like. How it would be different, how *I* would be different. I don't need to play that game anymore, I think, as I move down the aisles. Choosing cereal, pizza toppings, yogurt.

I like the person I am with Stella. She thinks I'm a hero instead of a coward. She looks at me like I matter, like I'm important. For the first time in my life, I don't want to be invisible.

So I want to hold on to that, even though it's wrong, because I can't have her. Not really. In nine days, everything will change. She won't want me then, not when she can hear me.

Because Kace is right. As much as I hate to admit it, he is.

Stella deserves better, and after she hears again, she will realize it.

And this will be over.

Until then, I can have this. And after a lifetime of misery, I deserve this. Even if only for a short time.

I pull out the list. Check it against my half full grocery cart. Only one thing missing: rice. I beat my record.

I can't help but smile as I realize that a box of rice had been in my hand—only I gave it to someone else.

I run through the self-checkout. It's faster. Scan and pay, throw the groceries into a few bags, and I don't have to talk to anyone. Within minutes, I'm out the door. I climb back into the truck. Stella's perfume lingers in the air. I breathe in, wanting to hold on to her a little longer.

As I drive home, I make one promise to myself. I will make sure Stella isn't hurt. The only way to do that is to hold back, to keep my distance so we don't get any closer.

Even though it's too late for me. I didn't know I had a heart to give. I thought it had been broken into too many pieces. But I know now. I have given Stella my heart.

And I will never get it back.

9

STELLA

When I wake up, the sun is shining. Which is exactly how I feel. Like liquid sunshine. I think I'll wear a dress today. Blue with tiny white flowers. I add brown boots and Hayden's daisy necklace. My hair is starting to grow back where they shaved it. I brush what I can until it shines. Leave it loose.

I pick up my phone. There are two texts. One from my dad and one from Lily. I will read them later. I drop the phone into my fringed leather purse, sling the purse over my shoulder, and head down the hall.

When I enter the kitchen, my sister looks up from her plate of eggs and raises an eyebrow. My mom winks at me. She writes on a piece of paper.

You look beautiful.

Mom and Emerson are dressed in their Saturday uniforms: Emerson ready to dance, Mom to garden.

I don't hear the doorbell, of course, but I see my sister

suddenly leap out of her chair. My mom shakes her head, no. She says something to Emerson that I can't follow. I have the sudden feeling that I'm being talked about, not behind my back, but in front of my face. Then Mom smiles at me and nods toward the door.

"See you later," I tell them both. I give my mom a kiss on the cheek before I practically skip out of the kitchen.

In the car, I study Hayden. He looks relaxed today. Happy. His hair is still damp at the ends, and I can smell the scent of his shampoo. Oranges and coconut. I breathe it in.

I don't ask where we're going. I used to hate surprises. The control freak part of me could never handle not knowing what was about to happen. But I like Hayden's surprises.

For a moment, I wonder if any of this would have happened if I hadn't been injured. If I ever would have spoken to Hayden. If he would have spoken to me. I know that we never would have had seventeen days together. Not like this. It's like the daisies. And the feather of hope floating through the darkness.

Hayden pulls onto the freeway. We pass buildings and fast-food restaurants. Fields and grazing cattle. Before long, Hayden exits and turns down a deserted road. At the end is a red farmhouse. He parks in the dirt.

"We're here," he tells me.

When I climb out of the truck, I breathe in fresh air. The sky is a pale blue, with white clouds scattered like sprinkles on an ice cream sundae. A warm breeze tickles my bare arms. A windmill spins lazily.

I turn to Hayden. He is watching me, a lopsided grin playing softly at the edges of his lips. "What do you think?" he asks as we walk to the small red building.

"I like it," I respond.

We're in front of a farmers' market. Bins of shiny, crimson apples and baskets of ripe strawberries. Racks of ruffled lettuces in jeweled colors, ripe tomatoes still on the vine. I smell the potpourri of heavenly scents. Hayden speaks to the stout, weathered woman behind the counter. She hands me a basket. Says something I can't understand.

"Thank you," I tell her then follow Hayden out the back door.

Horses graze on their hay, goats meander around in their pens, hens peck the ground. A peacock walks right in front of us, spreading its tail to reveal purple and green feathers like a blessing.

A group of children wait in line for a pony ride. Others climb into a wagon for a hayride. Hayden points to the fields just ahead. We walk through the white picket fence. Now we are surrounded by fields laid out in neat rectangles like a child's drawing. Hayden steers me to the left. Takes the basket from me. With his free hand, he curls his fingers around mine. His touch is gentle but strong. I feel safe. Calm.

We walk slowly. I watch the little birds dart in and out of the plants. The orange and white butterflies glide in front of me. Breathe in the scents of soil and plants growing. With no shade in sight, the sun spreads across the back of my shoulders like a heating pad. It relaxes me. I move forward, using my senses to explore. My feet sink into the dirt. Crunch against the gravel. Makes me grateful that I chose the boots instead of sneakers.

Within a few moments, Hayden pulls me to a stop. We are all alone out here, surrounded by rows and rows of crops as far as I can see. And on the ground, strawberries, red as rubies, sprout on vines.

Hayden leans over and picks a strawberry. He grins and bites into it. "Your turn."

I find a perfect strawberry, pull it off the vine. I take a bite. It is sweet as candy. Hayden chooses more and places them in the basket. I do the same. I look for the perfect ones. I am so busy picking strawberries that I forget about everything.

And that's when it happens. A melody begins in my head. And I sing. I don't realize it at first. Not until I look up and see Hayden frozen in place, watching me. A warm flush moves through my neck and up to my cheeks. But he isn't laughing. His eyes are filled with a happy surprise. It matches the surprise I feel inside myself.

I listen inside my head for another song. Hear it as clearly as if with my ears. I open my mouth and sing. The sound vibrates in my throat, my chest. Filling my lungs with air, with life. I hold the last note and then take a bow. Hayden applauds.

I never thought I would sing again, not like this. With abandon. With power.

Later, back at the market, we choose some sunflowers for my mom. Hayden pays for the strawberries and flowers, along with turkey sandwiches and lemonades. We find a giant tree with a view of the horses. And there we sit, side by side, our backs up against the tree.

"Having fun?" Hayden asks as he hands me a sandwich.

"So much fun," I answer.

"Good."

I offer him a strawberry from our basket. He bites into it, and the juice runs down his chin. I reach up to wipe it away. My fingers run across his skin. I lean closer. Closer. I let my fingers move across his scar. Trace it softly. Gently.

I want to smooth it away. Smooth the hurt away. Hayden pulls back. Flinches from my touch. My hand drops to my lap, and I look down, letting my hair cover my face like a curtain. Hiding me. I watch an ant crawl across the dirt. Wishing I could be like it, knowing exactly where I am supposed to go and what I am supposed to do.

Then I feel something. I don't move, don't breathe, as Hayden moves my hair from my cheek. He reaches for my chin and gently turns my face toward him.

I don't want to look at him. I just want to disappear.

But I look anyway; I can't help myself. His eyes have deepened to cobalt, like the bottom of the ocean where sunken ships are found. I can see the muscle in his jaw flex. He seems to be struggling with something, like he wants to tell me something but can't.

"Tell me," I say. An echo of his words at the beach. It's an offer of trust, of connection.

"I can't," he says. "I want to. But—" He breaks off, and his hand drops from my face. He looks away and his hand reaches for mine. "I just can't."

I don't know what to say. My thoughts whirl around my brain like a bird caught inside. Trying to find a window.

He doesn't trust me. I see that. Not like I trust him. And that knowledge pierces me. I want to pull my hand away from his. To retreat. To pretend this never happened.

But my accident has taught me something. Something I would never have understood before. The old Stella pushed and pulled until she got something she wanted. The old Stella looked at patience as a weakness. She had forgotten the butterfly touch.

The new Stella, waiting for her hearing to miraculously reappear in nine days, *this* Stella understands that some things are worth waiting for—and that some things take time.

Right now, I have time. So I say nothing. I don't pull away. I just hold his hand.

The drive home seems short. Too short. If I could hear, and the ride home was silent, I would feel like I had to fill it with conversation. To pretend like everything was okay. But this kind of silence seems reverent, somehow. Respectful and peaceful. There's a deeper understanding between us. So when he walks me to the door and says good-bye, it's with the promise of tomorrow. And the day after that. And suddenly, my days of silence no longer seem like such a bad thing. They seem rather like a gift.

I'm in such a daze, I don't notice Dad's car parked in the driveway. So when I step into the front hall and see him standing there, I am surprised.

"Hi, Dad," I say. My arms are filled with a carton of strawberries and a bouquet of sunflowers.

But Dad isn't smiling back. He is angry.

Mom is standing near the door to the kitchen, looking like she wants to escape.

I turn from her face to his. "What's wrong?"

Dad begins speaking. No, yelling. I can tell his voice is raised because the veins in his neck strain. He is angry. Really angry. But his lips are moving too fast, and I can't understand.

I shake my head back and forth. I am plunged from a calm peacefulness into the depths of confusion.

I don't understand.

My stomach clenches into knots just like it used to when they would fight. When he would yell at Mom like this. Only now, instead of crying and running from the room like she used to, Mom steps forward and places her hand on my arm. She is protecting me from his anger.

Someone in this house is always disappointing him in some way. I can't imagine what I've done. I hand her the berries and flowers.

Then I face my dad. "I can't *hear* you!"

Dad freezes. Mom watches me. Steady. Strong. Not leaving.

"I can't hear, Dad. I can barely read lips—and only when someone speaks slowly. Whatever you are trying to tell me, I can't understand it!"

So he pulls out his cell phone and begins typing. He glances up every few words to make sure I am still standing there. His fingers fly over the keys. I had no idea he could text so fast. He could win a contest against teen girls.

He hands me the phone to read.

I sent you a message to remind you. Today is my office picnic, remember?

Oh no. I completely forgot. I continue to read the message.

We were supposed to leave over an hour ago. But you weren't here. You don't answer your messages. And then I find out your mother has let you go running around with some boy. Unsupervised.

Unsupervised? What is this, 1810?

And he isn't *some boy* to me. But I know Dad will never understand that.

"I'm sorry, Dad. I forgot."

His expression softens slightly. But I know it isn't over.

"Can we go now?" I offer. "Even if we're a little late?"

Dad nods. He takes the phone and types again.

I don't care if this boy saved your life. You still can't go running around with him. The rules don't change just because you can't hear them.

Okay, now I'm angry. Really angry. I turn to look at my mom. I hand her the phone and watch her read the message. She looks from me to him and back again. I think she is trying to decide if she should step into the ring or not. She opens her mouth. Apparently she's stepping in this time.

I can't tell what she says, but whatever it is, it makes Dad furious. He argues with her, waving his hands around in the air for emphasis. Mom is surely sticking up for me, and I appreciate it. But I can speak for myself, too. So I do.

"You don't have to remind me that I can't hear, Dad. I live with it every single moment of the day. If it weren't for Hayden, I'd be sitting in my room in the darkness right now. Instead of trying to make the best of it. No matter what happens with my hearing, one thing is for sure: I will never ever be the same girl I was before. That girl is gone forever."

The looks on both of their faces say that I've surprised them. I've never spoken to my parents like this. And as I look at them, my words resonate with me. It's true. I'm not the same girl anymore. And not just because I can't hear anything. The accident has changed me. Hayden has changed me. I see more, feel more, maybe even understand myself more than before.

"I love him."

I told them before telling him. But right now, it matters. They need to know what he means to me. So I say it out loud. Even though I can't hear it. I say it. Mom doesn't look surprised. She already knew. Maybe before I did.

But Dad. He's another story. His face turns a deeper shade of red. But he doesn't say anything or write anything. He just stands there, speechless.

Mom puts her arm around me and hugs me close to her. I breathe in deep and relax against her. I close my eyes, wishing this were all over. But when I open them again, Dad is still here. He hands me the phone.

I still don't approve. But I will think about it. For the next few days, no Hayden. Then we'll talk.

Truthfully, it's more than I hoped. The dad I know never changes his mind. But a couple of days is too long to be separated from Hayden. Our seventeen days are not up yet.

I want to argue more. To convince Dad.

I look at Mom. She smiles and nods. It's going to be okay, she says with her eyes. I almost believe her.

I agree to go with Dad to his office picnic. Emerson is

ready, but she has been hiding this whole time. I find her in the kitchen, munching apples and licking peanut butter from a spoon.

"Thanks for all the support," I say sarcastically.

She shrugs. She doesn't need to answer. I already know that this is her way. She avoids conflict at all costs.

"Let's go," I tell her.

Then Emerson surprises me. She reaches out and embraces me. And for a split second, we are sisters again, bound together by blood and history. And by the experiences no one but she and I will ever understand.

"Thanks," I say.

She takes me by the hand, and we head outside to climb into Dad's car. I look out the window at Mom as we drive away. She is standing in the open doorway. For a minute, I can sense her conflicting emotions. Sadness, loss and something else. I watch from the window as she turns back into the house and closes the door.

And then I brace myself for the next two hours of Dad's colleagues and their families. Sometimes it is nice not to be able to hear anything at all.

Walls that crumble

HAYDEN

I can't spend the next few days with you. I wish I could, but I can't. It's my dad, and it's complicated. Or not really complicated, just really unfair. He's got these rules. In a few days, everything will be back the way it was. I hope.

I'm sorry.

I read her message over and over again, wondering if it's true, or just an excuse. She reached out to me, asked me to trust her—and I pushed her away.

I have never told my story to anyone, not even Gramps.

And as much as I want to trust Stella, my instinct tells me not to. It tells me to protect myself, to keep my secrets safe where they can't hurt me more than they already have.

I'm used to disappointment, so when I read her words, I imagine the worst. I see other words instead.

I can't do this anymore. You have this wall up, and you won't let me in. You won't trust me, even though you've asked me to trust you. Maybe after a few days of not seeing each other, we can step back.

I write her back.

I'm sorry too. Sorry things ended the way they did today. I didn't mean for it to be like that. I want to tell you. All of it. But I can't.

Stella must be sitting next to her phone. She writes me back immediately.

"Can't" and "won't" are two different things. But it doesn't matter. You'll tell me when you're ready. I'm not going anywhere.

It's the last sentence that breaks down the wall, leaving my chest open and exposed, wounds raw even after all these years. They might be healed by her. And maybe that's the reason for our twined destinies—healing, for her and for me. I have given her something, and she wants to give me something back. A salve for my open wounds. If only I could take that first step and speak the words.

If only . . .

8

STELLA

I cry myself to sleep the same way I did when I found out my parents were splitting up. My sleep is restless. Bits and pieces of nightmares jar me into semi-consciousness like someone is pinching me. Keeping me awake when all I want is to sleep. To escape into that quiet place where everything is exactly the way I want it to be.

I roll over. I bury my head in the pillow, and try to forget. But the nightmares continue.

A fog. I can't see anything. I am running. Away from something. I slam into a giant boulder. It slices my head open. Hot, sticky blood runs down my face like crimson tears.

I stumble. Confused. Disoriented. Blinded by pain. Fall into a bottomless lake. Black water sucks me in. Pulling me down. Deeper and deeper. I can't breathe. My lungs burn. I don't want to open my mouth. Don't want to let the blackness in. I clamp it shut, clenching my jaw. So the water seeps into my ears. Filling them. Weighing me down like a sandbag from within.

I shake my head to keep it out. But it's too late. My mouth opens to scream. And the darkness envelops me. Until I am no more.

I wake. Shaking. Soaked with sweat. Sobbing.

Mom rushes into my room. I must have been screaming. She pulls me against her. Cradles me in her arms and rocks me back and forth. I let her hold me, needing to forget. To chase the nightmare away with reality.

Mom releases me. Takes the pad and pencil next to my bed. Writes.

I'm here. I'm always here. I know you must be angry with me for letting your dad make rules in our house. But I have to at least try to co-parent with him. Just lie low for a few days while this blows over. Your dad is right about one thing. You have been spending too much time with Hayden. What seems like love when you are 15 won't seem that way later. What about Lily or your other friends? Why don't you see them instead?

"I don't have any other friends. Lily's changed." Correction: *I've* changed. And I'm not ready to talk to Mom about love. How she doesn't understand that the way I feel for Hayden will never ever change. Whether I am fifteen or fifty.

But her heart has been broken, so there's no sense trying to convince her. The only way to make her see would be to bring up things that would hurt her. Things that would remind her of my dad. What he did to her. To us.

Mom writes again. *What about all of those kids in drama?*

Kace Maxwell. He's a friend, I guess. But he asked me out on a date. According to Dad, that's off-limits. Quinn hates me. That leaves me with exactly no one.

I shake my head.

I'm sorry, she writes.

Sorry doesn't help me much. Sorry is just a word.

Suddenly, I'm exhausted. Whether I am really tired or just sick of this subject, I don't know. But I can barely keep my eyes open. Mom must notice, because she stands. Tucks me beneath the blue-and-white-checkered sheets. Kisses me on the top of my head like she used to when I was little.

When I wake again, the sun is shining. Today is Easter Sunday. Mom has chocolates for us. Little bunnies and eggs wrapped in pastel foil.

I help make tomato and jack cheese omelets. Then I wake Emerson with a plate of cinnamon rolls. She grins and dives for the plate. I hold it just out of reach, teasing her. She chases me around the room. And for a few moments, I forget about everything.

Mom has hidden plastic eggs in the yard for us to find. We're too old for these games, but we pretend to love it for her sake. Plus, the eggs are stuffed with jelly beans and chocolate. We'll never be too old for those. So we race around the yard in our pajamas, pushing each other out of the way when we spot an egg we both want. Laughing until our sides hurt.

Later, we go to church. We always get new dresses for Easter. Floral or pastel flowing dresses that make us spin in front of the mirror. Today, I spin a few extra times. Because Hayden may be at church. Dad said I couldn't go out with him. But he can't keep me from running into Hayden at church.

My dress is pale blue with a white lace overlay. It has a blue ribbon at the waist. I tie it on the side. Then I twist sections of my hair from the front and pull them back, off my face. I leave the rest of my hair down.

We meet in the foyer. Emerson's dress is yellow with white polka dots. She has left her hair down with a silver headband. Mom wears a white dress and tan cardigan. We look like one of those commercials for spring dresses.

Church is crowded. Every seat is taken. People spill out the open doors. Little girls dressed like princesses carry little white baskets and stuffed bunnies. Boys pull at collared shirts and vests, looking uncomfortable.

Hayden isn't here. I look for him during the service. And afterward, at the coffee and donut table. He isn't there, either. My stomach drops with disappointment. There are two other services today. He must be going to one of the others. All I wanted was to see him, if just for a few moments. With five days off of school for spring break, I won't have a chance to see him during school lunch, either.

We walk to the car. "You can sit in front today," I tell Emerson. "I'm kind of tired." It's not a total lie. I am suddenly really, really tired. Emerson is thrilled to ride shotgun. As the oldest, I am usually in the front seat. But I don't want Mom to see the tears welling in my eyes. The sag in my shoulders. Or the silent sobs that follow.

I check my phone every half hour. No message from Hayden. I finally break down and send him one.

Happy Easter. Hope u have a gr8 day! :)

I watch Emerson practice a routine for cheerleading tryouts. Emerson explains that the junior varsity squad tries out later than varsity, so the new cheerleaders can mentor the younger ones. I guess I should be happy that Lily wants to mentor my little sister. But it still gives me twinges. I smile at Emerson and clap for her when she does a spunky routine.

Emerson finishes with a series of jumps and then a perfect back flip. I give her a standing ovation. Not thinking about Lily now. Just Emerson.

Mom comes outside to see the routine. I stay and watch a second time. "You'll make the team for sure," I tell her. "I just know it!"

Emerson runs over and hugs us both at the same time. We're the three musketeers.

Then Mom hands me a pair of gloves and garden shears. She sets my vase on the garden path before moving into the garden with her own gloves and shears.

She wants me to fill the vase with flowers. I breathe deep, inhaling the scent of roses and lavender.

Then I start choosing flowers. I cut a yellow rose just beginning to bloom. I add sprigs of lavender and a bunch of pink peonies. One single white daisy with a yellow center. I arrange the flowers so the daisy is the centerpiece.

By the time Mom comes to check on me, I am finished. I hold up the vase for her to see. She nods her approval. Warmth spreads from her smile to mine.

I spend the next couple of hours side by side with my mother. We pull weeds, tie back roses and drag the hose around. I like watching the water slowly trickle from the hose into the flowerbed. Turning the brown soil black. Drenching it.

I forget for a while. Forget Hayden. Forget Lily. Forget everything. It feels good not to think. I just feel—the sun on my shoulders, the dirt underneath my hands, the ache in my legs from kneeling, the calm in my heart.

Later, we sit together on the sofa and watch cooking shows. It's easy to understand them without hearing or reading captions. Emerson makes a bowl of popcorn, and I empty our Easter candy into the bowl. The chocolate melts into the buttery popcorn and makes a tasty mess.

I keep my phone on the coffee table in front of us. I keep looking at it. Finally, at dinnertime, he responds.

Hope you have a great day, too.

Then nothing.

I can't blame him. When I think of things from his perspective, I even understand it. I am hollowed out, like one of the chocolate foil eggs. A shell on the outside. Empty on the inside.

I stay awake in front of the television. Afraid to go to sleep and revisit my nightmares. I wrap myself in a blanket, watch infomercials until I can't prop my eyes open anymore. And I fall into a dark, dreamless sleep.

Being in the moment

HAYDEN

With no hope of seeing Stella for the next few days, I pick up extra shifts at the nursery. There's nothing worse than sitting around—I'd rather be moving, working, sweating. I show up at 6 a.m. to unload shipments from the truck.

Yesterday, I needed to find something else to keep myself busy. So I helped Gramps clean out his studio—tearing down clay models that have been turned into bronze, recycling the clay, sweeping the floor, wiping the tables. We stopped only to go to church, the last service of the day. I didn't want to see Stella—too painful. Gramps didn't ask any questions and didn't pry. But he watched me, and I know he realizes something's wrong. He's waiting for me to share it with him, but I'm not ready.

I work at the nursery from 6 a.m. to 6 p.m., with only a short break to eat a peanut butter and jelly sandwich. I move bags of sod, rearrange rose plants, water everything twice.

Today, Jeremiah needs my help with customers. Sunny days bring crowds—good weather is like a banner that advertises planting and growing things. So today I load cars with fruit trees, carry flats of flowers to trucks, help people fit tall houseplants in their cars. I smile and nod, do as I'm told. I don't speak once all day. It's better that way, like I'm in a bubble—my own silent world.

I won't think about Stella; it's too dangerous. One trickle of emotion seeping through my façade will destroy everything. I block her from my thoughts completely.

I stay in the present, the here and now. Putting one foot in front of the other. That's all I can do. Just to get through this day, and the next, until I can see her again.

7

STELLA

The day moves so slowly. Each moment lasts an hour. Each hour, an eternity.

I bake oatmeal cookies.

Clean my closet.

Make friendship bracelets with Emerson.

Weed the garden.

Start *Persuasion* by Jane Austen.

Make tea for Mom.

Braid Emerson's hair like Katniss at The Reaping.

And it isn't even dinnertime yet.

Underneath it all, I'm angry. Angry with my dad for deciding all of a sudden to be a father. Just to enforce a punishment and then waltz back to his Number One Family. Angry with Mom for accepting it and allowing him to make rules for our household. Angry with Hayden for going silent on me. Angry with my ears for not working.

The only person I'm not angry at is Emerson, and that's because she's the only one who can make me laugh. She's my best friend.

Then I look at the picture, the one Hayden took of me with the butterfly. And I'm reminded about patience. This isn't forever. It's just a few days. A test to see if Hayden really means so much to me. If he does, time is immaterial. Because nothing will change my love for him.

So I sit on the floor cross-legged. Close my eyes. And breathe.

I breathe in life.

Love.

Grace.

Humility.

I find a place inside to be grateful. Full of thanks.

I let go of the anger. Fill myself with space instead.

Space for hope.

Possibility.

Dreams.

When I am fully relaxed, I pull out a notebook and a pen.

And I write.

Emotions begin in my heart. Flow through my veins and into my left hand. My fingers are the last stop. The pen carries the words forth. Giving them life. Ink gives them power.

I release it all. Freeing myself as I write. It's like nothing else. Because here, I have complete freedom to be anyone I want to be. Without judgment or criticism.

Each word is like a drop of my blood falling on the page. And while I write, I am aware that I am somewhere else yet right here. I once thought that only singing could create that dynamic for me. I was wrong. It was all here right inside of me. I just didn't know it.

She stands on stage
In the spotlight
Dressed in her dreams
Reaching for tomorrow

The unthinkable happens
Her dreams torn away
Leaving her naked
The spotlight extinguished

She is surrounded in darkness
Facing the worst of her fears
Mourning the loss of dreams
Unable to imagine tomorrow

A golden angel reaches out
Like a ray of sunlight
To pull her from the depths
With a promise of hope

Then she sees a rainbow
Braving the wind and rain
To touch the sun
Saying anything is possible

Finally, she sees a flower
Grounded in the earth
Reaching for the sun
Still there, always there

SILENCE

She sees outside herself
To the world beyond
Three beckon her step by step
With hope, faith and love.

Dreams reveal truth

HAYDEN

This morning I wake with dreams of Stella in the air, like the scent of her perfume—honey and wildflowers. I may be able to control my conscious mind and shut her out. But in sleep, my subconscious takes over, and I cannot lie.

Dreams trail through my mind like red ribbons all connecting back to her. I see her there in a red dress, on stage, singing to me. I am her leading man. Her voice soars over the audience with passion—and all of it is for me. I take her hands in mine and vow to never ever let her go.

Usually I can shake off my dreams. It's been a survival mechanism, dispelling memories of my mother, my past. Dreams that once haunted me in sleep, I learned to extinguish while awake. It's always worked before. Until today.

The dream of Stella will not disappear. It stays with me all morning, tormenting me. While I eat breakfast, get dressed, drive to work. Then more as I plant flowers, tend seedlings, move sod.

By noon, I know what I have to do.

I take a break to eat an apple, grab my phone, and send her this message.

I may not be able to see you. But I can still help you. So for today—day 6—shoot photographs. Tell a story with a camera. Challenge yourself. See things in a new way. Send me your best one. Here are two of mine.

I attach a photo of an apple tree laden with blossoms and another of a row of seedlings sprouting out of a red metal tin.

I add something: *I miss you.* But then I erase it. Instead, I sign it with an H.

I may not be able to be with her, but I can still keep my promise. I can still be there for her. Because like the red ribbons in my dream, I am tied to Stella, and nothing will change that.

Then I receive her response: *I was afraid you were never going to speak to me again.*

I write back. *I was just giving you space.*

I don't need space. I need you.

That makes me smile. I want to write back to tell her I need her too. But I can't.

Have to go back to work. Send me the pictures tonight.

All day long, no matter what I do, they are with me.

Red ribbons.

6

STELLA

I stand in the backyard, camera in hand. Looking for a way to challenge myself.

Hayden asked me to tell a story with pictures. But what story do I want to tell?

All I can think about is Hayden. And how even when we are apart, he is with me. I meant it when I said I need him. I do. I need him like I need to breathe.

I imagine him planting seedlings in the red tin. Tending the apple tree. Seeing his day brings me closer to him. Makes me feel like I am there.

Emerson sits in a chair, sipping a lemonade. Engrossed in a novel. Mom is working in her office. I sit on the ground. Observing.

Mom's garden is in full bloom. Bees fly here and there. I imagine they buzz as they move from flower to flower. Buds open to greet the sun. Daisies tip to touch the earth. Herbs spread their fragrant scent. The ground is carpeted with emerald grass.

I breathe in. Taste nature.

Lie back and look up. The sky sparkles like it is inlaid with diamonds.

I think of Hayden.

He cloaks himself in silence
If he isn't heard, he won't be seen
Guarding himself from memories
From a past he wants to forget

But his heart won't oblige
And refusing to be hidden away
It glows from within
Fighting for the chance to stay alive

His heart destroys the cloak
Leaves it in a heap
Silence is shattered
With the sound of his voice

More than one life he saves that day
Because his voice is a gift
Allowing him to reach out
To speak. To heal. To love.

This is the story I will tell.

I stand and move through the yard. I take a close-up of a red flower. So close, the petals begin to blur, making it look more like a heart than a flower. This will be Hayden's heart. The heart that refuses to be silenced.

I find a puddle. Take a shot of the water. Close enough to get the reflection of the sky. Infinite possibility. Hayden's gifts to the world.

Then I lie down and shoot through the blades of grass. So that it seems I am small enough to fit between them. And be lost forever. Invisible.

I need to find a way to express the concept of hiding. I wander around. Search the yard. I see nothing.

So I go into the front yard. Look at the street. The white picket fence in front of our house. The front step where I waited for Hayden that first day.

Then I see it. The oak tree. I tuck the camera into my shorts pocket. Boost myself onto the lowest branch. Nestle myself in. And look up. There. Between the branches. The bark of the tree separates, and I can just make out the tender wood underneath. Hidden by the bristly bark. I take the picture.

I climb down from the tree. Remove the daisy pendant from around my neck. Lay it gently on the front step. Then I move back. Take a photo of the step and the necklace. I sit on the step next to the necklace. Thinking how far I have come since that first day.

I'm still sitting here when Mom comes to get me. She takes me and Emerson out to lunch and then shopping for the rest of the afternoon. Something we haven't done together in a long time. I have so much fun that I forget I can't hear them talk. It doesn't even matter.

Later, I upload the photos to my computer. Then I type the words of Hayden's poem. I add the photos where they belong to tell the story. His story.

Then I send it to him.

Hayden's Song.

Eye to eye

HAYDEN

When I open the attachment to Stella's email, I know what I expect—photos of Emerson or a squirrel, or maybe a rose in bloom.

So I am not prepared for this—Hayden's Song.

As I read the words, and see the photos, I feel like someone has punched me in the stomach. I can't seem to catch my breath, and I have the sudden sense that I am falling into an abyss.

It's one thing to know that you are seen, but Stella sees me from the inside out, like she has climbed inside my heart. I read the poem again to let the images and words soak into my consciousness. So I can understand what she's saying.

The voice in my head that sounds like my mother begins to fade. Her words telling me I am worthless, a disappointment. Those words blur, become unintelligible, as though they no longer belong to me.

In their place, I hear Stella's voice—clear and deep. Reciting her poem.

More than one life he saves that day
Because his voice is a gift
Allowing him to reach out
To speak. To heal. To love.

It's all I can do not to jump in my car and drive over to her house, even though it's ten o'clock at night and her dad has forbidden it. An email isn't enough; there is so much I want to say.

Because I want to tell her.

Everything.

I want to tell her.

That she is healing me, that her voice is the gift.

And she has saved me.

I send her this message: *Stella, you are the gift.*

When I open my eyes the next morning, nightmares still roar in my mind like storm clouds heralding a thunderstorm. For a moment, I am five again, hiding behind the kitchen door. Bottles and jars being thrown at my head and crashing against the door.

My body shakes uncontrollably, teeth chattering. I breathe in, hold it, clench my teeth. Count to five, exhale, then again. Calm myself, the way the doctors taught me.

Breathe.

Breathe.

Breathe.

Something is wrong; I can sense it in the air. Splitting molecules in uneven patterns, a manic frenzy.

I climb out of bed and open my door.

I hear one voice. And it stabs me in the chest, piercing deep—opening scars.

My mother has returned.

I think about running, climbing out the window, escaping. I pull on jeans and a shirt, with my escape plan worked out in my mind. Gramps steps into my room, closes the door behind him. Eyes me—and the window.

"Going somewhere?"

I cross my arms over my chest. "Wh-wh-what d-does sh-she w-want?" I stammer worse than ever.

He shrugs. "Who can say? To see you, see me." His eyes say more, something he isn't telling me. It makes me nervous. The more nervous I become, the more my words struggle to be released.

I shrug too. "It's a-a li-little l-late for th-that," I say, panting with each syllable.

Gramps steps closer. "One thing I know about life is that anger has a way of turning on itself. Of eating you up inside." He places a hand on my shoulder. "If you face your mother, maybe you can start to let go of the past. That's all I want for you."

He's not asking me to forgive her, or even talk to her. Just to face her. I've never told him what happened all those years ago, but somehow, he knows. And that gives me courage.

I don't say anything; I just move past him and open the door.

When I walk into the room, she's standing at the kitchen window. My mother. The voice in my head, the author of the memories that haunt me, the reason I stutter and stammer.

The last time I saw her I was twelve years old—and silent.

Now I am seventeen. I may still bear the scars she gave me, but she can no longer intimidate me. I stand a full head taller than she does.

My mother turns when she hears us come into the room.

I stop still, watching her hands as they clench and unclench. Remembering them, how they would strike my face, my stomach, my back.

Again and again.

The past collides with the present, and I flinch. She stares at me for a moment without moving, not recognizing me.

Then, "Hayden Jagger."

No one has used my full name since she left, since I was ten. She opens her arms and moves toward me. I step back, shake my head.

She drops her hands. I look into her panther eyes, searching them for signs of intoxication. She has deep wrinkles around her eyes and mouth and her skin is sallow. Her hair isn't the blonde mass of curls I remember. Instead, it's short and tufted, dyed a bright magenta. She has a tattoo of a heart with an arrow on her arm, wears denim shorts made for a teenager, and feathers hang from her T-shirt.

"You look so grown up," she says, studying me. I squirm under her eyes, waiting for her to find fault. To call it out—expose it.

She tilts her head to the side, pulls out a pack of cigarettes. Taps the pack to pop out a single cigarette.

I am waiting for Gramps to tell her he has asthma and can't be around smoke.

She flips open her lighter, snaps it once, twice, before he finally speaks. "Dee, you'll have to step outside with that."

"Gotcha," she says. Walks out to the porch, the screen door clanging behind her.

My eyes flicker to the door, tracking her every move. Tensed in a fight-or-flight response, waiting.

Gramps pours me a glass of orange juice, hands me a plate with a bagel on it. I set it down on the counter.

Suddenly, I remember being in this same kitchen with her. Right before I turned seven—before the silence. It was Grandma's birthday. She had just blown out the candles on the cake. Grandma had promised me the first piece. I was still talking then, telling them about how I was going to be a professional racecar driver when I grew up.

My mom interrupted, said she needed to leave me with them for a little while. She wanted to sing background vocals for a new artist opening for someone in Asia. She didn't know when she would be back.

Now I remember something I had forgotten. My grandfather said yes, but my grandmother said no. My mother needed to be responsible, she said. Dreams of touring and singing on stage were over; she had a child to raise.

My mother began screaming, accusing my grandmother of being jealous, of not wanting her to be a star. And then she pulled me by the arm, dragging me right out of there. I never did get my piece of cake.

My mother finishes her cigarette. Grinds it into the ground with her high-heeled sandals and returns to the kitchen. The air is filled with the stale smell of smoke, reminding me of her and how she always smelled like this—smoke and alcohol.

She turns to me, lips stretched back over her teeth in a forced smile.

"Your grandfather says you're talkin' now. Says you're a real musician. Guess I gave ya somethin' good after all."

I still haven't said a word.

"You sing, too?" she asks.

I nod, still not willing to speak.

She smiles again. Then her smile turns bitter, sours before my eyes. "Remember, Haydie. Nothing wrong with being a musician. No matter what they told ya." Her eyes narrow, turn resentful.

I find myself gripping the edge of the counter, preparing for her anger. So attuned am I to her moods even after all these years, I can still read her.

She suppresses her bitterness, takes a long drink from my orange juice. I won't be finishing it now. "So, you got a girlfriend?"

I shake my head.

"You do like girls though, right?" She laughs at that, a coarse cough sort of sound that gives me chills.

I don't think I need to answer a question like that. Either way, it's offensive. Silence is my friend. I say nothing. Whether she takes a nonanswer as an answer, I wouldn't know, and I don't care.

I look at Gramps, willing him to say nothing. The mention of Stella is not allowed in this room right now. I won't touch her with any of this, even by speaking about her.

Then my mother sighs, as if this is all boring her. I'm not interesting enough to warrant further inspection. She turns to Gramps. "I better get goin'. King's waitin' on me. So . . ." She lets the word hang in the air, waiting for him to catch on.

My eyes flick back and forth between them. Gramps nods, reaches into his pocket, and hands her an envelope. She nods but doesn't thank him.

She turns to me. "You be good to your grandfather now. Stay out of trouble."

She moves to hug me again, and again I step just out of her reach. She shrugs, turns away.

And she's gone, in a puff of smoke.

Just like that.

I step to the screen door to look out. She climbs into the passenger seat of an old, beat-up Chevy. A guy with long hair and an armful of tattoos is in the driver's seat. This must be King. The car rumbles as he backs up. I watch as she drives away, gone for good.

I turn back to look at my grandfather, his eyes full of unshed tears. "Sh-she came f-for money, didn't sh-she?"

He nods, unable to speak the truth—the horrible truth.

"Wh-why did you g-give it to h-her?"

He shrugs, and his face crumples. For the first time, Gramps looks his age.

"She's my child after all."

I don't understand it, and I won't even try to. I leave the bagel on the counter, set the empty juice glass in the sink. "Y-you c-could've w-warned me." I speak without turning around.

"I didn't know. She rang the doorbell at 6:30 this morning. You were still asleep."

I turn to look at my grandfather. "Sh-she's n-never go-going to say s-sorry," I say finally. The smell of smoke still lingers in the room. Only now do I understand what I needed from her—what I needed and will never get. An apology.

Gramps runs one hand through his hair, a gesture I haven't seen since my grandmother was dying and he was helpless. "Would it matter if she did? Would it change things?"

I shrug. Maybe it would change things. Probably not. Gramps moves toward me then, reaching out to place a hand on each of my shoulders. I stand slightly taller than he does, but his grip is strong, powerful.

"I'm sorry, Hayden. For every single moment she didn't love you right. She's my daughter, so it's partly my fault. And it breaks my heart to think of the things she did to you. The ways she hurt you. I can never make it right. Never change the past. But I can tell you that I am so proud of you. You are the son I always wanted."

He's never apologized to me before, not for her behavior. And he's never called me his son before. It chips something away inside, a piece of the wall around my heart.

5

STELLA

I'm just getting dressed when I receive Hayden's message.

My mother was here. Today.

Within moments, my mother has agreed to let me see him. I don't give her the specifics. She already knows that Hayden lives with his grandfather.

"Hayden's mother showed up this morning. At his house," I tell her. "And I think he's really upset. Can I please see him? We'll stay here. Just for a little while?"

That's all it takes.

I reply to his message. *My mom says it's ok for you to come over. If you want.*

I'll see you soon, he says.

I wait on the front step, twirl the daisy charm back and forth in my hand. Wondering what I will say when he gets here. How I will help him. I hope I'll know the right thing to do.

I chew my lip as his truck pulls down the street. It stops in front of my house. I watch as he looks at me through the window. He gets out. Walks toward me. He looks so pale. Crumpled, like he is broken. He moves slowly, almost like he must control every step. Not his usual graceful stride. And I know exactly what to do. Because the expression of pain on his face connects with my heart. Instinct takes over. Moving for me. Speaking for me.

I stand and move toward him. I wrap him in my arms, and hold on tight. He trembles, like little earthquakes are rolling through him. He rests his chin on the top of my head as he lets me hold him. Lets me love him.

I feel him melt into me. Lean into me. The shaking subsides. I hold him tighter still. I don't know how long we stand there. It doesn't matter. Because he needs me as much as I need him. We need each other. We're stronger together. Better together.

When we break apart, I look into his eyes. They glisten. Seeing him so emotional does something to me. It makes me take over. As though I need to be stronger for him. To take care of him for once. So that's how I take his hand. Lead him around the side of the house through the gate. And into the backyard.

I walk him through the garden past the rosebushes and the lavender. Through the herb boxes. And to the little iron bench in the back. The one Mom bought at an antique sale years ago. It's nestled into the ordered chaos as though it's part of the garden. There, I pull him down beside me and finally speak two words.

"Tell me."

Hayden twines his fingers through mine, looking at our hands rather than into my eyes. I watch his mouth. Read his words.

"She was there when I woke up. I haven't seen her since she showed up with airport presents when I was twelve. Today, she showed up with a new boyfriend and a pack of cigarettes." His mouth closes in a line. Jaw clenching. He seems far away. No longer right beside me, but somewhere else. Someplace else.

Then he speaks again. "It was like I was seven again. I didn't say a word. Not one. Like I was still silent." His eyes raise to mine. Beseeching me to understand.

I can see how much he is hurting. I just want to be here for him, to help somehow. I place my other hand on top of our two hands. Run my fingers across the back of his. Letting him know that even if I can't hear him, I am listening.

He hesitates, then speaks. "She beat me. All those years ago."

I pull in a breath. Hold tighter to his hand.

"When she drank—and even when she didn't, she screamed at me. Blamed me for her failures, for her pathetic life. She wanted to be a famous singer and ran away from home at seventeen to join a band. Instead of a record deal, she ended up with me. I think my grandparents must have given her money to settle down so she wouldn't drag me around the country chasing her dream. But it made her so angry. She used to throw things. Bottles, cans, shoes. Anything within reach. Sometimes, she beat me with them." He breaks off for a moment as the torment catches up with him. He's unable to continue.

My heart is breaking. Tears slip down my cheeks as I imagine Hayden battered and pummeled. Punished for his very existence. I ache for the little boy inside of him who has been so damaged. His eyes are far away when he speaks again.

"One time, I was huddled behind a kitchen chair in a pile of broken glass. She picked up a broken bottle. Slashed it across my face. Said she wished I had never been born. I remember there was blood everywhere. How much it hurt. But I'm not sure now if the pain was coming from the wound."

The scar on Hayden's chin is so deep, it extends all the way to his heart. Now I understand why he flinched when I touched it. It represents her. And what she did to him.

"I called my grandfather and he took me to the hospital. Long sleeves and a story about a baseball couldn't hide what she had done. This time people started asking questions. And I didn't want to answer them. I'm not sure who I was protecting—my grandfather, my mother or me. But I stopped talking that day. I never talked about what happened. Not to her or anyone. Hours turned into days. Then months. The more she yelled at me to speak, the more I refused to. Silence became my only power. By then, I'd realized that I could become invisible. When you don't speak, people pay attention. Sometimes the absence of sound is louder than sound itself. But then, after a while, they give up on you. So months turned into years, and I disappeared."

Tears blur my vision. I wonder how he found the strength

to go on. The courage to keep fighting. To believe in himself. It would have been so much easier to give up.

"Is that when your grandparents took you in?" I venture.

Hayden shakes his head. "Not then. It wasn't until three years later, when I was ten."

My throat tightens and I forget to breathe. There is more. More he hasn't told me.

"It was another hospital visit that did it. This time with broken bones. Bones heal, but this"—he gestures to his scar—"is a constant reminder. She wishes I had never been born."

He wraps both of his hands around mine, looking at me. "And that's what I wished, too. Until I saw you for the first time—that day at school. Then I didn't want to be invisible anymore. I wanted to be seen. By you."

I can't breathe as he gazes at me. His heart is in his eyes.

"I've never told anybody," he says. "What happened that day with my mother. Until now."

Sharing his story with me is a sign of trust. He hasn't shared what happened with anyone, not even his grandfather. But he shared it with me. This is the moment I have been waiting for. The butterfly has come to me. Now I need to be gentle. Not scare him away.

The expression on his face shows pain, disappointment, and something else. In the set of his jaw, the lowering of his eyes. Guilt. There is something else. Something he needs to say.

"I can't forgive her."

That's what is tearing him up inside—he can't forgive her.

"Has she asked for your forgiveness?" I ask gently. "Has she ever apologized?"

He doesn't speak. Only shakes his head. Tears shine in his eyes, but he does not release them. I don't know how so many tears can pool in his eyes and not be shed. But he contains them. Holds them inside. The effect turns his eyes a pale blue, almost white. Blinding.

I lean into him. Look at the scar on his chin. The scar I now know is much deeper than the surface of his skin. It defines how he sees himself. A symbol of his worth. I wish I could erase his pain. Show him what he means to me. Before I realize what I am doing, I press my lips to his chin. I kiss his wound, trying to heal it. Heal him.

He doesn't flinch. Doesn't push me away. When I draw back, his eyes are wide with surprise. But he lets me see him. He doesn't pull back.

"I don't forgive her either," I say. "And one more thing."

He listens. Watches me.

"She can't hurt you anymore."

"She can't?"

I shake my head. "I won't let her." A beat. And then I finish. "Ever. Again."

That's when the sun shines on me. Because for the first time that day, Hayden smiles. "I believe you." One tear falls.

When Hayden leaves for work, I join Mom in her office. Offer to help with her work again. I need to immerse myself in mundane activities. My emotions need a respite. I spend the rest of my day assembling folders and stuffing envelopes. Making copies.

Mom doesn't ask for details, and Hayden's secrets aren't mine to reveal. I tuck them into my heart where they will stay safe.

I do thank her, though. For breaking her own rules—or Dad's rules, anyway. For letting me see Hayden. I tell her it meant a lot to him to be able to talk to me about it. "I was happy to be able to help him for once. He's helped me so much."

Mom nods and smiles. She writes me a note. "Hayden is lucky to have someone care about him the way you do. I think you've helped each other."

I grin at her. She just might understand, just a little bit.

Emerson needs a ride to dance class. Today, I offer to go along with Mom. I want to watch my sister dance.

I sit in the waiting room with all the dance moms, glad I can't listen to the gossip. My eyes are glued to the window between the studio and the waiting room. I proudly watch my sister leap and spin across the floor.

On the way home, we stop for pizza. The three of us share a pepperoni and olive jumbo. In the booth at the restaurant, I look at my mother as she smiles at Emerson. My mother, who has never blamed me for anything. Never raised a hand to me. Never abandoned me. Never done anything but love me.

She looks at me quizzically. I don't usually stare at her this way.

I try to explain. "You're a really wonderful mom. I love you." I turn to Emerson. "I love you too, you know."

Emerson leaps up, wraps her arms around us both. Kisses us on the cheeks. A wet pepperoni and olive kiss.

After we get home, I take up my favorite position on the sofa. Open up another Jane Austen favorite: *Sense and Sensibility.* I have finished the first twenty pages when I receive a text message.

All I knew this morning was that I needed you. I don't even remember driving to your house. But when I saw you, I could breathe. I will always remember.

My stomach flutters at his last sentence. Will I ever get used to Hayden's interest in me? Or will it always stir me this way?

A second message from him arrives.

My grandfather wants to invite you and your Mom and Emerson to be his guests at an art event tomorrow night. He's displaying some of his new works. I'd especially love to see you. H

Hayden has figured out another way for us to be together. I can't wait for tomorrow night. I run to tell my mom about the invitation. I know she will say yes. Now we just have to figure out what to wear.

Please thank your grandfather. We'll be there. Send me the address and what time. I miss you. S

Wings to fly

HAYDEN

I miss her too, every minute of the day—more than I want to admit.

My fingers touch my chin, run over the bump of my scar, the visible memory of my past. My secrets. I can still feel Stella's kiss there, her lips pressing against my skin, warming me, healing me.

Touching me.

Even after I told her everything—all of it—she didn't run away.

She holds my secrets now.

As she holds my heart.

My feet pound a rhythm into the asphalt as I run. Faster and faster, I pump my legs, as if controlling my body will help me control my emotions. I run without music. The thoughts are loud in my ears, and I cannot escape them. No matter how far I run.

I can never tell Stella how much she means to me, because then she wouldn't walk away. I can see that now. And I refuse to hold her back from all that she can become. I love her enough to let her go. I will never hold her back the way I held my mother back. I won't ever be responsible for destroying someone else's dreams. Not if I can help it.

In four days, she will hear again.

And I will tell her good-bye.

4

STELLA

Emerson and I spend the day with our dad. He tries to invite us to his house to go swimming. But I have Emerson tell him I am afraid of pools now. So we need to do something else.

I'm not afraid of pools or swimming. I just don't like to go to my dad's house and see the First Family.

And feel like a second-class daughter.

And pretend it's all okay.

When it's really not.

So we go to play tennis instead. Which is fine by me. Emerson is pretty good. So is Dad. Me, not so much.

The sun is shining on the court as we run back and forth, chasing the fuzzy highlighter ball. Dad hits every shot perfectly. Emerson leaps and dives, making some stellar points. I hit more balls over the fence than over the net. But at least we aren't fighting.

Afterward, we go to get smoothies. I am happy to ride in the backseat and leave Emerson riding shotgun. I look out the window and dream of tonight. Of seeing Hayden. Holding his hand. Just being near him. I can't seem to wipe the goofy smile off my face.

The smoothie place is crowded. We wait in line for a while. I know better than to try to bring up what's on my mind until Dad has eaten. Plus, he hates lines. I order a blueberry and strawberry smoothie. Emerson gets peach and banana, her favorite.

We find a table outside. Dad sips his veggie smoothie. Full of antioxidants, with three servings of vegetables. He offers a sip to me and Emerson, but we both decline.

If I am going to plead my case, now is the time. I meet Emerson's eyes, beg her to help me. She squeezes my knee under the table. And I begin.

"Dad, you said for a few days, no Hayden. Then we would talk." I face him directly. "Let's talk."

Dad raises his eyebrows, but he doesn't say anything. He sips his smoothie.

I'm waiting. I take a deep breath and lean forward. "You and Mom agreed I could date when I turned sixteen. My birthday is a month away. I'm only asking you to bend the rules for a few weeks. That's all. Hayden means a lot to me. I think if you would get to know him, you'd like him a lot. I know Mom does."

I cheated a bit invoking the name of my mother. But I'm not trying to pit my parents against each other; I'm just being honest. She does like Hayden.

I expect a lot of things from Dad. A stoic response. A non-response. A repeat of the other day. Frustration. Maybe anger.

I don't expect laughter. But that's exactly what he does.

He laughs. Then he pulls out his phone. His fingers fly across the keyboard.

You surprised me. I didn't think you could do that anymore. You are so much like me, you know that? You plead a great case. I hadn't even thought of the birthday argument—and it's a good one, I have to admit. But you're wrong thinking I don't like Hayden. I do. He saved your life, so he's not only brave but selfless. I saw him in the hospital, waiting for hours to make sure you were okay. I knew he had feelings for you then. I just think you're too young to be this serious about someone.

Dad surprises me too. In a good way. He reminded me for a moment that there is something I like about him. I had forgotten that.

But he still hasn't given me the answer I want.

"Are you still saying no?" I venture, tilting my head and wishing I could hear him instead of reading his answer. So much rides on this one word. Yes or no.

If he says no, I have already decided what to do. For the first time in my life, I will lie to my parents. I *won't* give up the last few days of Hayden's promise. I am counting down the days to my doctor's appointment, but I am also counting down the days to the end of our seventeen-day journey together. Because I have this foreboding sense that on that last day, something is going to change. And I don't want to give up any more time with Hayden before that.

Dad writes his answer. He sets the phone on the table. Spins it to face me.

Ok

I leap up from the table. Throw my arms around my dad.

And he hugs me back.

A few hours later, Mom, Emerson and I walk into the Picasso Gallery. It is located in the center of downtown. A red carpet is laid out on the sidewalk. Photographers snap photos. Glamorous people mingle.

I wear a navy dress with thin straps at the top and an inlay of navy lace. There are small ruffles of the same lace around the hem. It's the nicest dress I own. My hair is loose, with a small braid around the crown of my head, trailing into my curls. My shoes are gold strappy sandals. I wear the daisy around my neck.

Mom wears a fitted black dress with camel pumps and a camel scarf around her neck. Her hair is pulled back into a sleek ponytail. She looks stunning. Emerson wears a soft mauve dress that is shirred on the sides and ends in a flowing, uneven hem. She wears little brown and gold flats that tie around her ankles. I think she looks like a fairy.

The whole front of the gallery is open, as though the walls can be removed. We step into a wonderland of paintings and sculptures. My eyes dash from wall to wall. Not sure where to begin.

Hayden steps forward. Appears magically out of the crowd. I breathe in. Frozen at the sight of him.

For I have never seen him like this. He wears a navy

pin-striped suit with a light blue shirt. No tie. His hair is pulled back off his face. The blue shirt makes his eyes as bright as the sky on a spring morning. His skin glows.

And his smile is just for me.

"My grandfather is so happy you could make it," he says.

My mother gives him a warm hug. Emerson hugs him as well, though shyly. Hayden doesn't hug me. He simply reaches out and takes my hand.

"I'll show you his latest work," he tells us.

He turns us toward the sculptures. We have to wait for the crowd in front of us to finish looking. While we wait, Hayden leans in close. "You take my breath away." His expression is filled with admiration, appreciation. And something else. Sadness? Then it is gone, replaced with a dazzling smile.

I return his smile with one of my own. "I stopped breathing weeks ago."

Hayden understands my meaning; I know because his eyes deepen in color for a moment, turning a brilliant indigo. His gaze is more powerful than words. I forget where I am. I forget to breathe. I am completely his.

Mom touches my arm. And I remember where I am. The room is out of focus. I am dizzy. I blink, trying to clear my thoughts. Be present.

I breathe in and out. Look around. Mom catches my glance. Gives me a half-smile of understanding. I squeeze her hand. She squeezes mine back.

Finally, the group in front of us moves on. Hayden steps forward and gestures to the pieces in front of us.

We can only stare in awe. Humbled. Three white pedestals

stand in a line. Each holds a precious animal casted entirely in metal.

The first is a horse. Peaceful. Serene. Wide, calm eyes look at us as though they see us. The horse's mane flows in the wind, as smooth as if we could touch it. The muscles of the horse ripple. One hoof is raised, as though he is about to break into movement any second. He is majestic. The plaque underneath reads "'Freedom to Fly'—John Rivers."

The second is a bear. A rounded back with tufted hair rises in the air. The snout is long and curved. The nose smells the air, testing it. Claws grip the stones underneath his paws. He is so real, he makes my blood rush. "'Greeting Spring'—John Rivers."

The last is a mountain lion. Teeth bared. Front paws in the air. Hind legs bent as though ready to pounce. She is ferocious. Behind her are two cubs. Each has its own position and attitude. Each a different expression. One imitates Mama, posing just like her. The other is distracted, using a paw to bat something just out of reach. They are charming and wild at the same time. A family of three. "'Unbroken Chain'—John Rivers."

Mom is especially taken with the horse. I watch her move around the piece, looking at it from all sides. She had horses growing up. She's told stories about how she used to ride with my grandfather. Those are her favorite memories. If she could, she'd have a horse now. So it warms me to watch her face. The happiness there.

Hayden's grandfather joins us then. It's only the second

time I have seen him, so I marvel again at his strong resemblance to Hayden.

Hayden introduces his grandfather to Mom and Emerson. Gramps holds out his hand to Mom, but she surprises him by embracing him instead. Then Emerson does the same. Mom begins talking animatedly about the pieces—she points and gestures. Hayden's grandfather basks in her praise. Smiles as he talks to her.

Hayden translates for me. "He works in a method that is thousands of years old called lost wax casting. It is the same method they used in ancient Egypt, Greece, and Rome. He makes the figure out of clay first, then he takes the sculpture through many steps of creating different molds before the metal can be poured. The process itself is a traditional art."

I had no idea that Hayden's grandfather was such an artist, but it doesn't surprise me to know that Hayden is related to someone with extraordinary gifts. I look again at the horse. Marvel at the commitment it takes to make one piece.

Hayden turns to me. "Hi." But his eyes say so much more. He leans slightly into me. Nudging me with his shoulder.

Tingles like snowflakes dust my arm. "Hi, yourself," I return. Then I laugh. For the sheer joy of this moment.

We are interrupted by Hayden's grandfather. He has taken my mother by one arm and Emerson by the other. He weaves through the crowd. Heads for the other side of the room. Hayden grasps my hand in his, twisting his fingers through mine like a woven tapestry. We move together as one. We follow behind, relishing the time together.

I look around at the paintings on the walls. Ocean

landscapes seemingly washed by waves and sand. Rock formations teetering above a cougar ready to pounce. Horses running in herds, wild and free. American Indians, as natural as the scenery surrounding them.

I am absorbed by the images around me. Transported to other times and places. So much that at first, I don't notice. Not until I am right behind him do I see him: Connor Williams, with his arm wrapped around someone. Only it isn't Lily. My eyes flick to Hayden's. He sees it too. I hold his gaze briefly, but my eyes are drawn back to Connor and the girl who isn't Lily. She is turned sideways to me, so I can see her profile. I recognize her as one of Lily's posse.

I let go of Hayden's hand, try to side step away. To disappear into the camouflage of bodies. But at that moment, everything changes. As if in slow motion, Connor swivels around. Catches me. I freeze, poised to bolt. But I am already in his sights, clamped as though in iron cuffs. I see recognition register in his expression. And something happens to me. Darkness trickles through the glow of my happiness. Seeps like water into my ears. Throbbing. Triggering my fight-or-flight response. Flight is my choice.

But in the whirl of colors around me, I see no escape. Panic staggers my breathing. I have to get away.

Then—a hand on the center of my back. It's moving me away from Connor. Into the crowd. Hayden guides me in my flight. All I know is his touch. Anchoring me. Freeing me.

Saving me.

Within seconds, the encounter is over, though shivers still

run up my spine. And I still have the disturbing sense of being watched.

Hayden guides me to my mother, Emerson, and Gramps. And instantly, my mind clears. Mom stands as still as one of the sculptures. Her eyes are fixed on a medium-sized canvas on the wall.

A meadow of white and yellow wildflowers stretches lazily beneath the canopy of an azure sky. My eyes are drawn to the right side, where a golden horse stands in knee-high grasses, head raised, as though she has been waiting for us. Ears cocked forward, listening. Eyes luminous. Gentle.

And I know my mom is transfixed by this painting.

This looks exactly like her horse. The one she had when she was my age. I've seen photographs of it. Melody. It's like it was painted from my mother's memories.

I reach out for her hand. She doesn't turn to look at me. But she squeezes my hand. Telling me. I squeeze back. *I see it, too.*

A man steps forward. Medium build. Dark hair swept back as though he's just run a hand through it. Fine-lined olive skin. Wide open, chestnut eyes. It's his smile that defines him, though. He grins at Gramps. A sideways, almost impish, smile. Making him at once boyish and charming. He embraces Gramps and then Hayden. Gramps turns to Mom. She lets go of my hand so she can shake the man's hand. I watch as Emerson is introduced as well. Then it is my turn. Hayden makes the introduction, which makes me incredibly grateful.

"Stella, this is Christophe Durand. These are his paintings." I reach out to take the hand Christophe offers me. He smiles that engaging grin once more. His eyes glance mischievously to Hayden. As heat rises in my cheeks, I am gratified to see that Hayden is also blushing.

Then Christophe steps back to speak to my mother. She gestures to the painting, and I know, even without hearing her words, that she is telling him about Melody. Christophe steps closer to the painting, waving his hands over the horse as he speaks to her. I look to Hayden for help.

"He's telling her about his process. He has a few horses of his own, but he watches horses all the time then paints them from memory. This horse, though, was different. It came to him in a dream. And he painted the dream."

Something happens then. In a brief, earth-stopping moment. My mother and this painter look into each other's eyes. And Hayden doesn't need to translate for me, because no words are spoken. But the meaning is clear. To my mother. To Christophe. And from the glance that passes between me and Emerson, to both of us. I cannot remember ever seeing my mother look like this. She glows. That's what she must have looked like when she was my age. Christophe points to another painting, one of a herd of wild horses running through a canyon. Their hooves churn the dust into a cloud behind them. Their manes are tangled, heads thrown high to catch the wind. Wild and free.

Emerson walks to stand next to me. She looks at Mom then back to me with raised eyebrows.

"I know," I say.

Gramps motions to Hayden, needing him for a moment. Hayden turns to me. "I'll be right back."

Emerson drifts back to stand next to Mom. And I find myself alone. I spot an open door to my left and make my way toward it.

I step onto a balcony. The night air bites my bare shoulders, slaps my cheeks. Tiny lights overhead illuminate the small area. I see no one else. Leaning over the edge, I look up at the stars. Wish I knew the name of even one constellation.

Suddenly, I know I am no longer alone.

I don't hear someone approach. I feel it on the back of my neck. Warning me a split second before I realize that even though my senses can now operate independently of my hearing, I am incredibly vulnerable. Without hearing, I cannot protect myself from someone sneaking up on me.

I glance over my shoulder. Connor. Alone. Somehow I already knew it was him.

I try to appear casual as I turn to face him. "Hi, Connor. I thought that was you." His eyes narrow. He takes a step toward me, closing the gap between us. He is tall. Broad from years of sculpting his body. Strong. His eyes are so dark they reflect the balcony lights. Eyes of fire.

He speaks. And I understand his words as clearly as if I could read his lips. I understand them from his body language. His menacing posture. Narrowed eyes. Strained neck muscles in the space where his shirt opens at the top. And from the scent of sweat and the tang of adrenaline he wears like cologne.

Connor is threatening me.

Without realizing it, I have backed up. I am now pressed against the stone banister. I lean back to keep distance between Connor's face and mine.

I can't back up any more or I will fall over the top of the balcony.

He says something else and leans in even closer. His hands are now on the railing. His arms closing me in on both sides.

Warning bells ring in my head. Bells I can hear.

I turn my head to the side and duck at the same moment. My sudden movement gives me the advantage of surprise. Split seconds to slide under his arm and around him. To free myself.

"I won't tell Lily about this," I say. "Any of it."

He has a gleam in his eyes. Anger or frustration. Maybe even shame. But I don't want to find out which. I turn and rush for the door. Fling it open and step back into a world of light and color.

I find my mother and Emerson quickly. They are sampling an assortment of desserts. Mini chocolate cakes and tiny raspberry cheesecakes. Emerson offers me a cup of lemonade. I take it and drink it down, suddenly exhausted.

Hayden and Gramps join us. "What's wrong?" Hayden asks immediately. I am a fool to think he doesn't know me well enough to tell when I am upset.

I shake my head. Not now.

"Did something happen?" His eyes narrow as he looks at my expression. Trying to read me. Hayden waits for me to answer. Not willing to let it drop.

I nod. Lean in close to speak to him. Tonight he smells like cool ocean breezes. I breathe him in. Then I speak. "Connor followed me outside. I think he was afraid I would tell Lily that he is here with someone else."

"Did he hurt you?" Hayden asks. His jaw tenses. He is fighting with himself. He is fighting his feelings for me.

I shake my head. "I forgot for a moment," I tell him honestly. "I forgot that without my hearing, people can sneak up on me. I have to remember that." It makes me sad. Just admitting it makes it more real. And the fact pains me even more when he doesn't argue the point. Hayden nods.

Emerson offers me an oatmeal cookie. Glad for the distraction, I take it. Turn to find a napkin. I don't see Hayden walk away. I don't see Connor on the other side of the room.

So I am too late to stop him. Too late to call him back.

Instinct overpowering reason

HAYDEN

I see fear in her eyes, color on her cheeks—and something snaps inside me. Something that has been buried for so long, I didn't even know it existed.

It's more than anger; it's something more powerful, potentially deadly.

Rage.

Connor stands across the room from me, arm around his date. His parents speak with one of the artists. He watches me out of the corner of his eye, just as I watch him. We are like two wolves circling each other, each waiting for the other to strike.

Stella's accident wasn't entirely Connor's fault, but he didn't help her, and neither did Lily. I was there, and I remember the things she didn't see. Connor and Lily ran around, making the tragedy about them while Stella was carried away on a stretcher.

At school I hear all the things Stella cannot hear. People blame Connor, even if Stella doesn't. If someone took a poll of his popularity before the accident—and after—they would find he is no longer worshipped like he was before.

Connor will graduate in June, and I won't graduate for another year, even though I will be eighteen this summer. I lost an entire year of school back in third grade. I wish I were graduating, moving on, so I wouldn't have to see Stella every day next school year but not be with her.

My hands clench into fists at my sides, and I breathe deep to contain my emotions. I know what I am capable of, and I fight to keep control over the rage that threatens to explode. This room is filled with priceless art, patrons of my grandfather, and Stella. But Connor has threatened Stella—and I cannot remain silent.

Connor breaks away from his parents and his date and saunters toward the bar.

I find myself walking toward him before I am conscious of having made the decision. He stands with his back to me, ordering a soda. As he turns around, his face registers surprise, and I don't give him time to recover.

I step very close, close enough to be intimidating. He has to look up at me. I keep my voice low, because I don't want to make a scene. Not here, in the middle of an art gallery. "Watch yourself, Williams."

Connor juts his chin at me. "You wanna take this outside?" he challenges, fixing a bright smile on his face as though he'd relish a fight.

I'd like nothing more right now than to smash my fist

through his toothy grin. But I refuse to be like my mother, even now. Even when it's to protect someone I love. "You aren't worth it," is my answer. But I'm not finished. "Just leave Stella alone."

Connor sizes me up, considering his next move. He glances around to see if anyone is watching him. Rolls his shoulders back one at a time while he decides. His eyes dart back and forth rapidly, fear displayed in the movement, if not in his expression. I watch, alert to every move. Still not sure this won't end in a fight. The seconds drag as I stand in silence. Now, I'm not silent because of fear, I'm silent in strength and power. Connor shifts his soda from his right hand to his left, and extends his right hand as an offering.

"Sorry, man, I lost it earlier. Won't happen again." He's defusing the situation by backing down.

My hands are capable of inflicting serious harm, this I know. They are exactly like my mother's hands. Anger can turn them into weapons. They can destroy. I will not let that happen. I force my hands to uncurl and stretch free, releasing the rage. I channel it into my words.

"No, you didn't 'lose it.' You knew exactly what you were doing—and so do I. We both know you were an idiot that night, and you did nothing to help her. What if it was you that night, instead of her—and you could never play football again? What if you lost that scholarship to Michigan? What then?"

Connor drops his eyes to the floor, and when he raises his face to me, it is drained of bravado, of arrogance. What I see now is shame.

"High school is almost over for you. You know how many

people will remember you next year? Not many. But you will remember you. So try to make choices you can live with." I glance at Connor's date, who is standing a few steps away, and then back at him. "Personally, I'd start with honesty."

I watch his expression as my words register. He understands my meaning.

"Don't ever threaten Stella again, or you'll have to deal with me. Understand?"

Connor nods. Looks me fully in the eyes, speaking words he looks surprised to say. "You made your point."

"Then we're done here," I answer, ignoring his hand. I wait for him to walk away first.

I have won. Not with my fists, but with words. I have won with the power of speech.

And it is at this moment I realize that I spoke my words to him clearly, without faltering. The words didn't fight to be released, they did just what I asked them to do: protect Stella.

The thought triggers a memory, something I had forgotten until now. The night Stella fell into the water, I also spoke without hesitation—without tremors and stutters. I was in control. My speech didn't falter.

I don't know why I didn't remember that until this moment.

But now I know.

I know possibility exists.

And where there is possibility, there is hope.

3

STELLA

I wake Friday morning to see a gray sky.

Slate clouds. Ominous. Dark.

I roll over and go back to sleep.

Dream of kissing. Of Hayden. The person who protected me last night. Who knew what I needed and took care of me. No one has ever taken care of me like that before.

I wake hours later. Still thinking of Hayden. Last night, I didn't see him walk away. I didn't notice until it was too late. Until he was already talking to Connor. Hayden's back was to me, so I couldn't read his lips. Couldn't see what he was saying. But I could read his body language. The way he challenged Connor. There was a moment, a split second, when I thought Hayden might punch him. But he didn't. His words must have been powerful, because I've never seen Connor look so scared. He practically ran away from Hayden. When I asked Hayden what happened, he didn't want to tell me. Just that he wanted to be sure I was safe.

His words fill me with sunshine. Make even this gloomy day bright. Bright with the thought of seeing him again. Until Emerson hands me a note.

Lily is coming over to help me with my cheer routine.

So much for my happy day.

Two hours later, I am pacing in my room. Door closed. Trying to figure out so many things at once. All I know for sure is that I have a blazing headache. Right between my eyes.

Mom opens the door. I wave her in and sit down on the bed with a heavy sigh.

She grabs the pen and paper next to my bed.

The hardest thing in life is to forgive. But we need to forgive to move on. Lily isn't perfect, but she was your best friend. There are things about her that you respect and admire, or you would never have chosen to be close to her. She's here now, helping Emerson. And I don't think it's really for Em. I think she's helping your sister to reach out to you. I'm not saying to forget. I'm just saying that when you open your heart, you let the light in.

I finish reading. Look up at Mom. I wonder if she has finally taken her own advice. If meeting Christophe last night showed her that she needs to move on. Even if she never sees him again, that she deserves to move on. Let the light in.

I stand and curl my arms around her. Gather strength.

And then I go outside to see Lily.

She is sitting under the big tree, Emerson seated beside her. The clouds haven't spilled their drops yet, but the air is scented with perfume heralding rain. The chill drifts across my bare arms. Tickles my nose.

As I draw closer, Lily looks up at me. Her face is damp, her eyes swollen. She runs a hand under her nose. Even like this, Lily is beautiful. Her hair is tangled chaos. Her makeup is smudged. She looks vulnerable. Her expression unguarded.

I sit on the opposite side of Emerson. We bookend Lily.

"What is it?" I ask her.

Her mouth opens. And speaks one word. I read her lips. *Connor.*

I didn't want her to know, didn't want her to get hurt. I wanted to protect her.

Mom's advice lingers as I slide an arm around Lily's shoulders. She leans against me. Her head touching mine.

She hands me a folded piece of paper. A note. The sentences run together as if she wrote too quickly to remember punctuation.

Connor broke up with me Said he needed to be honest He's seeing someone else He was cheating on me all this time I wish I had broken up with him Then maybe it wouldn't hurt so much You know I probably only made the cheerleading squad because of him I lost my BFF because of him I'm so sorry Stella

Things have a way of working themselves out when you least expect it. At least, that's how it happens for me. Because, finding Lily here, apologizing, is the last thing I expected today. And my reaction to it—complete and utter forgiveness—is a total surprise. But that's how I feel. I forgive her. For all of it.

I think about telling her about last night.

But I don't.

Because it's over. Telling her more bad news will only hurt her more. So I keep it inside. One day, maybe I will tell her. But I doubt it. Some things are meant to be kept silent.

Lily has reached out to me. The real Lily. So I reach back.

I turn to look at her. "You made the cheerleading squad because you were the best. Not because of your boyfriend. I was there, remember? You deserve better than Connor. But it's not even about that. It's about you, Lily. You have so many gifts. Stop pretending to be someone you're not. Be yourself. Trust in you."

Lily's eyes widen. I think I have surprised her. Maybe I have changed more than I thought. I never would have spoken to her like this before, but now it seems natural. Comfortable. With the sleeve of her sweatshirt, Lily wipes tears from her cheeks. Manages a small smile.

With her finger, she writes three letters in the dirt. *BFF.*

I grin and add an exclamation point. Then I laugh as Lily throws her arms around me.

Emerson watches us hug, clearly happy that we have made up at last.

Maybe Lily has changed. Or maybe she has learned not to change. Our friendship is damaged; there's no way around that. But perhaps Mom is right. Perhaps by opening my heart to forgiveness, I can allow for rebuilding. By accepting Lily for who she is—and by being her friend.

By midafternoon, rain begins to fall. Hayden sends me a text.

Want to take a walk in the rain?

When? I return.

After dinner?

Ok. I answer.

It's pouring outside when he arrives, but he's not wearing a jacket. He has on a sweatshirt and jeans. Raindrops bead like diamonds on his long hair.

"Ready for that walk?" he asks.

"In the pouring rain?"

Hayden nods, his grin looking slightly mischievous.

I tilt my head and look at him with a raised eyebrow. "Okay," I say doubtfully.

I open the closet and take out an umbrella. Grab my red jacket from the hook near the door. "Mom!" I call.

Her head pops out of the kitchen. I'm sure she's been listening the whole time, but just in case . . . "Hayden and I are going for a walk. We'll be back soon."

Mom smiles and waves at Hayden. She says something to him. He grins at her.

"We will," he answers.

The sky is pewter and silver. Rain comes down in sheets. Unrelenting. I breathe in the smell of damp cement. Wet grass. And somewhere, orange blossoms. Hayden removes the umbrella from my hands. Holds it over our heads with his right hand. Then he takes my right hand in his left. And we walk out into the night.

Puddles slosh against my boots. Seep through the soles to dampen my socks. A chill sneaks through the open collar of my shirt. Water gathers on the sleeve of my jacket. Runs down my arm in little rivulets.

In the dark, I can't read his lips, so we can't talk. But it doesn't matter. We walk side by side. I feel his hand, warm against mine. His skin is smooth but not soft. His hand is strong, safe. I breathe in and out, tasting the wet air in my mouth. My eyes adjust to the milky darkness, and I see the lights in the houses as we pass them.

Some people are sitting down to dinner around tables in their dining rooms, eating as a family. The way my family used to eat together. Others are watching television. The blue glow from the screen flickers gently. A few cars drive down the street, their lights illuminating the shiny sidewalk in front of us. A sense of calm floods me. Peace.

Then we reach the end of the street and a small park here. Just a grassy area with a tree and benches in the middle. Streetlights that burn amber. Hayden walks me to the tree. The leaves and branches form a shield from the rain. He releases my hand so he can close the umbrella. Sets it down.

Then he places one hand on my waist. Takes my other hand in his. I shiver. Not from the cold. From the closeness. Hayden pulls me against him. I raise my left hand to his shoulder. Look up at him. In the glow of the lights, I can see his expression. Rapt. Focused only on me. As I am focused only on him. And then he begins to move. Dancing with me under the canopy of leaves. Dancing in an empty park. Without music. In the rain. I am drenched, but I don't even care. I am warmed by him. By the heat of his body against mine. I am pressed close to him. Wrapped in his arms.

I follow his lead, moving with him. Then he starts spinning me. Around and around. Until I am dizzy. And laughing. I look up at him, his face glistening. He looks down at me, and I am mesmerized. Suspended. I don't even realize we have stopped moving at first.

I don't know how long we stand like that, neither of us moving. But then I shiver. I am soaking wet. And suddenly freezing. Hayden pulls away and picks up the umbrella. He opens it and holds it over me with one hand while he pulls me close with the other. And that's how we walk home.

At the front door, I stop to look at him. I don't want this night to end.

"You need to get inside," he tells me.

"I don't want to say good-bye," I say.

"Tomorrow," he promises with a soft kiss on my forehead. "Six o'clock."

And so I go inside. Mom takes one look at me and shakes her head. I just laugh and go take a hot shower. I am asleep in less than twenty minutes. A smile on my face.

The sound of silence

HAYDEN

Tomorrow.

Our last day together.

Our last day in silence.

Tonight she was more beautiful than she has ever been. She makes my heart race and ache at the same time for what I have found and what I will lose. But I have kept my promise—I have taught her to imagine a different life, one filled with sensations she's never noticed. I have done for her what no one ever did for me. I have given her the tools to survive no matter where her journey takes her.

And she has given me something even greater. She has healed my heart. In the mirror of her eyes, I can see myself, the me I always wanted to be, but was too afraid to try to become. Hiding behind stutters, anger, bitterness. She has melted all of that away.

Tomorrow night.
Our last day together.
I only hope I can stay silent.

2

STELLA

Six o'clock. I have been counting down the minutes all day. As if all the hours leading up to now were standing between me and this moment. As if I had to conquer them rather than live them.

I am wearing my Easter dress, the blue one with the lace overlay. I had hoped to see him the day I first wore it. Hoped he would see me wearing his eyes. The dress I chose is the exact shade of Hayden's eyes when they look at me.

I leave my hair loose in a side part. Tuck the front section back with a silver butterfly bobby pin. I wear the daisy pendant around my neck.

I don't know where we are going tonight. Only that this is my first official date with Hayden. The first time I have been given permission from both parents to go out with him.

I wait in the living room, holding a small wrapped package on my lap. My present to Hayden. I spent hours searching for it today. I knew what I wanted. I just didn't know if I would find it. But after hours of searching through endless shelves, I discovered the perfect gift.

I run my fingers over the silver and white diamond shapes on the wrapping paper. Think about the past seventeen days. A short time to cradle so much change. I have grown to love Hayden. Not for what I see on the outside, but for the complicated and beautiful person he is inside. Without my ears, I have learned to see, to touch, to taste, and to feel. I have reached outside myself. I have learned the lessons Hayden wanted to teach me. I can imagine myself differently. Because I am different.

The countdown to April tenth has changed from being the countdown to something I anticipated—the return of my hearing—to something I fear—the end of Hayden's commitment to me. Will he disappear once he has fulfilled his promise to me?

At five to six, Mom opens the front door. Hayden steps through. Wearing a crisp white shirt tucked into dark jeans. Hair loose, like it was the first day I saw him leaning against the lockers. Watching me.

He turns to me. His eyes reach me first. I can read him now. So I view the myriad of emotions that cross his face like a poem.

Cautious optimism
Barely contained
Overflowing at the edges
Wanting so much
Yet still unsure

Questions unanswered
Words unspoken
Emotion colliding with reason
Waiting so long
Always waiting

"You look just like the butterfly," he says as he closes the distance between us in three smooth strides.

I know exactly what he means. The butterfly on our walk through nature. The one in my photo. My continual reminder of the rewards of patience. It seems fitting that I should be one with the butterfly.

Hayden's gaze drops to the present in my hands. He cocks his head to the side, asking the question without words.

I glance down. Then back at him. "It's for you. For later," I tell him.

A small grin touches his face. And his hand reaches for mine. As we move toward the front door, I see Mom and Emerson standing side by side. Smiling. Watching. Being happy for me.

"Nine thirty," Mom reminds me. I nod. I would agree to anything she asks as long as she lets me walk out the door with Hayden.

"Where are we going?" I ask. The truck rolls along. The silver knot swinging back and forth.

"It's a surprise," Hayden answers. He can't hide the joy on his face. And I can't hide mine, either. This feels like a celebration.

I don't try to figure out where we are going. I don't want to know. I want to be surprised. To relish the delight of someone caring enough to surprise me. To plan something just for me.

I watch the houses we pass. Let my mind drift. Flow.

Hayden's hands wrap around the steering wheel. Eyes on the road ahead of him. At a stoplight, he reaches out. Runs his hand down my arm. Ending with my fingers. Tracing them one by one. As though he is drawing a handprint on a piece of paper. As though he is memorizing it.

Then the light changes. And he lifts his fingers from mine.

Hayden pulls into a driveway, climbs out of the truck. Opens a metal gate. Then he drives through. Plants overflow into the driveway. Trees with pink flowers. Beds of flowers. Statues. Fountains. I read the sign, "Flores' Nursery."

"It looks closed," I tell Hayden.

Hayden nods, a knowing grin lighting his features. "It *is* closed."

I don't understand. But I don't have time for more questions, because he has jumped out of the truck again and is already walking around to my side.

Hayden opens the door. I step out. My feet hit the ground closer to him than I planned. So as I stand, he brushes against me. Tiny bells ring inside of me.

I take the package in my right hand as Hayden grasps my left. "This is where I work."

"It's beautiful," I say.

"Sometimes, working here is like escaping. Plants are forgiving like that. They don't ask questions."

Like a rosebud reaching for the sun, Hayden is opening to me.

But it makes me wonder. In my silence, speech is the least important of my abilities. Conversation is at a minimum. Has this been the secret of my appeal? It is a sobering thought. One that clouds my view and dims the brightness of the flowers in front of me.

As if he understands, Hayden stops. Turns to me. "You can ask me any question you want. And I will answer anything you ask. But only you."

And just like that, the cloud is lifted. I am certain I have never been this happy.

Hayden gives me a tour of the garden. Flats of flowers give way to herb gardens in rectangular boxes. Then to shrubs cut into shapes of diamonds and circles. Beyond are fruit trees. Groves of palm trees in containers.

Nestled in the middle of the rose bushes are an iron table and two chairs. The table has been covered with a red-and-white-checkered cloth. Two place settings.

Candles are scattered on pillars surrounding the table. The sun is setting as the two of us sit down to dinner. Hayden has a picnic basket filled with chicken, Caesar salad, strawberries, and French bread. Chilled sparkling water.

"It's beautiful," I say as Hayden pulls out a chair for me. "Did you do this all by yourself?"

Hayden moves around the table to sit across from me. "I had some help. Turns out my boss is quite the romantic."

I laugh, loving the idea that Hayden and his boss have talked about me. Made these plans for me.

"Now, whenever I come to work, you will be here with me," Hayden says as he offers me a glass of water.

"Is this what you want to do, work with plants?" I ask. "You said I could ask any question I want and you would answer."

Hayden's eyes crinkle at the edges. I can tell he is laughing. Then he answers me. "This is just for now, just until college. I want to be a social worker."

I didn't expect this. Musician. Marine biologist. Something else. Not a social worker.

"That's really specific. You know that already?"

He nods. "So many kids out there grow up in homes they shouldn't be in. I want to do something about it. I may end up going to law school to be a child advocate. Whatever lets me help the most."

I speak my first thought aloud. "There's no one like you," I say. "You inspire me."

"We inspire each other." He reaches for my hand across the table.

"All I've ever thought about is being able to connect with people through my voice," I say. "Now, of course, it's different." I fall silent.

Hayden shakes his head, not willing to let the subject drop as I would like. "You can still sing. You did it the other day. And after tomorrow, who knows?"

I tilt my head. Watch him. The way his eyelashes curl at the ends. The dimple in his cheek. "Even if I can sing again, I can never go back. Not to the way it was before." I pause. "I'm different now. You taught me to be different, to imagine being a different me. I never thought I would write. And *poetry?* I didn't even read poetry before. Even if I had wanted to write,

I'm not sure I could have without losing part of myself first. In losing myself, I found myself. Does that make sense?"

Hayden doesn't answer me in words. Instead, he turns my hand over, palm facing up. He traces my lifeline. "You can do anything, Stella."

I'm not sure I believed that before this moment. But right now, in the flickering light of the candles, breathing in the aroma of lavender, roses, orange blossoms, and jasmine, it's in this quiet moment that I know. I know something for the first time since the accident.

I am going to be okay.

Whatever happens, I will be okay. Because I'm stronger than I thought I was—and I can do anything. I didn't know that before. But I know it now. And that knowledge fills me with a sense of peace like nothing I've ever known. Like I am drifting on a cloud. And even if that cloud collides with a thunderstorm, I will survive. I know I will.

I reach for Hayden's wrapped gift. "For you," I tell him.

The soft smile plays on his face again. And I understand it now. Hayden hasn't received many gifts in his life. This means more to him than I realized. He studies it. Doesn't tear the paper. Just holds it. As though he is savoring the moment. Holding it close before he lets it go. His eyes meet mine.

I nod. "Open it."

And he does, gently running his finger underneath the tape on the edge to release the paper. Then turning the package to do the same on the other side. Folding it back. Carefully. As though the paper itself is the gift.

Inside is a book of poetry. Poems by Whitman, Dickinson,

Wordsworth, Blake, Poe. The book is an old volume. Leather bound with gold-tipped pages. Hayden opens it. His smile broadens. He looks through the pages as if looking for old friends. And perhaps some new ones. Then he comes to a marker I tucked inside, a small, ivory card marking the place. He takes the note in his hand. Reads my words.

He looks back at me. Says nothing but stands and moves around the table. Lifts me to my feet.

My face tilts to meet his. Drawing together, our lips seek each other. Meet in a kiss.

His arms close around my waist as I reach to his shoulders. My hands clasp behind his neck, pulling him into me. Closer. Our kiss deepens. Reaches into my soul. Where he has always been. Where he will always be.

When we pull apart, I have broken through the surface of the water. No longer treading. I'm floating.

Hayden doesn't release me right away. He keeps me locked against him. When he is sure I will not move, his hands take my face. Bring me closer to him. He kisses me again. Once. Softly.

Then we stroll through the garden again. Marvel at the peacefulness of the flowers in the moonlight. Darkness blankets us. We sit on a small bench near a fountain. I cannot hear the water trickle into the basin decorated with stone birds. But I can imagine it. I rest my head against Hayden's shoulder.

"I don't want this to end," I tell him. I don't want to go home.

In the shadows, I can't read Hayden's lips. So I don't even try. I just thread my fingers through his. Close my eyes. And make a wish.

Speech of the heart

HAYDEN

I don't want this to end either, and that's what I want to tell her—but I don't.

I take her home, walk her to the door, and wait until she is inside.

When I get home, I sit outside on the porch, not ready to go in. The book of poetry is open, my eyes scanning lines I remember from long ago. Sentences memorized to practice my speech, the speech that was the destruction of me.

That same speech allowed Stella to read my lips. Brought us together in a world where only we can connect. Poetry isn't afraid of emotions. It isn't afraid to challenge, to question, and sometimes, to admit.

The cat rubs against my legs, purring. Kittens weave around my shoes, trying to get my attention. The littlest one, an orange tabby, separates from the rest and moves to the center of the porch. She sings to me, meows turning into a melody. I reach down to pet her, then scoop her up and set her in my lap. The others look on enviously.

I pick up the card from Stella, which marks a poem she wanted me to read by Robert Frost: "The Road Not Taken." I read his words, think about my life. About the roads I have and have not taken.

I chose to save her from drowning, and then I chose to save her from herself. Life would have been simpler if I had walked away, never allowed myself to get close. But then I wouldn't have known her—I wouldn't have held her hand, shared poetry with her, walked with her by my side. I wouldn't have kissed her. I wouldn't be the same without her. Just as she wouldn't be the same without me.

I turn the card over and over in my hand, looking at it for the hundredth time tonight. There, in her rounded handwriting, are the words I have memorized.

Words I could have written to her.

If I had dared.

You have given me the gift of myself. I owe you my life.

And my soul.

Always,

Stella

Her words stop my heart every time. Because she tells me something I already know but have been too afraid to admit.

The connection between us has grown as strong as the roots of a hundred-year-old tree grounded in the earth—unbreakable. Capable of standing against hurricanes, tornados, and earthquakes. I will have to sever it to free her, to let her go.

But a small voice in my head poses a question. The question that I have been hearing for the past few days but have been afraid to answer.

What if I don't let her go?

1

STELLA

Today is the last day.

The last day I will live in the unknown.

Wondering.

Waiting.

Silent.

Tomorrow morning I will receive my processor. I already know it may not work on the first day, or even the day after that. It takes time to get used to the implants, time for my brain to adjust. But because my hearing has been lost for only a short time, the doctors say I am a good candidate. Some people can even hear music again.

I sit at the kitchen table. Work on homework. I have a test Wednesday on *Hamlet.* And a geometry quiz. And at some point, I have to do something for my drama class, though I have no idea what.

Wisps of last night float through my thoughts, disrupting

my focus. Bringing a smile to my face. Now I understand what all of those romantic movies are about. I understand how my mother fell for my father. And even why Lily was willing to give up everything for Connor.

Because in those moments of deepest connection, everything else disappears. All you know is the beat of your heart. The touch of his hand. The incredible sense that you both feel the same way. And for that one split second, you are not making this journey alone. You have someone by your side.

Hayden promised me seventeen days. And in those seventeen days, he showed me so many things I could do even if I could never hear again. The beach, painting, eating junk food, helping others, baking, playing board games, writing poetry, making friends, experiencing music, enjoying nature, hiking, dancing in the rain, even kissing. Most importantly, he showed me that I can love. With my whole heart.

I meant what I wrote on the card; he did save my life. He also saved my soul. No matter what happens tomorrow, I am a better person today than I was before the accident. I wouldn't change a moment of this journey.

I am still sitting there, lost in daydreams, when Emerson taps my shoulder. Waking me. I blink. She writes on the top of my homework page.

H is at the door.

I look at her in confusion. We didn't have plans for today. Not that I know of.

I am still in my pajamas. Pink-and-white-checkered pants with a white Eiffel Tower tank. My hair is in two ponytails knotted into little buns. Hayden may not notice, but I don't want him to see me like this.

I point to my clothes. Wide-eyed, Emerson nods. Our silent communication at its finest, she dashes into the laundry room. Returns with a slightly damp, turquoise floral tank and a pair of pale blue jean shorts. Emerson must have been doing her laundry. In seconds, I am dressed.

"I owe you," I say as I kiss Emerson's cheek and head for the front door.

Hayden sits on the front step. His back to me. I step close. Sit down beside him.

"Hi," I say.

"Hi, yourself." Our favorite greeting. But he doesn't meet my eyes.

"Is everything okay?" I ask. Has his mother returned? Did something happen?

No answer.

His eyes finally meet mine. And I see it.

The curtain has dropped. He's looking at me, and he may be able to see me. But I can no longer see him. His feelings are hidden from me behind the curtain.

My heart plummets to my stomach. Fills me with dread.

"Brought you something." A forced smile parts his lips. The same lips that were kissing me just last night.

Was it just last night?

How could so much change so fast?

"Something you can do while you're adjusting to your hearing." Hayden has said the unspoken words.

This is the last day. The last day of his promise to me.

The end.

"You've done so much for me already." I remember my first thoughts about why he was helping me. The stray-puppy scenario. "You don't have to do anything else."

I want to scream. To shake him. To find out why he is acting this way.

Instead, I sit there, clown smile pasted on my face. Every second an eternity.

Hayden walks to his truck. I watch as he opens the passenger door. Removes a small basket. He returns to sit beside me once more. Sets the basket on my knees. I open the top.

Inside is a small orange kitten.

My eyes seek him. For a split second, he drops the façade. For a split second, I think he is here with me right now because he wants to be here. Not because of a promise.

"We have this tabby cat. Sleeps on our porch. It's one of her kittens."

I scoop the kitten into my arms. Cradle it. Stroke its tiny head. The kitten looks up at me. With bright blue eyes.

What will my mom say? We don't have any pets. Not that there's a specific rule against them, per se. But Dad took our dog with him. And ever since, the subject's never really come up.

As if he reads my mind, Hayden speaks. "I already asked your mom. She said it would be okay."

"Really?" I'm not sure what I am responding to. The fact that my mom agreed to let me have a kitten, or the fact that Hayden asked her permission.

Hayden shrugs. "I asked her the other night at the gallery.

She was so happy. I figured that once she met Christophe, she'd have said yes to a pet elephant."

I laugh. Marvel at how easy it is to be with him. How comfortable I am speaking to him like this. The ebb and flow of conversation is so natural. Free.

"She has a date with him tonight," I say. "Weird to think of my mom going out with someone. Weird in a good way."

"He's been alone a long time. It's good for both of them."

We're quiet then. I pet the kitten. Hayden stares out in front of him. From time to time, I glance at his profile. A muscle in his cheek twitches. His eyes barely blink.

Finally, he turns to me with eyes as deep as lakes. I lean closer, wanting to fall in. Drown in them. Then he says five words. "Tomorrow, everything will be different."

"Not really," I respond. "I won't be different."

Hayden's stare is unreadable. "Yes, you will," he argues. "You can't see it now, but you will. And this—" He waves his hand in the air. I am not sure what the gesture is supposed to mean until he speaks again. "Won't be important anymore."

What is he saying? That *he* won't be important anymore? Or that he won't need to help me anymore? My brain is twisting and turning like a ball of yarn the kitten has knotted into an impossible mess.

I seize one thread. Try to pull my way out. "You won't have to help me anymore, true. And you've kept your promise to me. For seventeen days, you have shown me so many things I can do. You've opened my mind to possibility. To hope. I'll always be grateful. Even if you don't want to hang out with me anymore."

Now Hayden is the one who looks confused. He shakes his head as if trying to make sense of my words. "That's not what I meant. But we end up in the same place anyway."

This is madness. I want to scream. To stand and stomp my feet. Anything to stop talking around what we both want to say. I close my eyes. Breathe in deep. And I jump into the deepest part of the water. Whether I sink or swim, I'm taking this chance.

"From the first moment I saw you, I sensed it," I say. "You and I are meant to be. If the accident is the reason we're together, then I'm grateful. I wouldn't change one moment. Not one breath." I don't realize I am crying until I finish speaking. I taste tears.

Hayden leans toward me. Kisses the new tears as they fall. One by one. Touching the rain with sunshine and leaving a rainbow in its wake.

Last, he kisses my lips, gently, like he is afraid to show too much. To give too much. I pull him closer. Opening my heart to him. Giving him my love. Then he pushes away. Touches my lips with his finger. Traces them. As if he is memorizing their shape.

"Stella, there's a reason you can understand me. And no one else. It's my speech. You can read it because it's slow, repetitive." He shrugs. "I guess it was good for something. But that's all. Because once you can hear it, you will want to cover your ears. You will wish you couldn't hear it."

All at once, I understand.

And my heart swells with compassion.

"I know why I can understand you. And it's a gift. *You* are a gift."

I take his face in my hands. The face that is so incredibly beautiful to me. The face in my dreams. I hold it gently as though it is made of glass. "I love you, Hayden."

I lean close. Kiss the scar on his chin. His cheeks, also wet with tears. The eyes that see my soul. I kiss his lips. With all my heart.

Bleeding with truth

HAYDEN

She kisses me like nothing else matters—and I believe her.

I believe her when she holds my face in her hands, tells me that I mean so much to her. As much as she means to me.

When she tells me she loves me—the most beautiful thing I have ever heard. And I want to tell her the truth. I want to say the words.

But I can't.

Because she doesn't know yet, doesn't know how she will feel tomorrow when she hears me stutter and stammer. When she hears the things people say about me. When she realizes that she is better than I am, that she deserves better. She's too good to hurt me like that, too good to break my heart. One day, she will resent me for that. Just like my mother resented me.

So instead of saying the words I want to say, I say the words

I know I need to say. Words to free her. "I c-can never l-love you. Or an-anyone. Ever."

Then I stand and walk away before I can see her cry, before I can see that I have broken her heart, before I change my mind.

SOUND

STELLA

I cry. More than I ever have before. More than when my parents split up. More than when my dog went to live at my dad's with his new family. More than when I came home from the hospital and couldn't hear a thing.

I cry until I am sobbing but the tears have run dry. Wondering where the tears come from. And how I can make more. Because I want to drown in them.

Sometime before the sun rises, I fall asleep.

And dream of him.

Mom wakes me at 9:00. It's time for my appointment. The kitten is curled up on the pillow next to me. She lifts her tiny head. Yawns. And curls up once more. I suppose I need to give her a name. But right now, my mind is empty.

I drag my legs to the edge of the bed. Push myself up. And

stand. Forcing one leg to move at a time across the room. It's easy when I don't think. When I force my mind to go blank.

So that's what I do.

I think of nothing. Absolutely nothing.

I get dressed without thinking. Brush my teeth without thinking. Eat a bowl of cereal without thinking. Get in the car without thinking.

Mom holds my hand, lets me know she is there if I need her. But she can't fix this. No one can. No one can except Hayden.

We are back at the hospital but in a different building. Mom and I cram into an elevator packed with people. She presses the button for the seventh floor. Mom never lets go of my hand.

The office is bright yellow. A happy, hopeful color. Mom checks me in. I sit next to a giant fish tank. Watching the fish swim around and around. I still think of nothing.

Dad walks through the door. I had forgotten he would be here. His gray-striped shirt is perfectly pressed. I hug him hard enough to wrinkle him. He hugs me back, oblivious to his shirt.

The audiologist comes to get us herself. She is petite, with light brown hair that sits on her shoulders. Her eyes are dark brown. Warm and friendly.

We follow her into her office. This one is light blue. That's when the first thought sneaks in. Past my guard. This is the color of Hayden's eyes when he is sad.

Dad and Mom take the two chairs in front of the desk. I sit in the chair next to the audiologist. The desk has a computer and lots of papers. Photos are taped on the wall behind her. A little girl with light brown hair. Drawings are taped on the wall, rainbows and unicorns. They remind me of my rainbow girl. The thought gives me courage.

My name is Gretchen, she writes on a white board. I nod.

"Nice to meet you."

We'll be working together today to map your processor. Mapping is basically programming. Setting the levels so you can hear comfortably. Some people don't hear much at first. It can even sound strange. You have been without hearing for a short time, so your brain should adjust quickly. I imagine you will be able to hear your parents speak before you leave here today.

I nod. I've read all of the paperwork from her, so I know what to expect.

She shows me the part I am to wear above my ear. It looks like a Bluetooth earpiece. I was able to choose the color before the surgery. Of course, I chose blue. I look at the piece now. It's the color of the deepest part of the ocean.

Hayden's eyes just before he kissed me.

The piece fits around the back of my ear. Gretchen adjusts it until it is comfortable and I give her a thumbs-up. There is another piece, a small disk attached to the earpiece. It needs to go on my head. It clings there against my hair. The dark pewter blending into my hair.

I am going to start the programming now. I will send you a series of beeps. Give me a sign when you hear them. Raise your hand, like you did for your other hearing tests.

Gretchen moves back to her computer. I watch her fingers tap the keys. Mom grips my left hand, her face drawn, lips clenched. She wants so much for this to work. I smile at her. Tell her it's okay. She relaxes a bit. Her grip loosens.

It's at that exact moment I hear the first beep.

Then I realize—it's because of his mother.

Beep.

The reason.

Beep.

Her.

Beep.

Hayden's mother blaming him.

Beep.

For her lost dreams. It was her.

Scarring him.

Breaking his skin.

His bones.

His heart.

But not his will.

Her.

Beep. Beep. Beep.

I raise my right hand, signaling them. I can hear.

Mom's cheeks are wet with tears of relief. Of joy.

Dad nods his encouragement. His eyes shimmer.

Gretchen beams. *Now I am going to use these levels to help you hear us.*

I watch the clock. Wait for something to happen. Minutes go by. Nothing.

Still silence.

Still in my bubble.

But it's different from before. I don't hate it anymore. It's a part of me now. And always will be. Silence.

"Stella . . . can you hear me?" My mom's voice. It's scratchy, like she is speaking through a metal tube from far away. I strain to make out the words.

But I can hear her.

I can hear.

My father speaks to me, but I can't quite make out his words. The sounds are jarringly close and far away at the same time. I lean closer to my parents, wanting to hear more.

Gretchen slips an arm around me. Congratulating me.

There's much work to be done. Hours of therapy. More mapping. I know this. I know we are only at the beginning. But it is something to celebrate. This is the day I have been waiting for—to hear again. To be able to listen to music. To sing. This is what I wanted.

Isn't it?

For so many years, singing has been the thing that made me special. The thing that made me who I am. That's what I used to think, anyway.

Before.

Before I woke in a hospital bed.

In silence.

Before I realized that I am more than my voice. That what I do doesn't define me. That it's who I am that matters. The girl I was before—the girl who dreamed of Someday Broadway. That girl is gone. She was lost on the bottom of the pool. Who I am today is the real me.

That night in the pool, I was given the chance of a lifetime: Silence.

Without the silence, I would have stayed on the same road. Never veering. The silence let me take a different road, one I hadn't traveled before. A road that unfolds because of *who* I am. Not what I am.

I hear myself crying, before I feel tears rolling down my cheeks. Muffled sobs shake me.

I'm not sure if I am crying because I am happy.

Or sad.

In losing my hearing, I found Hayden.

In regaining it, I may lose him forever.

Knowing, just knowing

HAYDEN

My fingers fly across the piano keys, the melody mournful, plaintive.

I am alone on stage. The theater is empty and dark. If I keep playing, I won't have to think about the first moment I saw her. Unaware of her beauty, her charisma, oblivious to her power.

Pulling her from the water, holding her body against mine. Breathing for her, willing her to live.

Watching her find her way like a colt learning to stand for the first time. Unsure, but determined—triumphant.

Looking into her amber eyes and seeing myself reflected back. The me I have always wanted to be.

I am willing to let her go so she can fly.

I am lost in the music, in thoughts, in Stella.

And then I know she is here. I sense her presence even though I cannot see her.

I feel her. I knew she would come here. The same way I knew I would save her life that night.

As much as I tried to push her away, to pretend I can go on without her, I know that it is impossible. It would be like trying to separate the waves from the sea. Stella and I are bound together. Forever.

My hands drop from the keys, and I turn to watch her walk across the stage.

"Don't stop," she says. "It's beautiful."

She can hear.

She can really hear.

Elation mixes with regret—a combination of emotions so powerful that a weight presses on my chest. I struggle to breathe as though I am underwater and cannot reach the surface.

Still she moves toward me. I watch her.

Confident, strong, brave.

Before I can stand, she speaks. "She was wrong—your mother. She had it backwards." She stops in front of me. Waits while I stand to face her. "Hayden, *you* are the dream. I know you don't want to hold me back. But if you walk away from me, that's what will happen. Because I need you. And you need me. More than you realize."

She takes a step closer. In the shadows, it's just the two of us. "We counted down to this day. Seventeen days together. You waited with me for this day. And it's here. I can hear again. I have a long road ahead of me. I may not be able to sing again for a long time. And maybe never the way I used to. But I'm not even sure I want to sing anymore. I want to write. To tell stories. To share feelings with words. I don't have to be on Broadway to be happy. The accident taught me that. *You* taught me that. I thought I was counting down to this day because it would determine the rest of my life. But when I heard the first sound, I realized something. It was the journey. Not the destination. You are my journey. And if hearing again means I lose you—then I don't want it. I'll turn this device off. Throw it away. I don't need it. I just need you."

SONG

STELLA

I stand before him. Give him everything I have. For the first time in my life, I know that dreams are for today, not for someday. They are for here. And now.

I wait for him to say something. To say the words I have longed to hear. He doesn't speak. Doesn't move.

We are close enough to touch. But we don't. Our hands remain at our sides.

Finally, he speaks. "Are you sure?"

I hear him. I am sure of it. I'm not reading his lips. I am really hearing him.

Only there is no stutter. No stammer. Just Hayden's beautiful voice. In my ears.

"Yes."

He is silent again. Thinking. Torn between his past and his present.

"Hayden," I say softly. "The past is behind us. We can't

change it, no matter how we may want to. And we have no way of knowing what tomorrow may bring. All we know is today, this moment. Be in the moment with me. Trust your heart. Trust me."

Hayden reaches for me then. Pulls me close. Holds me like he will never let go. I cling to him.

Giving and receiving.

And then he says the words. The ones I have longed to hear. Three words.

"I love you."

I don't know if I hear them, or if I read his lips as they move against mine.

But I know I understand.

And in the silence between the words, I hear music.

Acknowledgments

Thank you for reading *Silence.* I am so grateful to you for taking this journey with Stella and Hayden. I hope their story filled you with hope.

I want to thank my agent, Stacey Glick, for being with me since the beginning of my career. You have always believed in me, even when I didn't believe in myself. Thank you for reading and rereading countless drafts of Stella's story and for working so hard to make this possible.

Thank you to everyone at Shadow Mountain for embracing *Silence* and falling in love with Hayden and Stella. Heidi Taylor, your enthusiasm and appreciation for this story is a writer's dream. Chris Schoebinger, thank you for believing in *Silence* and seeing its potential. You have both given me a home at Shadow Mountain, and I am eternally grateful. Lisa Mangum, thank you for your encouragement and honesty and for sharing a love of the beauty of language. Annette Lyon, thank you for your insightful and thorough copyediting.

For the beautiful layout of the book from the cover to the subtle chapter headings which so embody the story, many thanks to Richard Erickson. A big thank you as well to Heather Ward for coming up with a gorgeous cover design. Thank you to Rachael Ward for the stunning typography. And thank you to Karen Zelnick and Michelle Moore for the publicity and for making all the marketing of the book run so smoothly and for always making me feel so welcome. Ilise Levine, I am so thankful for your insights and your support with sales and marketing. You have made it possible for readers to experience this story. Thank you for all your hard work. I appreciate everything you have done for *Silence.*

I had help with my research on the book from some really generous people who responded when I asked and received nothing but my thanks in return. Any mistakes are truly my own.

Rosalind Cook, thank you for answering all my questions about sculpting in bronze and for teaching me about the Lost Wax Casting process. Jennifer Howard, M.S., CCC-A, and Erin McAlister, AuD., CCC-A, from the House Clinic, thank you for helping me with research on Stella's injury, her cochlear implants and her recovery. Lauren Crosby, M.D., and Jennifer Snyder, M.S.N, P.N.P., thank you for talking through head injuries with me and answering my medical questions about Stella's resulting hearing loss, surgery, and recovery.

Thank you to all my writer friends for all your critiques and pep talks, but especially, Sydney Salter, Suzanne Morgan Williams, Kathryn Fitzmaurice, Cynthea Liu, Susanna Leonard Hill, and Cynthia Leitich Smith.

I also want to thank Jimmy Powell at Stellar Media Group for my beautiful website and Laron Glover at Ninth Moon for her lovely designs.

A special thank you to all the teachers and librarians who have supported my work. Thank you for sharing my words and for making a difference in the world, one student at a time.

A giant hug and kiss to my entire family. Thank you for your love, encouragement and prayers, for bringing everyone you know to my book signings and being the first to buy my books. Your support means the world to me.

Thank you to my daughters, Ava and Caroline, for believing in me, for reading everything I write and for sharing this dream with me.

Most importantly, I thank God in whom all things are possible.